"Rick Collignon's last novel, *Perdido*, r~~eceived wide~~ ... ~~er~~ work seems bound for even higher prai~~se~~ ... *García*, Collignon fully commits himself ... does so to fine effect, avoiding that hok~~ey~~ ... ~~grow~~ so tiresome in lesser writers. . . . What ~~makes~~ ~~Collign~~on's use of magic realism in this novel particularly successful is that he does not merely paste it on top of his narrative; the magic runs deep because the novel takes on as subject the difficulties involved with knowing what is real and what isn't, what has happened and what has been imagined. In the world of Guadalupe, almost everything and its opposite might be true."

—*The San Diego Union-Tribune*

"Collignon deftly blends history and magical realism to create a moving account of the last day of family patriarch Flavio Montoya. . . . Throughout, Collignon pays homage to the power of storytelling, framing the central story with the tales that elder relatives and neighbors weave about the town's history. A fitting and evocative end to his trilogy."   —*Booklist*

"*Chiaroscuro* is not a term ordinarily used to describe writing, but Rick Collignon's most recent novel, *A Santo in the Image of Cristóbal García*, can be read only as movement between light and dark. . . . In an imaginary village in northern New Mexico, contemporary events slip helplessly from one disaster to another while from the past, goodness and kindness appear as shimmering islands in a destiny of implacable currents of madness and harm. How Collignon manages this without being overwrought or didactic is a measure of the control in his writing."   —*The Santa Fe New Mexican*

"Collignon's final installment in his Guadalupe Trilogy . . . takes place as a mysterious fire envelops the narrator's fictional New Mexico village. . . . Dreamlike and melancholy, it is a worthy read."   —*Publishers Weekly*

"A self-contained mythic world nonetheless tightly tethered to reality. As in the earlier works, the narrative carries strong strains of the oral tradition: vivid and exact descriptions, an episodic approach to storytelling, and precisely drawn . . . characters. The story re-creates the earlier history of the town from its initial settling until its final immolation. Especially reminiscent of Garcia Marquez's magical realism."   —*Library Journal*

continued . . .

Perdido

"Driven by Collignon's decisive prose, his strong characters, and his deep knowledge of New Mexico folklore, *Perdido* is a one-sitting read, a novel that captivates and surprises all the way to its chilling end."
—*The New York Times Book Review*

"Mr. Collignon has created a distinct and meaningful world."
—*The Atlantic Monthly*

"Mr. Collignon has taken readers back to the village he wrote of in his first novel. It is a happy return." —*The Dallas Morning News*

"Satisfying, unpretentious . . . a natural storyteller." —*Missouri Reviews*

"Intriguing . . . compelling . . . The novel succeeds admirably with its deception of a peaceful way of life abruptly hurled into dangerous havoc by unwonted curiosity. . . . Collignon's male characters are masterfully drawn, as is his rendering of the stark New Mexico landscape, with its harsh, unforgiving climate." —*The San Diego Union-Tribune*

Also by Rick Collignon

Perdido

The Journal of Antonio Montoya

A Santo in the Image
of Cristóbal García

Rick Collignon

BlueHen Books · New York

BLUEHEN BOOKS
Published by The Berkley Publishing Group
A division of Penguin Group (USA) Inc.
375 Hudson Street
New York, New York 10014

Copyright © 2002 by Rick Collignon
Book design by Meighan Cavanaugh
Cover design © 2002 Royce M. Becker
Cover photograph of doors and wall © Michael Gesinger/Photonica
Cover photograph of man © Gildo Spadoni/Graphistock
Cover photograph of butterfly © Elisa Katz/Photonica

First BlueHen hardcover edition: October 2002
First BlueHen trade paperback edition: October 2003
BlueHen trade paperback ISBN: 0-425-19313-6

The Library of Congress has catalogued the BlueHen hardcover edition
as follows:

Collignon, Rick, date.
    A santo in the image of Cristóbal García : a novel / Rick Collignon.
      p.   cm.
    ISBN 0-399-14921-X
      1. Spanish Americans—Fiction.   2. New Mexico—Fiction.
    3. Villages—Fiction.   I. Title.
    PS3553.O474675 S36   2002   2002071134
    813'.54—dc21

Printed in the United States of America

10   9   8   7   6   5   4   3   2   1

To Guadalupe

Acknowledgments

Although the process of writing a novel is basically one of solitude, I found that my mind was often full of those who had helped and encouraged me over so many years. I'd like to thank, after so long, Marsha Skinner for her wisdom and her ability to make me see when I felt blind. Thanks to Modesto Cisneros for his friendship and the fifteen years we spent either huddled from the cold or burning from the heat on one jobsite or another. And thanks to my editor, Fred Ramey, who has always taken what I've written and only made it better.

Thanks also go to Niki Baptiste, Ruth Lemansky, Sheila Guzmán, David A. Leffel, Sherrie McGraw, Mary Dwight Olson, and David Wheeler, who all read the manuscript in bits and pieces. I don't think any of you truly knew how much your encouragement meant.

Thanks to my son Ollie, who ended up immersed in typing page after page, and also for giving of himself and for his will to always be there. To my son Nick, for his commitment to what is true in himself and those around him. And to my youngest son, Eli, who was so good with an often exhausted father and who loved the witch story so much. I'd also like to thank Shana, who was with me through much of the writing of this book. I am so proud of all of you.

And last of all: Thank you, Jennifer. It was a hard time and you filled it with your heart. I thank you so much for your strength and your patience and your love. Without them I might have been lost in Guadalupe forever.

A Santo in the Image
of Cristóbal García

The morning the mountains caught fire and the village of Guadalupe began to burn, Flavio Montoya was once again standing beside the irrigation ditch behind his sister's house.

"This field is turning to dirt," Flavio said, and then he turned his head and looked at the foothills. There had been no moisture in Guadalupe for four months, and the hills were dusty and too dry. The trees had grown faded and listless as if they had forgotten altogether what rain was. There was a shadow moving between the piñons, and Flavio thought idly that it seemed too large and moved too haphazardly to be a deer.

"My sister's field," he said again, to no one but himself, "is dying."

It was just past dawn, and the sun was still far below the mountains. Flavio had been trying to irrigate Ramona's field for the past twelve days, and he had come to wonder how such a simple chore as moving water, a thing he had done all his life, had suddenly become so difficult. While it was true that there had been no rain for months, it was also true that the ditches in the village were running full from the heavy snows the winter before. More than enough water to keep the fields wet. Where the ditch ran, the alfalfa was green and sturdy, but stretching away from it was cracked earth and a scattered army of stunted yellow plants. And although the drought and the harsh spring winds were much to blame, Flavio knew that he, too, was at fault.

Each morning, long before dawn, Flavio would come to the field. But after just a few minutes of digging, he would tire and then stand motionless with his shovel as if both were spaded in the ground. He would stare blankly at the dark shadow of the mountains or at the back of Ramona's empty house with its small curtained windows and think about nothing. And then, suddenly, as if there were no such thing as time, he would wake and find himself standing in the heat of the sun. Then he would walk slowly to his truck and drive home.

This morning, the morning Flavio saw the shadow of Felix García moving between the piñons and the morning Guadalupe began to burn, Flavio and his shovel were again standing quietly beside the irrigation ditch. He had once again forgotten how dry his sister's field was, and staring absently at the foothills, he remembered the time his Grandmother Rosa told him that Demecio Segura had been born into a snowbank.

"Demecio was just a little man, mi hijo," Rosa had said to her grandson. "Almost no bigger than you. And for all his life the only luck he ever had was poor at best."

It was early October and snow had fallen for the first time on the village of Guadalupe. Flavio had walked that morning from his own house on the other side of the valley to his grandmother's. He had never walked that distance by himself before, so when Rosa opened the door and saw him standing proudly in the snow with wet feet and no hat on his head, she had shaken her head and smiled. Then she told him that, although she was happy he had come to visit, if he ever did such a thing again she would have his grandfather sit him down and they would have a little talk. Rosa and Flavio sat in the kitchen together, Flavio ate biscochitos and drank warm milk with coffee while his grandmother told him about Demecio Segura.

"Demecio had always sworn," Rosa said, "that he could remember distinctly the moment of his birth. And he would tell this story over and over to anyone who would listen.

" 'It was the coldest night of the year I was born,' Demecio would say. 'When there is no daylight and Christmas has just passed and there is no reason to live. I was born on that night. Although it was my mother's good luck not to endure the severe pains of childbirth, it was my bad luck to be born into a snowbank.'

"Demecio's luck was always like that," Rosa said to her grandson. "His cows were not only sickly, but grew to the size of large dogs and were so mean-tempered that when Demecio was near they would bark and try to bite his feet. His wife, who was not from here, was fond of climbing trees until one day she fell while picking piñon and broke the bones in her neck. Not long after that, Demecio went to live with his nephew, Luis, a man who never spoke but only grunted. It was said that Luis would hit Demecio with a stick whenever Demecio complained, which was always. He was not a happy man, hijo, and he went about his life as if the air was full of stones.

" 'I remember clearly,' Demecio would say, 'that life before this life was warm and without trouble and that the first time I took a breath it was snow.'

"Demecio's mother, who was named Demecia after her own mother, became pregnant one spring night. She was forty-six years old and unmarried and an only child who lived with her old parents. Demecio's mother told no one she was with child because she did not know she was pregnant until the moment her son sprang from her womb like a fish jumping from the river. Although Demecia was a good-natured woman, there was, since her own birth, a blankness about her eyes and around her mouth and in her movements as if a fire inside her had never been lit. She did not know she was pregnant for the simple reason that she was unable to comprehend the idea of yesterday.

"On the day of Demecio's birth," Rosa had said, "Demecia was returning home from the church where she had dusted with a dry rag, as she did every Thursday evening, the fourteen stations of the cross. As she neared her parents' home, a sharp spasm racked her lower stomach and Demecia gasped in pain. Her feet slipped out from under her, and she fell hard on the frozen path. She wrapped her arms around her belly and moaned, and in that instant, Demecio, in his haste, burst into the world and landed face first in the snow. He lay there half buried without moving, his voice shocked into silence. If he'd had one coherent thought it would have been that life is full of surprises and none of them can you see coming."

Rosa leaned back in her chair and folded her hands in her lap. She looked across the table at her grandson. "So you see," she said. "You must always be careful and never walk across this village until you're old enough."

Flavio, who'd had no idea his grandmother's story had anything to do with him, suddenly saw the village full of small vicious cows and men who did not speak but only hit you with sticks. A place where babies could be found in snowbanks.

"Grandmother," Flavio said. "Will those things happen to me?"

"Which part, hijo?" Rosa said, and she smiled.

"All of it."

"No, mi hijo," and she leaned across the table and touched her grandson's hand. "It is someone else's story. Not yours. But that doesn't mean you should ever ever forget."

Seventy-five years later, Flavio stood in the field behind the house that had once been his grandparents' and then, after their deaths, his sister Ramona's. His mouth was half open, and his breath came and went gently. He slowly became aware of the water rushing through the ditch, away from him and away from his alfalfa. It occurred to him that all he had really done for the past twelve days was drive across the village to torment his alfalfa, which deserved better. It was then, out of the corner of his eye, that he saw Felix García, a man too old and sick to be out by himself, walking through the piñons.

Felix García hadn't walked anywhere for the past eight years other than to shuffle along with his son, Pepe, from his bed to a table in the café that carried Felix's name. A vein had burst in Felix's head one morning while he was preparing beans and chile in the kitchen of his small restaurant. And though Felix had always been a quiet man who kept to himself, the stroke left him utterly mute and slow and vacant, as if whatever had once been inside him had suddenly left. He now spent his days sitting alone in the far corner of the café while his son cooked in the kitchen.

Flavio and Felix had known each other all their lives and, before Felix's stroke, Flavio would often stop at the café before going to his fields. He and Felix would sit and drink coffee, and through the smoke of their cigarettes they would watch light come to the village. Flavio had continued to go to the café after Felix fell ill, but in truth, the trembling that never left his old friend's hands and the soft sounds that came from the back of his throat made Flavio feel uncomfortable, as if the two of them had become lost in the same place.

One day, a few years ago, Flavio had sat beside Felix and without even looking could see how badly Felix's back was now bent and how he stared straight ahead with wide open eyes even though his head dipped low to the table. It was then Flavio realized not only that he no longer knew who this man was, but that he couldn't bear to continue watching him approach death in such complete solitude.

That was the last time Flavio had been inside Felix's Café. Even now, when driving past the restaurant, he would look elsewhere and think of his fields or of the wood he was to get at the lumberyard. He would think of anything and pass by the café as if the place was not quite real and those inside were only thoughts he used to have.

The first thing that went through Flavio's mind when he saw Felix stumble to the base of the foothill and into the sagebrush was that what he was seeing couldn't possibly be happening. The Felix García he remembered had difficulty walking just a few steps, and that only with help from his son.

"I am seeing a trick," Flavio muttered. He closed his eyes and felt the sun hot on the back of his neck. He wondered how long he'd been standing in the heat, and he realized that somewhere along the way he had become an old man. Along with too much sun, that could make someone see things he would prefer not to. Flavio took a deep breath and let it out slowly. But when he opened his eyes, he could still see Felix wandering slowly through the sage as if lost in each step.

By the time Flavio had hurried and tripped his way through the brush to Felix, Felix had stopped moving altogether and was standing stone still staring straight ahead. His clothes were a mess. His trousers were ripped at the knees, and his shirt was torn where it had snagged on piñon branches. His hands were stained with pitch and crusted with dried blood. Flavio thought that he looked as though he had spent the morning not walking, but rolling up and down the foothills.

"Felix," Flavio said hoarsely, out of breath from moving so quickly through the sagebrush. He reached out, almost more to steady himself, and touched his friend's arm.

"Felix," he said again, "what are you doing out here? This is no place for you." Felix's lips moved without making a sound. His face was streaked with dirt and saliva and was badly scratched, a thick clot of blood on one ear. Flavio shook his head and looked at the foothills. "Where's Pepe?" he said. "How can this be?" The hills were empty, and with no breeze it seemed to Flavio as if nothing had ever lived there except loose rock and piñon and scrub oak whose leaves were now curled and yellowed with no rain.

Flavio leaned forward and in a whisper said, "Are you better, Felix?" As soon as the words left his mouth, he realized how foolish they were. No one as ill as Felix ever got better, and if they did the whole village would have heard. Even if Flavio had not been told such news, no one in Felix's condition would suddenly get up one morning and go hiking in the mountains.

"I'm sorry, Felix," Flavio said. "I didn't mean to say that. Venga, primo," and he reached out his hand again and took Felix's arm gently. "Let's get out of the sun."

Flavio found that if he pulled Felix's arm slightly, Felix would shuffle his feet and follow alongside him. They made their way slowly through the sagebrush and over the warped timber spanning the irrigation ditch into the alfalfa field. At times, Felix would stop and Flavio would talk to him about anything, as if his words carried the rhythm that would make Felix move his feet. By the time they crossed the field to Ramona's house, the back of Flavio's shirt was stained with sweat. He felt as though he had been walking in the sun for hours.

When Flavio pushed open the door of his sister's house, he felt a rush of cool air against his face and could smell the heavy odor of dampness and musk. He had not been inside the house in the five years since Ramona's death, and the place was exactly as it had been on the day she died.

A week after her funeral, Flavio had driven to her house with the intention of packing away her things in boxes, draining the pipes of water, and boarding up the windows. He had parked his truck under the cottonwoods in her drive and sat in the cab smoking. It was late spring that day. The leaves on the trees had just opened, and the air was warm. Looking at the house, he thought that this was where his grandparents had once lived and where his father had been raised. The earth around the house was full of their footsteps, and the old adobe walls were seeped with their scent. After he finished his cigarette, he had started the truck and left the place as it was.

There was talk in the village, especially among those who were older, that Flavio had left things the way they were just in case Ramona was to return, that he thought she would be upset if her favorite dress or her coffee cup was stuffed away in a box somewhere. Sometimes children would peer in the windows, in the thin space between the curtains, and they would see Ramona's shoes on the floor beside the bed that was unmade or the pots still sitting on the stove. When they would see her paintings hanging on the walls, they would decide that there were better places to be than in this house.

Over time, the house became a place people gradually stayed away from, as if its emptiness was full of things that made them uneasy. Even Flavio, who had spent much of his youth there and later had drunk coffee with his sister in her kitchen, had come to feel uncomfortable when walking too near the house on his way to the alfalfa field.

Now Flavio stood before the open door and looked inside. He could see the sofa across the room. Hanging on the wall above it were a number of Ramona's paintings, the oils dulled with dust. He thought that maybe it wasn't such a good idea for him and Felix to stop here, that it was possible they would catch some disease from the air that had been trapped inside the house for so long. He wondered how much longer it would take the two of them to walk the distance to his truck. But he could see how ragged Felix's breath came and went and how dry and cracked his lips were. Who knew how long it had been since he'd last had water. Flavio patted his arm.

"Come inside, my friend," he said. "We'll take a little rest in my sister's house and then I'll drive you home," and they walked together inside the room.

Sunlight was coming in the small window above the sink in the kitchen. There was enough light in the room for Flavio to see that the surface of all the counters was thick with rodent droppings and the dirt that fell like mist from between the boards in the ceiling. The walls were stained a dank yellow from roof leaks and were so bad in one area that the plaster had swelled out away from the adobe. Bowls and pots and silverware that had once been his grandmother's lay strewn on the countertops. On a small table was a stack of old books that mice had gnawed at, bits of pages lying on the floor. And here, too, were more of Ramona's paintings, some of them streaked with dirt and water, the paint smeared and blurred. The room looked small and sad and used up and made Flavio feel even more tired than he already was.

"This house is becoming lost," he said softly, his words not much more than air. After a few seconds, he walked across the room to the sink. He turned on the tap and was relieved to find that the pump in the well still worked. He let it run until the water ran clear and then he drank deeply from the faucet, washed out a glass, and filled it again for Felix.

Felix was sitting on the sofa in the front room. Other than the dirt and scratches on his hands and face and his torn clothing, he looked just as if he were sitting as usual by himself in the corner of Felix's Café. His hands, trembling slightly, rested in his lap. His shoulders were hunched and he stared forward with his head drooping. Flavio sat beside him and held the water to Felix's lips as the old man took a few sips.

"This has been some morning, Felix," Flavio said and leaned back against the couch. "To see you walking out of the mountains." He shook his head and settled a little deeper into the sofa. "I don't know what I thought."

Across the room was a painting of the same alfalfa field Flavio had been trying to irrigate for the past twelve days. But in this painting the field was full, the alfalfa green, the blossoms a rich purple. Two men and a small boy stood in the distance with shovels where Flavio knew the ditch lay. Beside it hung a painting of the old village office, which still stood not far from Ramona's house—a crumbling adobe with cracked windows and a bellied roof that sat in a field of dry weeds and twisted, rusted-out vehicles.

"My sister," Flavio said, "painted these paintings. You remember Ramona, Felix? She would paint like there was nothing else to do—even as a young girl, when we were children. And every painting was a painting of this village." Felix's head had begun to shake slightly, and again Flavio wondered how this man who could barely sit up had come wandering out of the hills.

"I don't know why she did this either, Felix," Flavio said and looked back at the painting of the alfalfa field. For a brief second, he almost knew who the two men and the small boy were, but then, like a breath, the memory left. "It's true, though," he went on. "She painted the church and the cemetery and old twisted juniper trees and even once I remember she painted a painting of mud. A whole road of mud she painted and not even one flower or a blade of grass."

For the most part, Flavio thought that what his sister chose to put on canvas was foolish. One painting after another of a tired village that not only had seen better days, but was a place Flavio saw only with familiarity. But at other times, if he stared at her paintings longer than he should, he could almost hear the creaking of vigas or smell the thick odor of dirt on the blade of a shovel.

Moving his eyes across the rest of the paintings on the far wall, Flavio thought that this house was too full of his sister, as if she had just walked off one day and forgotten to return. He grunted softly and lowered his eyes. It was then that he saw the seven santos standing like shadows in the corner beside the door.

Flavio had first seen the santos thirty-five years before. They had appeared in this house as if from nowhere, and seeing them now standing in the corner made him suddenly feel as if they were the only remaining members of his family. Unfortunately, of all the family that had passed through his life, these were not relatives he had ever been fond of. They were too old and too coarse and seemed to hold secrets that Flavio knew in his heart he hadn't the slightest inclination to hear.

"I'd forgotten they were here," he said. He turned his head to look at Felix, whose eyes were now closed, beads of saliva at each corner of his mouth. "Don't look at them, Felix, if they bother you. They are only things Ramona used to have."

Flavio had walked into Ramona's house one day and found her washing dishes in the kitchen. It was not long after the death of their brother and not long after their brother's son, Little José, had come to live with her. Behind his sister, crowded together on the small table, were the carved figures, one of which had been merely touched with a knife. All stood with their hands at their breasts, and they stared straight ahead without a smile. One was older than the others, the wood split with age, the paint on her gown and on her face cracked and peeling. Flavio had suddenly felt awkward, as if he had interrupted a conversation between people he did not know.

He had stopped just inside the kitchen, and eventually he had scraped his feet nervously on the floor. When his sister turned to look at him, he had waved his arm and said, "What are those things, Ramona?"

"They are santos, Flavio," Ramona said and turned back to her dishes.

"I know what they are. What are they doing here?"

"They're not doing anything here, Flavio," Ramona said. "I found them and brought them into the house."

"You found them?" He looked at the figures again. He thought that they resembled small children who had grown far too old. "They were lost?"

"No, Flavio," Ramona had said, and in her voice had been the same tone he remembered hearing often as a child. "I found them in the crawl space above the ceiling."

Flavio walked over to the table. On the one that was only partially carved, he could see fresh markings on the wood. At her feet were curled splinters as thin as paper. "This one's just been carved," he said.

"Yes," Ramona said. "That one is Little José's. He works on it a little each day."

"José is making a santo?" Flavio said. Then he reached out and touched the oldest of them, and a chip of paint flaked off and fell to the surface of the table. Where the paint had been, the wood was smooth and black. He looked up at the vigas overhead.

"How did they come to be in the ceiling?"

Ramona wiped her hands on her pants and turned to face her brother. For a moment she said nothing, and then she smiled. "I don't know, Flavio. I only know that they were there for a long time."

It occurred to Flavio that through all the years he had been in this house, just above his head had stood these seven Ladies, cloaked in cobwebs. He looked back at them and wondered what they had been doing up there all that time. Then he realized that this, too, might be something that he would rather not know.

"What made you look up there?" he asked.

Again Ramona paused before speaking. "To see," she said finally, "what was behind the door grandfather had nailed shut."

Flavio turned to her. She was leaning back against the sink, her arms folded beneath her breasts, a slight smile still on her mouth. Flavio thought that though his sister was answering his questions, she was saying nothing.

"What are you going to do with them, Ramona?"

Ramona closed her eyes and shook her head gently. "I don't know, Flavio," she said. "I only know that I'll keep them here."

The santos stayed with Ramona, usually out of Flavio's sight, until she died. And after that they had remained in the house by themselves. How they had come to be in the space above the ceiling or why Ramona had thought to look there was something Flavio and his sister never talked about. Flavio had almost come to think that the seven Ladies had stopped for coffee one morning and chose, for their own reasons, never to leave.

Flavio could feel that Felix's weight had shifted against him and that the old man's breathing had slowed. There wasn't a sound in his sister's house, and he thought that if he didn't get up soon, he would fall asleep and all of this day would be lost.

"We should go, Felix," he said. "To find your son who is probably worried sick." Through the open door he could see the cotton-

wood trees where his truck was parked and, beyond that, the Sangre de Cristo Mountains that sat still and dusty in the heat.

"How can it be so hot?" Flavio said to no one. "I can never remember it like this." Then Flavio felt Felix move his hand and reach
over and cover his own.

In a voice harsh and low and unused, Felix said, "Flavio, I can see
Guadalupe dancing in the snow."

2

Guadalupe García was crazy and even Flavio, who was nine years old, could see that. Worse, she was crazy and old. Flavio wished that he and his friend, Felix, were anywhere else than in her kitchen eating stale tortillas that went down his throat like dirt.

"Sometimes," his mother had told him not so long ago, "there are people and places that are not what they seem. While it's true, hijo, that the García house is no more than mud and sticks like ours, it's also true that the spirits of her whole family are seeped into the walls, and not one of them was ever in their right mind." His mother had been lying in bed, a pillow propped behind her head. She had reached over and taken his arm in her hand. "If some of the children in this village want to throw rocks through the windows of that house, that's their business. You, Flavio, are never to go near there. Do you understand?"

"Yes, Mama," Flavio had answered, without a second thought. He was a boy who knew instinctively that there was an easy way to go through this life, and disobeying either of his parents, or anyone else for that matter, was not a thought that occurred to him. Besides, even looking at the García house from a safe distance made him feel as if he were standing in shadows.

The house Guadalupe García lived in was the same house in which her great-great-great-grandfather, Cristóbal García, had once lived. It was built, as Flavio's mother had said, of mud and sticks and sat on the hill not far from the church. The roof was dirt and—if there was enough rain in the spring—weeds and grasses and even small apricot trees would grow atop the house. Although the walls were thick and the corners of the house were buttressed to the earth, with its small canted doorway and few windows and the way it leaned with the ground, it often seemed to Flavio as if the house was not only on the verge of falling over, but was secretly thinking about leaving the valley.

The house was not only the oldest in the village but also the largest. It sprawled over what seemed to be an entire acre. Rooms branched everywhere off the original structure as if not one of Cristóbal's numerous descendants ever wished to leave home, but just built their own rooms, attaching them haphazardly wherever they liked. There was no semblance of order to the place, and to Flavio it looked as though it had been built by children with whom he would not have had one thing in common.

"There are rooms in this house that I have forgotten," Guadalupe said, looking at Flavio. "If you come back, I'll show you. I'll show you the room where my great-grandmother, Percides García, was kept. When she died in her small bed, the priest left this house and never came back."

Flavio lowered his head and looked down at the table. The surface was built of heavy wood and it was rough and scarred and, in places, burned black. The floor it stood on was hard-packed adobe, and Flavio could see the shape of large rocks beneath it. After so many years of sweeping, the earth itself was being uncovered. He glanced back up at Guadalupe. She was sitting across from him and Felix, and again Flavio thought that he was in the house of a crazy woman. If his mother could have known that, he would have been beaten. It wouldn't have mattered if it had been his Grandmother Rosa who had sent them here.

"Take this, hijo," Rosa had said, handing Flavio a burlap bag of halva beans. "I want you and Felix to go to Guadalupe García's house and give these to her."

Flavio's eyes had widened. "But . . ."

"I know what you are going to say, hijo. That your mother would not have wished this." Flavio's mother had died gently in her sleep the previous winter, and now he and his little brother, José, spent much of their time with Rosa while their father worked.

"Don't worry yourself, hijo," Rosa had said. "Your mother would have understood."

"But Guadalupe García is crazy."

"So?" Rosa had said, and then she had gone back to the dishes in her sink. "Now go."

Guadalupe was sitting with both her hands on the top of the table, smiling in a way that made Flavio feel uncomfortable. Her hair fell far down her shoulders and was white—not gray like Flavio's grandmother's, but white, the color of snow, the color of clean paper. But her face was clear and smooth and her eyes were too wide, as if she were an old woman and a young girl at the same time. She was wearing a nightgown that fell to her knees and her arms were bare. There seemed to be so much of this woman that Flavio wished he were outside with grass and sky around him.

Guadalupe moved a strand of hair away from the side of her face. Then she leaned back in her chair and folded her hands in her lap. "I can tell you boys something that no one else knows," she said.

"What?" Felix asked. He was sitting close beside Flavio and staring at Guadalupe, his mouth full of tortilla. His foot kicked against one leg of his chair.

"It's a long story," she said, staring over the boys' heads and out the open door. "Have you the time to listen?"

"We're not doing nothing, are we, Flavio?" Felix said, and Flavio, who knew that what Guadalupe had asked was more than a question, lowered his head and half closed his eyes. Deep scratches were etched on the table, and with his eyes squinted he thought they looked like rivers that ran everywhere and nowhere.

"My great-great-great-grandfather was Cristóbal García," Guadalupe said. "He was the first man to ever set foot in this valley. And with him came Hipolito Trujillo and Francisco Ramírez."

Hipolito Trujillo stood among the loose rock and dwarf piñon on the slope of a foothill that overlooked the valley below. Standing beside him was his first cousin, Francisco Ramírez, and behind the two of them, his arms wrapped around his stomach, his shoulders slumped, was Cristóbal García. All three were thin and unshaven. Their hair was long and matted. They wore wide-brimmed hats pulled low on their foreheads, and their clothes were stained with dirt and sweat and the fat of small animals they had killed and butchered. Their raw and blistered feet were wrapped in cloth and strips of leather.

"All we could ever wish for is here," Hipolito said. He looked at his cousin and the two men smiled. Then they lowered themselves to their knees and bowed their heads, their arms hanging slack. "By the blessed virgin," Hipolito went on as his eyes filled with water, "this will be our home."

Cristóbal García looked over their heads. Although the valley below was bathed in a soft light from the setting sun and the air was still and warm, he felt chilled, as if the world had turned to ice. We have come too far from where we belong, he thought, and this place does not want us here.

They had set out from the village of Las Sombras twenty-eight days before in search of a place where they and their families could begin a new life. They had left on foot with Francisco's burro to carry their supplies: flour and dried meat, blankets, and a few tools. The burro, which had never been named, was small and so old it slept lying down and had to be hit with sticks each morning to stand. And, as it had gone blind years before, it was led by a thin rope.

At first, they had traveled slowly along the base of the mountains, thinking that surely in a land so empty it would not be difficult to find what they were looking for. "After all," Hipolito had told Francisco and Cristóbal just before leaving Las Sombras, "beyond each ridge lies a valley untouched and waiting for us."

They had stopped in each place they thought held the possibilities of enough water and shelter and pasture. But each time one thing or another was lacking. The creeks, running full in the mountains, suddenly disappeared beneath the ground or became dry, dusty arroyos, or the foothills lay flat and bare, offering no protection from the cold and wind. In one small valley, they had found markings that the Indians had left behind, pots full of colored powder, the hides of deer and bear stretched between trees, and circles of stone with strange clay figures propped up in the center with sticks. Though there had been no sign of life there, they had left quietly and quickly, leaving no trail behind them.

After ten days, they began to wander aimlessly. They would find themselves walking through old snow high up in the mountains or far out in the valley that stretched forever to the north and held only cracked earth and spindly grass.

We are lost, Cristóbal would think, stumbling behind his companions, in a land that cares nothing for us. When they would stop for the night, he would sit huddled close to the fire and voice his fears to Hipolito and Francisco.

"You cannot get lost," Hipolito would say, "where no one has been."

"That is what lost is," Cristóbal would answer.

"To find our way back, we need only to return the way we came."

Cristóbal would shake his head and look into the fire. "We have been walking in circles for days. To go back the way we've come would only bring us here."

Hipolito would lean toward Cristóbal and place his hand on his shoulder. "With luck," he would say, "tomorrow will be the end of our journey. You must have faith, my friend."

But whatever faith Cristóbal once had was now gone. He didn't know what he was doing in the middle of a vast wilderness, especially with two men who spoke to him as if he were a child and who shared none of his fears. Worse, he could barely remember what had prompted him to leave the safety of Las Sombras in the first place. All he truly wanted was to be in his small house surrounded by his eight daughters who loved him dearly and his wife whom he had known all his life and who cared for his children and was never out of sorts. How could a man, he thought, who had so much, give it away for something that couldn't be found?

Each morning, the three men would wake in the cold, their blankets stiff with a thick layer of frost, and again, as he had the night before, Cristóbal would begin to complain. Francisco would look at him is disgust, as if there were little difference between his burro who refused to rise without being beaten and Cristóbal, who sat hunched and motionless by the fire, his blanket wrapped tightly around his shoulders. Hipolito would begin to talk as if Cristóbal had forgotten his past and what had happened in it.

"They were killing the priests," Hipolito would say. "That is why we left, my friend."

And each morning, his head bowed, Cristóbal would stare at the smoldering fire and answer the same. "There are too many priests."

Francisco would grunt and shake his head and feed small sticks into the coals. "They were shot with arrows, like animals," he said. "Then they were beaten with rocks and their clothes were stripped from their bodies and thrown in trees. How could you have forgotten all this, Cristóbal?"

"It is the fault of the priests. If they would leave the Indians to themselves, none of this would have happened, and we would be home in Las Sombras where we belong."

"The priests will never leave the Indians alone," Hipolito would say softly to Cristóbal, and although Hipolito knew that what Cristóbal had said was true, this was the closest he or his cousin would ever come to speaking out against the church.

The village of Las Sombras was at the end of a long trail that wound and twisted and sometimes disappeared altogether south, far into Mexico and beyond. The village sat, with its small, mud plaza and scattered ranchitos, just a few miles west of a large Indian pueblo. Even though they were so near each other, other than chance encounters while gathering wood and the sporadic trading of meat or cloth or seed, there was seldom any contact between the two. It was as if each village had somehow come to believe that the other did not exist, and that if it did, it was in everyone's best interest to ignore that fact. And Cristóbal was right, whenever problems did arise, it always seemed to stem from the doings of the priests.

"As soon as a new priest arrives," Cristóbal would go on, "does he stay in our church where he belongs? No. He takes a large cross and his rosary beads out to the Indians and upsets them." Cristóbal would raise his eyes and look at Hipolito. "Do the Indians come into Las Sombras and force our children to dress in the masks of animals and dance in their dances? Do they make us sit down and tell us stories about their gods? If they did, we, too, would throw rocks at them."

"It is more than just the priests and the Indians," Hipolito would say. "You know that."

"No, I don't know that any longer."

"Why must we talk about the same thing each morning?" Francisco would ask. "And in the evening, we have it again." Then he would walk away and stand looking off into the distance at nothing.

Hipolito and Francisco had known Cristóbal nearly all their lives. The walls of their houses were built against and grew out of each other's and their children, who were numerous and close in age, lived as if all shared the same family. Of the three men, Cristóbal was always the most outspoken, especially when it came to the village. Hipolito and Francisco often agreed with his complaints, but it was one thing to hear his words within the village and another to hear them in a place where each step took them farther from home. Cristóbal's words not only were a plea for them to abandon their search, but also made Hipolito and Francisco feel as if their reasons for leaving Las Sombras in the first place were only a trick they had played on themselves.

"It was you, Cristóbal, who first mentioned leaving the village," Francisco would say over his shoulder, and Hipolito could hear the anger in his voice. "Besides, do you not remember the winter two years ago?"

Following a summer of drought where the corn was empty in its husks and the alfalfa grew coarse and stunted, that winter had brought snow and cold and disease to Las Sombras all at once. Snow began to fall in late October, and it continued for months, until the houses sat buried to their roofs and everything outside the village became just a memory. When it wasn't snowing, a cold came to the valley so intense that tree limbs cracked with ice and the chimneys could not draw air.

Soon after the first snowstorm, villagers, especially the old and the very young, began to fall ill with a sickness that dulled their minds, took the strength from their bodies, and finally brought on a fever that rose so high they would forget how to breathe. Those who died, among them Francisco's young son Pablito and his daughter Sophia, were wrapped in thin cloth and carried to the plaza. There, one of the priests would crouch stiffly against the wind, say a brief prayer, and then cross himself before hurrying back to his room beside the church.

The dead were placed together on the ground beneath a large cottonwood, and there they remained under so many feet of snow until late in the spring when the earth was no longer like stone. Livestock not brought into shelter froze standing in the fields, and those that didn't were butchered for food. Seed stored for the following season was ground between rocks and boiled in melted snow and fed to children.

When the weather finally broke in mid-April, the hollow-eyed people of the village straggled out from their homes and found only mud and slush and the dead, stacked on the plaza like cords of wood.

The following summer, Cristóbal began to complain bitterly and incessantly about life in Las Sombras. While Cristóbal had always complained about one thing or another, Hipolito and Francisco knew that he had no real intention of ever leaving Las Sombras. But what he said made the thought of remaining in the village unbearable.

They would listen to Cristóbal and agree with him that there were other places in this country where they could choose the best land for themselves—where there was enough pasture and game that a winter such as the one that had just passed would not be so crippling, and where they could have just one priest who would stay with them and not cause trouble by foolishly bothering the Indians. Hipolito and Francisco would take what they heard from Cristóbal back to their families. Almost without realizing it, they began to plan to leave Las Sombras for a place that would be their own.

After the murder of the three priests, rumors began to spread that the pueblo and other pueblos in the south were threatening to unite. When they did, they would rise up as one and drive the Spanish and their God that could not mind his own business from the entire territory. Although these rumors had occasionally surfaced in the past, it was what finally prompted Hipolito and Francisco to leave. By then, there was no doubt in their minds that Cristóbal would go with them.

Five days after the priests were buried, the three men left Las Sombras before dawn. The night before, Cristóbal had told his wife, Ignacia, that he would go only a little ways with his friends so that they would not become lost and, with luck, would be back by nightfall. Ignacia had helped him pack his things, and before he left, she had taken his hand in both of hers and smiled. "Be careful, Cristóbal," she had said. "We will wait up tonight until you return. Never forget that we love you."

"Eee," Felix said suddenly, startling Flavio so much that he jerked in his chair. "I wish I was Cristóbal García." He reached out to the plate in the center of the table and broke off a piece of hard tortilla. "Then I could have been the first García to ever be here."

Flavio had been listening to Guadalupe in a state that was close to sleep. He had almost forgotten where he was and had followed the tone of Guadalupe's voice as if it were a hand that was leading him. He looked over at Felix. "Don't you listen?" he asked.

"Cristóbal García was crazy. And even if he wasn't, every morning he was covered with frost and he didn't even have any shoes."

"So?" Felix said, chewing his tortilla with his mouth half open. "You don't know everything. Besides, I'm a García, too. Maybe Cristóbal García was my grandpa."

There were Garcías scattered throughout the village and, as far as Flavio knew, not one was related to Guadalupe. "I think Cristóbal should have stayed home," Flavio said. "Whenever someone says be careful, something bad is going to happen."

"Don't worry, Flavio," Felix said. "Nothing bad is going to happen."

"What about the priests being shot with arrows and the frozen cows?" Flavio said. "That was bad."

"It's just a story, Flavio. Besides, it's almost over."

"They walked all over this valley," Guadalupe said. She was leaning back in her chair, staring through the space between Flavio and Felix. She was still smiling slightly, and when Flavio glanced at her, he could see that her nightgown had pulled a little off of one shoulder. He stared at her for only a second and then quickly lowered his eyes.

"The three of them," Guadalupe said. "Where you boys live, Cristóbal and Hipolito and Francisco once walked. They breathed the same air you do and cut fence posts from juniper that still grow in these hills." Then she moved her eyes and seemed to look at Flavio and Felix at the same time. "This is just the beginning of the story," she said.

"There is room here not just for us," Hipolito said excitedly, "but for a whole village." He pointed at the mountains. "Look at the aspens running in the canyons. There is so much water, and the peaks are still white from last year's snow."

The valley was cradled on three sides by low-lying foothills and on the east by the Sangre de Cristo Mountains. It is sheltered from the wind, Hipolito went on, and the mountains reach high enough to catch the clouds that bring snow for irrigation and rain in the summers.

Three large creeks flowed out of deep ravines and joined together at the base of the mountains. From there, the water wound its way through the center of the valley. High grass grew everywhere, and Hipolito and Francisco could see where deer and turkey had beaten down trails when coming to feed.

Although a part of Cristóbal could see the beauty of this place, he felt only uneasiness at how jagged the mountains were and how they seemed to loom over the valley rather than protect it. He didn't like how the twisted junipers and thick cottonwoods grew along the creek. They seemed to be hiding something and reminded him of the shadows he sometimes dreamed of at night. As he stood on the foothill amid the small piñon and scrub oak, two things went through his mind and then left before he could fully grasp them. One was that he could never live in this place, and the other was that he would never leave.

They camped beneath the limbs of a tall juniper where the grass was not so high. The burro was staked near the creek, close enough that coyotes or the small wolves that roamed in packs would stay away. Cristóbal had wished to spend the night in the foothills rather than even set foot in the valley, but Hipolito and Francisco had chided him and talked to him until finally he had followed them out of the hills and into grass that came to his waist.

They ate in silence the same meal they had eaten for the past twenty-eight days: a tortilla with dried rabbit meat and beans that had been heated over the fire. Occasionally, a slight breeze would move the flames, and the shadows made it seem to Cristóbal as if the juniper itself was moving. He would close his eyes and tell himself that he would be here for just one night. In the morning he would leave. By the time he reached Las Sombras, he would not even remember this place.

Hipolito finished eating and put his plate on the ground. He leaned forward and tossed a small branch on the fire. Sparks flew into the darkness.

"When it's light," he said, "two of us will begin the walk home. The third will remain here and wait for us to return. If we leave the burro and take only what we need, we can be in the village in six days and then back here eight days after that."

Cristóbal stopped eating and looked at Hipolito. "We should all leave," he said. "There is no reason anyone should stay here."

"It's what we planned before leaving Las Sombras," Francisco said. "If we found what we were looking for, then one of us would remain behind to claim it as our own."

Cristóbal, who had no intention of remaining anywhere and who wished only to live the rest of his life in Las Sombras, glanced at Francisco. "Who would ever come here?" he said. Besides, he thought, this valley wants no one. It only wants to be left alone.

"Those were your words, Cristóbal," Francisco said. "You spoke them over and over in Las Sombras."

The burro suddenly let out a deep sigh. Cristóbal watched as it lowered itself to its knees and lay down in the grass. When he looked back at Francisco, he said, "I will tell your wife and children that you are well and miss them."

Francisco smiled and said, "You think it is me who is to stay behind?"

It had been Hipolito who had led them from Las Sombras and even if many of his decisions had been poor and cost them days and miles, still, it was he that Cristóbal and Francisco had followed. Cristóbal had no desire to be led out of this valley and into the wilderness by Francisco, who only made decisions about how much his burro should carry, which was usually little, or what they would eat at night, which was always the same.

"Cristóbal is right, Francisco," Hipolito said, looking at his cousin. "You are the one who should stay."

Sometimes at night, after Cristóbal had finally fallen asleep, Hipolito and Francisco would sit close to each other and talk in whispers. As they had traveled farther and farther away from Las Sombras, both had come to fear that Cristóbal was losing his mind. He would wake every morning refusing to go on, and when he did, he would talk to himself and stare at the ground as he walked. At times, as he stumbled behind with the burro, Hipolito and Francisco would hear him moaning as if weeping. Neither knew what to do about their companion, and some nights when Cristóbal was more upset than usual one of them would remain awake by the fire until dawn. Hipolito had told his cousin he was afraid that if Cristóbal woke he would wander off by himself and who knew what would happen to him then. What troubled Hipolito the most, however, and what he did not tell Francisco, was that he realized once they returned to Las Sombras Cristóbal would never leave again. It was Cristóbal's own words spoken before they had left the village that haunted Hipolito.

"My daughters," Cristóbal had said, "and your sons, Hipolito, and yours, Francisco, will be raised together, and when they grow older they'll marry. Our families will be as one, and our descendants will receive what we found. Then, truly, we will have a place that is ours and where our names are known."

Hipolito would sit up through the night and watch Cristóbal sleeping fitfully. He knew in his heart that they needed Cristóbal's family far more than they needed Cristóbal himself. He would sit by the embers of the fire, and a blackness would come over him as if he, too, knew that what they were looking for was already lost.

Hipolito looked across the fire at Francisco. "We will be gone only a few weeks," he said. "When we return, all our families will be with us. We'll bring the corn and the grain and the hides we've stored, and once here, we will build a shelter to protect us through the first winter. Our sons will hunt deer and turkey, and the meat will feed us until spring. And if, by chance, Francisco, anyone should wander into this valley while we're gone," and here Hipolito turned to Cristóbal, "you are to tell them that this place is ours and that it is named Guadalupe, in honor of Our Lady."

Hours after Hipolito and Francisco had fallen asleep, Cristóbal lay awake, staring up into the limbs of the juniper. Through them he could glimpse the stars and the sliver of a new moon. He could hear the sound of the creek. Even the wail of coyotes at the other end of the valley now seemed comforting to him. For the first time in weeks, Cristóbal felt at peace. He thought of his wife and how he longed to be near her. He thought of his eight daughters and how it would be to hold each one, even the youngest, who was but an infant and only cried when he came near her. When he finally fell asleep, a thin mist of clouds had hidden the moon. In his mind Cristóbal saw himself walking into Las Sombras, and all about him was his family.

Cristóbal didn't wake the next morning until it was light. The sky was a pale white and looked thin and fragile to him, as if it were something that might break. He lay quietly for a moment staring into the limbs of the juniper, and then he wondered why Hipolito had not already roused him to begin the journey home.

"If we travel like this," he said aloud, "we will not be back home until spring." He smiled and when his words went unanswered, he turned his head. He could see that the fire had burned out long ago and that the burro was still asleep in the grass, his sides heaving slowly with labored breaths. He could also see that not only were

Hipolito and Francisco nowhere about, but their packs and their blankets were gone.

Cristóbal threw off his blanket and sat up. Other than depressions in the grass where Hipolito and Francisco had slept, the place looked as though just one man had ever been there, not three. Beside the ashes of the fire were a small pot and one plate and spoon. Cristóbal's pack was at the foot of his bedding as were the hatchet and the one gun they had carried with them from Las Sombras. Everything else was gone. For a few seconds Cristóbal did nothing but stare about him in disbelief, his eyes wide and his mouth half open. Then he leaped to his feet and ran out of the trees and into the meadow.

All he could see in every direction was grass that stood tall and motionless. He cupped his hands to his mouth and yelled Hipolito's name. A large flock of ravens picked up in the foothills and then disappeared up a canyon. He yelled again and again, looking for movement in the piñons. He yelled until his voice was harsh and until the sun had risen high up above the mountains.

It took Hipolito and Francisco seven days to make the walk from the valley of Guadalupe back to Las Sombras. They had traveled as quickly as possible, leaving each morning in the dark and walking until long after the sun had finally set. Neither spoke of Cristóbal or of what they had done to him. Francisco, because for the most part he was relieved that he no longer had to listen to Cristóbal's constant complaining, and Hipolito because he could not even bear to speak Cristóbal's name. He envisioned his friend lost in his own confusion in the valley they had found, and he knew that the responsibility was his alone. The only thing that eased his mind was the thought that if they returned to Guadalupe quickly enough, all could, in the end, be set right. Unfortunately for Hipolito and Cristóbal, that is not what happened.

When the two men walked into Las Sombras, not only did they find everyone who had lived there gone, but the entire village had been burned. Each house was no more than charred adobe, the walls lying in heaps or at best half standing. Ceilings had collapsed and the latillas and vigas were only black ashes. The sole structure unharmed was the church. It stood in the middle of all the debris as if it had left the village when the fires had begun and not returned until it was safe.

On the thick plank doors of the church was nailed a piece of white cloth and on it was written:

We have left this village for the safety of Santa Madre. All those who read this must know that the church has abandoned these lands and this territory and all those who live in it.

In peace,
Padre Martinez

Weeks later, in a howling blizzard, Hipolito Trujillo and Francisco Ramírez stumbled into Santa Madre and began the search for their families. In the small valley of Guadalupe, which lay so many miles to the north, Cristóbal García stood in snow that came to his waist. He had lost his mind not long after Hipolito and Francisco had left, and all that had once been part of his life was now lost to him.

3

Flavio and his wife, Martha, had been married fifty-six years
when Flavio came home one morning to find her dead on the floor
of the kitchen. He had just returned from irrigating and had taken
his boots off by the front door and hung up his cap. Then he had
walked through the quiet house to the kitchen. When he saw his
wife sprawled on the floor, his first thought was that while he had
been working peacefully in the sun, his wife had gone through
something terrible all by herself.

He had hurried to her side and crouched down. Her dress had
pulled up above her thighs and so he pulled it back down to cover
her legs. Then he touched her face with the back of his hand. Her
skin was still warm, but beneath it he could feel a chill like a pocket
of cold water.

"Martha," Flavio had whispered, as he shook her shoulder

gently. He moved her hair from her face. Her eyes were half open and her mouth was slack. "Martha," he said again.

Martha Montoya had been a small, round, quiet woman who, much like her own mother, had been blessed with a good nature. She had been an only child, and her mother, besides having an even temper and a soft smile, had entered the world speechless. So the sounds Martha remembered of her childhood were not voices, but the sounds of things. She remembered the scraping of spoons, the dry limbs of juniper cracking in the woodstove, the swish of her mother's dress as she moved through the house.

Martha's father was much older than his wife, and he had left the village in search of work far to the north before Martha was born. He was a miner and had left on foot one morning, carrying with him only a worn leather bag that held a few tools, a change of clothes, and a framed picture of his wife. No one in the village ever saw him again, but on the first Monday of every month a letter would arrive for Martha. In it would be a few dollars in coins and a note, the words printed in a childlike hand on yellow paper. It almost always read:

To my daughter, Martha,

I am fine and still far away
and the work I do is very hard.
Always I think of you and your mother
and of the day I will finally come home.
I know you will be a good girl
And in my prayers I am with you.

Your loving father

Martha and her mother would sit at the kitchen table as Martha read the words aloud. They would sit close together and count the coins, and then Martha would take a pencil and paper and write to her father. She would tell him how far she walked to school each morning and if it was cold or windy or if there had been snow. She would tell him how she and her mother made tortillas and biscochitos and, in the autumn, picked gooseberries and sour cherries and apricots for jam. Even if she was ill, she told him that she was well so that he would not worry. She said that she missed him and hoped that he would finish his work soon and come home to them. Later, at night, Martha would lie awake in bed and see her father far away, with a piece of paper clasped in his hand.

The last letter Martha received from her father was the day after her mother's death following a long illness. Martha was a grown woman herself, married just one month to young Flavio Montoya, and she had found the letter on the small table beside her mother's bed.

To my daughter, Martha,

I have grown old and I fear
that this is my last letter to you.
And if that is so, I want to say that
I am so proud to have you as my daughter.
I pray that you will always lead your life well
And never forget me.

Your loving father

Beside the open letter on the table were scattered a few coins and a pencil.

In all of Martha's fifty-six years of marriage to Flavio, she had not one regret. She had married a man who cared for his cows and kept the house in good repair and who never once raised his hand in anger. While it was true the two of them seldom spoke of things of importance, other than the lack of rain or a cow that would not grow, the silence in the house comforted her. She would listen to the sounds of their forks while they ate or the hiss of the beans on the stove, and she would feel that the fullness in her life always came from the things not said.

Each morning, she rose with Flavio to prepare his breakfast: eggs and chile and a warm tortilla with butter and honey. She would drink a cup of coffee by herself and look out the window at the apple trees that grew along their drive. Then she would begin cooking dinner. When it was done she would cover the pan with foil and leave it on the counter to cool. She would straighten the kitchen then and sweep the floors and make the bed. In the summer months, she tended a small garden near the house where she grew corn and yellow peppers and small red potatoes.

She sometimes thought that her life with Flavio was like a season, although she wasn't exactly sure just what season it was. Not spring with its winds and late snows, or autumn when the aspens streak gold across the mountains and the light is too thin. Martha's life was more like the thick heat of summer, or the flat frozen days of winter when it seems as if nothing will ever change.

If there had been any difficulty in their marriage, it was the absence of children, and even that was not for lack of trying. In truth, she and Flavio had tried so hard and so often to conceive a child that eventually their efforts became a habit. Far past middle age the two of them would make love quietly and Martha would close her eyes, her hands light on Flavio's hips, and listen to the sound of his breath. Sometimes she would cry softly at the thought of Flavio's seed swimming lost inside her, and Flavio, who seldom knew the right thing to say, would pat her arm awkwardly until they both fell asleep.

On the morning of her death, Martha was preparing Flavio's favorite food, enchiladas with cilantro, when her heart caught in her chest. She stood by the stove for a moment as if waiting for someone, and then she felt her knees buckle. As she fell slowly to the floor, she thought that there was something she should tell her husband, but she couldn't quite grasp what it was. Her eyes closed and she could smell the scent of garlic. Through the open window she heard the wind moving in the leaves of the apple trees.

Two days after Martha's death, her Rosary was held at the church. Flavio sat alone in the front pew, just a few feet before the altar. He was dressed in a black suit that was a size too small for him and black boots that pinched his feet. His head was bowed slightly and his hands were in his lap.

Behind him, the church was filled with his friends and their families, but among them was not one relative of his or Martha's. For the first time, he realized that somehow he had managed to outlive his entire family.

Martha lay in her coffin on the altar, and as the priest led everyone in prayer, Flavio raised his head and looked at his wife. He could see that her eyes were closed. Her hands were folded together on her chest. She was wearing a soft white dress that had once been her mother's, and her hair was brushed in a way that Flavio couldn't remember. She looked younger in her death and also different, as if she were someone he had once known but then forgotten.

The thick wood planks beneath his feet had worn to a shine from people kneeling for so many years, and he remembered all the other Rosaries for the dead he had attended. Then it occurred to him that when the priest was done, everyone in the church would pass by him to give their condolences. He had no idea what to say to so many people. Flavio suddenly wished he was in his fields staring at the mountains, listening to the water in his ditch and knowing, without thinking, that his wife was home waiting for him to come for dinner.

For months after Martha's death, it appeared to everyone in Guadalupe that nothing had really changed in Flavio's life. He still rose early each morning and went to his fields. He kept the house clean and neat. He even watered and weeded the small garden that Martha had planted in the spring. The talk in the village was that it was good Flavio had recovered so quickly from the death of his wife, rather than complaining constantly and weeping by the side of the road as Onecimo Romero had done, making everyone else feel bad. It was best to let go of the dead, most people thought, not let them hang around and cause trouble.

At one time, Flavio would have readily agreed with all of this. He had always been a man who thought little about things, content to go through his life much as one of his cows would have, wherever his feet took him, which was usually from his field back to his house. Unfortunately, although it was true that on the surface Flavio appeared to be fine, not only had he quietly become lost, as if in a place he no longer knew, but he began to dream without sleeping.

Flavio would be in his fields with his cap pulled down low on his forehead, his arms loose, his shovel leaning against his body. He would stand by the ditch and suddenly he would find himself having long conversations with people who were not there. What made it worse was that when he was done visiting with these people, he would barely remember just who it was he'd been talking to, let alone what it was they'd been talking about. He would think that he had dozed while standing, but when he glanced about he would see that the field was wet and his boots were stained with mud and water.

Flavio began to feel as if he were living in two places at the same time. Although he took some pleasure in the knowledge that his body was smart enough to keep irrigating in his absence, it made him uneasy to think that his mind could leave without him knowing it. All that would remain with him when he came to his senses was a faint memory that was more like a scent. Sometimes it was the vision of his father splitting wood in the winter, his breath a cloud, his large hands chafed, or his brother walking backward as an infant, his eyes seeing only where he'd been. Sometimes what he could remember was only something he had once heard: the sound of coyotes in the winter when the air is dead. The harshness in his sister's voice when they were children. His grandmother calling his name just before dark. Flavio was living in the past, and the present had become lost to him.

On a day in late autumn, Flavio left his field earlier than usual. He was tired and there was a deep ache in his bones. He thought that rather than stand in his alfalfa and feel poorly, he would go home and rest. Although it was not cold that day, there was a hollowness in the air and a thin feel to the warmth. The leaves on the aspens and cottonwoods had already fallen, and the gray patches of woods high up on the mountains wavered like smoke.

As Flavio climbed into his pickup, he realized two seasons had passed since Martha's death and he could barely remember either one. He also realized that October had come and gone and he was still irrigating plants that had no use for water, but only wanted a little peace before the onset of winter.

Halfway home, as he drove through the center of town, Flavio began to cry. As tears ran down his face, he suddenly found himself making strange gulping noises. When the road became blurred, he slowed the truck and then lowered his head so no one passing by would see him in such a state. He could not remember the last time he had wept, and a mile later when his tears ended so abruptly, it seemed to him as if it had happened to someone else, some other old man driving alone in his pickup.

Outside his house, Flavio stood in front of Martha's small garden. Although there was not a weed to be seen anywhere, the corn and peppers and potatoes had been left unharvested. The stalks on the corn were yellow and brittle, and they moved slightly even with no wind. He would take a nap, he told himself. When he woke, he would come back outside and dig up the potatoes his wife had planted just before she died.

When Flavio pushed open his front door, he saw a shoebox sitting in the middle of the room. It was a gray box with a faded blue lid. The last time he had seen it, it had been sitting on the top shelf of Martha's closet. It had once held a pair of small red shoes with slender black straps that Martha had ordered from a city in the east just before their marriage. She had worn them only once, then put them away, saying they made her feel foolish, not like a woman who was about to be married. She had taken the shoes off carefully, placed them back in the box, and covered them with delicate white paper. Then she had placed the box on a shelf in her closet, where it had sat for five decades.

Flavio wondered if someone had entered his house while he was gone. If they had, why had they done nothing more than move a box that was worthless from one place to another? Then it occurred to him it was possible he had actually moved the box without remembering, for himself to find later. The thought made him even more tired than he was, so he shook his head and closed his eyes.

Four hours later, Flavio woke on the couch in the living room. It was almost sunset. The light coming in the windows was pale and flat. He sat up slowly and brought his hands to his face, feeling weak and tired, as if he hadn't slept at all. He took a deep breath and rubbed his eyes with his fingers and realized that the day was nearly gone. He realized, too, that all the evening held for him were two tortillas, cold beans, and the same magazine he read each night before falling asleep. His eyes fell on the shoebox a few feet away. It bothered him again that it hadn't stayed on the shelf in the closet where it belonged. I'll put it away, he thought, pushing himself up off the couch, and then see about dinner.

Flavio knelt beside the box and took off the lid. What he saw inside was not a layer of thin white paper covering Martha's shoes, but six neat stacks of envelopes that completely filled the box.

"What is this?" Flavio said aloud. "Where are Martha's shoes?"

The top layer of the envelopes that faced him were all identical. There was a stamp in the upper right-hand corner and printed on each of them in Martha's handwriting was:

To Flavio Montoya
Box 17
Guadalupe, New Mexico

"What is this, Martha?" Flavio said again, as he reached down to pick one up. He slid his finger along the seal and opened it.

To my husband, Flavio
April 3, 1996

The apple trees are full
of blossoms this morning, and
I can hear the noise of so many bees.
It is a warm sweet morning.

your loving wife, Martha

Flavio stared blankly at the writing. His mouth was half open and he squinted, trying to comprehend not only the meaning of the words, but the fact that it was his wife who had written them. In all their years together he and Martha had seldom shared words such as these. Besides that, he couldn't remember her writing anything other than a recipe or a few, hurried lines on a pad of paper that, more often than not, said, "Flavio, I have gone to the store and will be back soon, Martha."

Flavio placed the letter he had read on the floor. Then he reached into the box and took one from another stack.

To my husband, Flavio
January 6, 1952

When you come home tonight,
I will tell you I am
carrying our baby.
Be careful, my husband,
it is so cold.

your loving wife, Martha

Flavio's breath caught in his throat. He could remember that day forty-nine years ago. His cows had broken their fences, and he had found them walking the road at the south end of the village as if they had a place to go. It had taken him all day to chase them back where they belonged and then to fix the fence. By the time he had returned home, it was dark and his toes were swollen and purple from the cold. Martha had greeted him at the door, her face flushed. "I am pregnant, Flavio," she had said laughing.

"We made love that night," Flavio said out loud. Afterward, they had lain close together and stared at the ceiling, neither of them talking. It was a few days later that Martha found out she'd been mistaken.

Flavio put the letter on the floor with the one he had already read. Once more he reached into the box.

To my husband, Flavio
September 1, 1945

Today I buried my poor red shoes
beneath the apple tree.
When I told this to Grandmother Rosa,
she smiled and said that maybe an
empty box is of more value than one
with shoes.
We have been married one month and
it is like a second.

your loving wife, Martha

Suddenly, Flavio found himself standing. He ran into the kitchen and filled the coffeepot with water and enough grounds to make mud. He stood impatiently by the counter while the coffee brewed, every so often peering into the other room at the box on the floor. He ate a cold tortilla and, between bites, told the coffee to hurry. When it was finally done, he took the whole pot and a cup and went back into the living room.

Flavio began reading backward through his life with Martha, and in each letter he, too, had something to say. More often than not, he would remember what Martha had written about, but when he didn't, he would shake his head and say, "Eee, you should have told me." Once he began arguing with a letter and when he heard how loud his voice was, he lowered it to a whisper and chided Martha for making him so angry.

Flavio read and talked until it was dark and then on through the night. When morning came, not only was Martha truly gone, but she was all about him. She was sitting on the sofa, her hands together in her lap. She was in the bedroom straightening the blankets and folding his clothes. She was in the kitchen at the small table by the window with a pencil and a piece of yellow paper. She was in the air Flavio breathed. From that moment on, although Flavio never stopped dreaming while awake, whatever it was he had lost in the months after Martha's death, she had returned to him.

Inside Ramona's old house, Flavio and Felix sat together on the sofa. They leaned heavily against each other and Felix's hand still lay upon Flavio's. Flavio's chin had sunk down low on his chest and he was staring blankly at the floor. At first glance, the two of them looked more like brothers napping on a warm morning than anything else. Suddenly, Flavio took in a sharp breath. He blinked rapidly and then raised his eyes and looked out the front door. A slight breeze had picked up, and the leaves on the cottonwoods stirred. The door creaked a little back and forth. He could feel a cramped muscle in his neck and he moved his head gently until it eased.

"I must have fallen asleep, Felix," he said out loud. And for a second he almost remembered what it was he had dreamed, or thought he dreamed, and then it flew away from him. With a groan he pushed himself up to the edge of the sofa and sat there quietly for a moment. His hand still lay beneath Felix's and he could feel the constant trembling of Felix's fingers. He spit out some air and shook his head. "I dreamed you talked, Felix," he said. "That's what happens when you stand in the sun for so long. And then to be in this house."

Flavio rose to his feet and stretched out his back. The day outside looked hotter than ever and, worse, now a dry wind was beginning to blow. In his mind, Flavio could see Ramona's alfalfa field wilting and dying in such heat while he sat inside doing nothing. "I should take you home, Felix," he said. "Back to Pepe where you belong."

Behind him, Felix leaned forward and reached out and touched the back of Flavio's leg. "My feet hurt too much, Flavio," he said, "and I don't feel so good."

And, without thinking, Flavio answered, "That's what you get, hombre, for walking through the mountains at your age." Then, he fell silent.

A sudden chill ran through Flavio's body so deep that his legs nearly buckled. The rasp of Felix's breath filled the room, and again Flavio felt the brush of Felix's hand. As if he were still a child, Flavio thought that what was happening couldn't be and that it was possible one of them had died while dozing on the sofa. What he should do, he thought, was walk out of the house and get in his truck and drive home—even if it was he who was dead. He actually took a step toward the door before he stopped and turned around.

At first, not one thing about Felix seemed to be any different. His hands still shook, his back was badly bent, and he seemed to be no more than bones inside his clothes. But, now, his eyes stared straight up at Flavio without wavering.

"Where have I been, Flavio?" Felix asked, and this time, though his words were still harsh, they came out of his mouth in a way Flavio remembered.

"Felix," Flavio said, and his voice broke. "Are you back, Felix?"

"I don't feel so good, Flavio."

"I can't believe my ears," Flavio said. "You're talking, Felix. It's like a miracle." He grinned and suddenly felt like running in small circles about the room. "Wait until Pepe finds out. Wait until the village hears. It's so good to see you again, Felix."

"Where have I been, Flavio?' Felix asked again.

Flavio looked down at him. "When?" he asked.

"When?" Felix asked. His eyes moved away from Flavio and went nowhere. "I don't know when," he said. Then he began to cry silently. Tears ran down his face and, mixed with blood and dirt, dropped to the floor.

Flavio took the two steps back to the sofa and sat down. He put his hand on Felix's leg and gave it a little pat. "It's okay, Felix," he said. "Quiet yourself now. You've been sick for a long time, but now you're better. I don't blame you for being so upset."

Felix shook his head. He opened his mouth to say something, but all that came out was a cough so deep and full of phlegm and tears that Flavio clenched his teeth and shut his eyes until it passed.

"A little water," Felix said. "I could drink a little water, Flavio."

"Oh sí," Flavio said. He picked up the glass from the floor and held it to Felix's mouth. "There," he said, "but don't drink too much, my friend," and he took the glass away.

Felix sat there swallowing water and air. Then he turned his head, and the two men looked at each other. "I'm so happy to see you, Felix," Flavio said, his own eyes filled with water.

"It was a pot that made me sick," Felix said. "The big pot that my grandmother had cooked in. This pot had been in my family since before I was born, and it was one I always trusted."

Felix talked staring straight ahead, his words not much more than ragged air. Sometimes, as he told his story, he began to tremble so badly that Flavio would put his arm around his shoulder as if to hold him together.

It was early on a late winter morning that Felix had his stroke. It was still dark out and the only one in the café was Paco Duran, who was sitting by himself, smoking and drinking coffee by the front window. Outside, old snow was crusted along the side of the road and the moon was shining in the melted ice on the highway. Felix's son, Pepe, was rolling out tortillas in the kitchen, and Felix had just begun to prepare his beans. A small radio on one of the counters was turned on low, and as Pepe sprinkled flour, he sang a little with the music.

Felix had slept badly the night before, dreaming of things that disturbed him and that he couldn't remember. He could feel grit beneath his eyelids and his shirt felt too heavy and too close to his skin. He thought that after he put on a large pot of water for his beans, he would step outside to feel the cold air on his face.

As he took the pot down from the hook on one of the vigas, he glanced inside it to make sure that Pepe had cleaned it well the night before. The light from the ceiling danced on the bottom of the pot, and in that instant, with the sound of Pepe's singing in his ears, Felix's life passed before his eyes.

"It was like eating," Felix said to Flavio, "and in one bite is your whole life."

He saw his grandparents, bent and stiff and always arguing about anything, walking together on the path that led to the church. He saw his mother and father cooking beans and tamales and canning chiles in their own kitchen, and he understood the look his mother would sometimes give his father when she would bend over to pick up something she had dropped. He saw his wife, Belinda, as a young girl in school before he had ever kissed her or touched her face and then, later, on their wedding night when he knew in his heart there was no such thing as death. He even saw his sad little baby with the twisted foot that Belinda had lost giving birth to, and he remembered the sound of Belinda's crying, which he had worried would never end.

Felix saw things that he thought he had forgotten. Then, with the pot still in his hands, he turned to his son. "Pepe," he said, "my life is too full"—although the words his son heard him say were,

"Your mother's breasts, hijo, are the reason I cook so well." Then, as Pepe stood shocked into silence, and without even the thought of catching himself, Felix fell to the linoleum floor.

Felix stopped talking and looked up at Flavio. "That's what happened to me, Flavio," he said. His head was going through such a myriad of motions that he appeared to be shaking it. "I can still see my grandmother cooking chickens in that pot."

Flavio didn't know what to say. He had never seen anything in the bottom of a pot but rust and old food—which, it now occurred to him, was probably a blessing. He also thought that if he saw all of his life at once, there would be little to see.

"You said eight years?" Felix asked.

"Sí," Flavio told him. "Eight years, Felix, and in all that time you never said a word."

Felix looked down at his hands. They were filthy and marked with scratches and dried blood. He turned one over. "This doesn't even look like my hand."

Before his stroke, Felix had been a solid man. His hands had been thick and callused from cooking and his arms strong from lifting. If his hands had ever been dirty, the dirt had come from food, which bothered no one. There was little that resembled that Felix in the one now sitting beside Flavio.

"What was it like, Felix?" Flavio asked.

"How should I know?" Felix said. "I was asleep. You should be telling me these things. What's happened here since my stroke?"

For a moment Flavio was quiet. He thought that in the eight years Felix had been somewhere else nothing had changed. "A lot of the viejos are gone now," he said slowly. "And my sister, Ramona, died también. And Martha. Many of our old friends."

Felix looked down at his hands without speaking. Finally, he said, "This is too hard, Flavio. I'm sorry you had to go through that alone. Martha was a good friend to my wife, and she could cook biscochitos like no one else. They were so soft I remember they tasted like warm snow. Eight years is a long time. And what of the village?"

"The village?" To Flavio, the village was not a thing that ever really changed. It was something that just was and always would be. But not even he was blind to all the things that had been happening in Guadalupe and in the hills around the village.

People from other places had begun to move north out of Las Sombras and into the mountains surrounding the valley. From the center of town you could look into the foothills and on the ridges, where the land was full of rocks and there was never enough water, stood sprawling adobes. No one knew who these people were or what had brought them to such a place, and sometimes there was talk, especially at Tito's Bar after too many beers, that all of these outsiders should be burned out and sent back where they came from. They had no respect for the old ways and drove through the village as if it were just a stretch of highway to get somewhere else. Besides, the men in Tito's Bar would say, that land was once ours. It was where our grandfathers cut fence posts and firewood and picked piñon and hunted deer and elk.

But Flavio had lived his whole life in the village, and he knew that what he heard people complaining about could also be said about many of them. It was obvious to him, too, that the hills would still be empty if the people in Guadalupe had not sold their land.

On top of all that was the copper mine that sat just five miles to the east. The village had fed off of it for so many years that few kept cows anymore and most fields were left fallow. All of these things made Flavio feel as if the village were shrinking and becoming less of what it once was and more of something he couldn't understand.

He didn't know how to answer Felix's question. So, he shrugged and said, "The village is the same as always, Felix. But maybe you shouldn't hear so much all at once. You should take it easy for a while and get strong. Soon things will be as they were."

"I don't know, Flavio," Felix said. "I think the fire could be a big problem."

Flavio grunted and jerked his head back. "Qué fire, hombre? There's no fire."

"No?" Felix said. "Maybe you're right, but I have a bad feeling that already the mountains are full of smoke."

Flavio stared at Felix for a moment. Then he took his arm from around Felix's shoulder. Suddenly, he felt exhausted and empty. He had spent the morning tricking himself into believing that if you went backward in life everything would be the same. Half of what Felix had said was crazy, and here he was, calmly listening to talk of pots and fires as if these were things he heard every day. Who knew what Felix had gone through in the eight years of sitting hunched over in the café. Flavio pushed himself to the edge of the sofa and stood up.

"I guess we should go now, Felix," he said.

"I don't blame you for not believing me, Flavio," Felix said. He was staring past Flavio though his head drooped so low that his face almost touched his knees.

The door creaked in the breeze, and Flavio felt a vague disquiet come over him. Hanging on the wall above the sofa were two of Ramona's paintings. One was of a washed-out arroyo, a trail of muddy water running past bone-white rocks. The other was a picture of three horses standing so still in the rain that they seemed dead. Flavio thought Felix looked more like one of Ramona's pictures than anything else, and one that she probably would have enjoyed painting.

"Go outside and look for me, Flavio," Felix said. "Let me rest for a little while."

Flavio stood looking at Felix as he grew quiet. Then, he turned and walked across the room to the open door.

Even with the wind doing nothing but blowing heat around, Flavio felt better as soon as he stepped outside. He took the steps down off the porch and walked across Ramona's yard. His pickup was parked in the shade beneath the cottonwoods, and he nodded at it as he passed by. He walked into the middle of the dirt road where he was nearly run over by Sippy Valdéz, who was driving too fast.

Sippy hit the brakes hard, and the truck pulled to the right and bounced to a stop. The cloud of dust that had followed Sippy down the road got caught in the wind and blew off toward the foothills. Sippy stuck his head out the window. "Cuidado, Flavio," he said. "I'm glad I didn't run you over."

"No," Flavio said. "I should watch where I'm going." He glanced at Sippy and then looked away. Half of Sippy's face was stained red from a birthmark, and as his eyes were too light in color and slightly crossed, it was difficult to talk to him without looking somewhere else. Sippy lived just up the road from Ramona's in a double-wide trailer. It was rumored that he made his living selling drugs around Guadalupe and down in Las Sombras.

Sippy and a number of others from the village had been dragged from their homes a few years ago when the state police, one helicopter, and thirty other cars that bore no markings came quietly into Guadalupe one morning before dawn. Flavio had been irrigating his own field that day, and he'd seen the helicopter flying low over the valley and the caravan of cars stopping, seemingly at random, at people's homes. At first, he'd thought it was an invasion, but he had no idea by whom, let alone why. He had stood in his field with his shovel and watched as they'd pulled into Celina Mondragon's drive and taken her away in handcuffs. Her four children, none older than twelve, were crying in the open doorway, and Celina had yelled back at them to call their grandma and not to worry. Then she had been shoved in the backseat of a car, and in a few seconds they had all driven off.

Later, Flavio had heard it all had to do with drugs, and though some in the village were glad the problem had been dealt with, others wondered if things were done this way in other places. But since Sippy and Celina and everyone else taken away that morning all returned a few days later, the controversy soon died down and the village forgot about it as if what had happened hadn't.

Sippy was smiling a little. His arm was hanging out the cab window and his fingers tapped on the outside of the door. "What are you doing in the middle of the road, Flavio?"

Flavio took off his hat and then shoved it back on. "I'm looking for a fire," he said, and he looked up at the hills. All he could see was what he had seen for months, mountains that were dusty and faded and too dry. He shook his head. "I thought the mountains were on fire. Pero, don't even ask me why. Where are you going so fast, anyway?"

"Didn't you hear?" Sippy said. "My Tío Petrolino died a couple days ago. The funeral's this morning."

"No," Flavio breathed out, and he walked over to the side of the truck. "I didn't know that."

Petrolino Valdéz had been a few years younger than Flavio, and though the two had never been friends, they had known each other all their lives. Ever since Petrolino was a young boy, he had walked up and down the highway picking up things that other people threw away. He would carry two large burlap bags and walk the length of the valley in both directions. His house, which was small and dark, was cluttered with crushed aluminum cans, glass colored by the sun, various car parts and bottle-cap sculptures, and other things he had thought valuable. He was someone everyone saw each day and had for so long that Flavio couldn't imagine not seeing Petrolino stooped over on the side of the road.

Flavio let out another long breath of air. "Petrolino's dead," he said. "I didn't even notice."

"It's hard to miss something when you see it every day," Sippy said. "But don't feel too bad, Flavio. Ever since those cows, I think he'd been in a lot of pain."

One morning, just before dawn, Petrolino had been found in the ditch beside the road buried beneath two cows. All that could be seen of him was the little hat he always wore and one of his feet. Ray Pacheco, who had been the Guadalupe police officer back then, said that one of those trucks that hauled hay had plowed into some cows and thrown them on top of Petrolino. But after he'd been uncovered, Petrolino said there had been no truck. He said that God had dropped them for him to find and it was only his own bad luck that they'd fallen on his head.

"Everyone thought he was dead," Flavio said.

"And that was one of my tío's better days," Sippy said. "We ate hamburger for a long time." He pulled a cigarette out of his shirt pocket and when he lowered his eyes to light it, Flavio glanced at his face. The birthmark ran halfway across his lips before fading away and down through one eyebrow to the bridge of his nose. Flavio remembered Sippy as a small boy who had few friends and who would often walk with his tío and help him carry what he had found.

"I'm sorry about Petrolino," Flavio said.

"Yeah," Sippy said and blew a lungful of smoke out of the cab. "Well, he got old and he never was an easy man to be with. I better get going, Flavio. They're waiting on me at the church. I hope you find your fire." Then he looked past Flavio at the hills. "Or maybe not. I can't remember the last time it rained." He slapped the side of the door with his hand. "Come by the house later," he said, "and have a few beers." Then he shoved the truck into gear and drove off.

Flavio stood in the road and watched as Sippy drove to the stop sign and then turned right onto the highway. The breeze tugged at his cap, and he pulled it down lower on his forehead. He had left Ramona's house halfheartedly to look for Felix's fire, but what he had found was one more viejo who had died. At one time, he had thought that one's death and the life one had led would hold some importance, but it seemed to him now that what death meant wasn't much more than a curtain moving in a draft or a reason for others to drink a few beers. He watched the dust from Sippy's truck twist away from the road. Then he walked back to Ramona's.

"Petrolino's dead," Flavio said, standing in the doorway. Though his eyes were still half blinded by the sun, he was able to see that Felix had straightened up and was actually leaning back against the sofa.

"No," Felix said.

"Oh, sí," Flavio said as he walked across the room and sat down. "He died a few days ago in his bed."

"That's too bad," Felix said. His hands were folded in his lap and they lay still now without trembling. "I never liked him, but he always knew what he was going to do each day. And he kept the roads clean."

Flavio leaned back beside Felix, took off his hat and put it on his knee. "Sippy said we should come by his house later and have a beer."

"I don't know," Felix said. "Maybe I should wait a little before drinking beer. Besides, the fire's going to be trouble."

Flavio turned his head and looked at him. "There's no fire, hombre. I just looked. The only smoke in the mountains is dust."

Felix was breathing quietly and though his head still shook slightly, even those tremors seemed to be easing. Finally, he said, "We were just little boys, who didn't know nothing."

"What are you talking about, Felix?"

"She told us that this place was named Perdido, because everyone in this valley was lost."

4

I'm glad you came back to see me," Guadalupe García had said.

She was standing at the cookstove, pouring hot water steeped in mint and chamomile into three cups. The wall behind the cast-iron stove was pocked with small nichos, all of them empty and woven with cobwebs. Flavio wondered why anyone would put so many holes in a wall and then, instead of filling them with photographs of plaster saints, would leave them empty. He thought it was just one more reason that he had no business coming to the García house for a second time in so many days.

Across the room, opposite the cookstove, a long adobe fireplace swelled out from the wall. To one side above it were three wide shelves that looked more like beds where children would sleep than a place to keep food. The ceiling was supported by thick vigas, which were spanned with gray, twisted aspen latillas. In the spaces between them, Flavio could see dirt and sharp chunks of adobe. He felt as if he were in a hole above the ground rather than a house. Everywhere about him was dirt and mud.

Unlike his Grandmother Rosa's house, where the kitchen walls were covered with colorful pictures of saints and crucifixes and dried flowers, the walls in Guadalupe's house were bare. There wasn't even a pot hanging from them. In Rosa's house there were so many things, that Flavio seldom noticed anything in all the clutter. Here, where there was nothing, Flavio found that his eyes would rest on the slant of the doorway as it ran with the ground or on the one wall that bellied out so badly it appeared on the verge of collapsing.

"I don't know the last time someone stopped by here to see me," Guadalupe said. "Other than when you boys came yesterday." Her back was still to Felix and Flavio. Her hair was knotted and long. It looked as if it had never been brushed. "This is not a place people come to visit."

"Why not?" Felix asked. Flavio glanced over at him. He knew why no one came to this house, and he couldn't believe that Felix had asked such a stupid question.

Guadalupe carried the cups carefully to the table. "When I was a little girl," she said, "my mother told me that people stayed away because they thought they were too good for us. But my grandmother said they didn't come because we frightened them, even if they had forgotten why." Guadalupe placed the cups on the table and slid one in front of each boy. Then she sat down across from them. "What do you think?"

Felix shrugged. "I don't know," he said. "But I'm not scared." Flavio stared down at the mint and chamomile in his tea and didn't say anything.

It had been Felix's idea to come here, and somehow he had managed to do it without even telling Flavio. They had been fishing at the creek and their path home had taken them past the church and up the hill and then across the field not far from Guadalupe's house. They had caught four small trout, which they had strung together through the gills and mouth with a thin willow branch.

When they came near the house, Felix had stopped walking and said, "If I had been Cristóbal García, I would never have stayed here. I would have got on that burro and rode to Albuquerque."

Flavio, who had been thinking about how his grandmother would put the four small fish in tortillas and smother them with garlic and chile, kept walking and said, "There wasn't any Albuquerque, jodido. There wasn't anything anywhere back then."

"Still," Felix said. "I wouldn't have stayed here with nobody around."

Flavio didn't care what Cristóbal García would have done. In fact, he had been so relieved finally to leave Guadalupe's house that he could barely remember the story she had told.

"None of it was true, anyway," Flavio said. "No one could know what happened so long ago." When Felix didn't say anything, Flavio looked back over his shoulder. Felix was halfway to the García house, the trout flopping from his arm as he ran. Flavio watched him run up to the door and then he saw Guadalupe appear in the doorway. A few seconds later, they both stared at where he was standing. And now, once again, he was sitting in the kitchen inside the García house.

Guadalupe took a sip of her tea. She moved the hair that had wandered in front of her face back behind one ear. "There is a room in this house," she said, "where bones are buried in the wall. It's a small room with just a banco for a bed and a small table with a kerosene lamp. I would play there as a child because it was a room where no one would find me. One day, in the mud above the bed, I saw what I thought was a stone. It was hard and white and smooth. I tried to dig it out with my fingers, and as I scraped away the dirt, I found set in the wall a small bone like those in the hand."

Flavio felt a chill rise up his back. He looked down at Guadalupe's hand resting on the table. Her fingers were long and thin and the nails were broken. There was a scratch across her knuckles that had healed in a dark ragged line. He looked at his own hands and then closed them into fists and put them under the table in his lap.

"After that," Guadalupe went on, "every time I played there, I would scrape more plaster away and always I uncovered more bones. I think the bones are those of Emilio García the bandit. He was my great-grandmother's first cousin, and he was hung from the cottonwood tree that stands beside the church." Guadalupe stopped talking. She took another sip of tea and smiled.

Neither Felix nor Flavio said a word. Then they both spoke at once.

"Why did Cristóbal García go crazy?" Felix said

"Why did they put his bones in the wall?" Flavio said. He thought that if he lived in a house where there were bones in the walls, he would sleep outside.

"Tell me first," Felix said.

"I'm older," Flavio said, which was true. Felix was still only eight years old.

"You always say that," Felix said, glancing at Flavio. "It doesn't mean anything."

"Why did they hang Emilio García?" Flavio asked, louder this time.

Guadalupe turned her eyes to Flavio. "He was a bandit and a García," she said. "That was enough. They hung him in the rain from the cottonwood beside the church."

There was just the one tree that grew by the church, and its thick limbs spread high up over the roof. In the spring, when the branches leafed out, the tree shaded half the structure, and in the summer, on hot days, people would stand beneath it and talk after mass. Flavio couldn't even grasp the thought of someone hanging from its limbs, even if he was a bandit. On top of that, although violence was not unheard of in Guadalupe, it always came suddenly like when Andres Cortes went to shoot the dogs bothering his cows and ended up shooting his neighbor, Tito Medina, in both feet. Though this had made some people unhappy, especially Tito, who didn't even own a dog, nothing much was ever done about it. Guadalupe was a small place, and people knew that life was easier if you ignored most things. Besides that, it was almost impossible to get those in the village to agree on anything, let alone on hanging someone. Flavio thought that Guadalupe must be mistaken, that what she was saying must be part of another village. Not this one.

"But what about Cristóbal García?" Felix said.

"That's a different story," Flavio said.

"No," Guadalupe said. "It's the same story." She looked at both boys and then stared past them, out the open door. "Cristóbal García," she went on, "was never meant to be alone. The first mistake he made, other than leaving Las Sombras in the first place, was not following after Hipolito and Francisco. The second mistake he made, which was far worse, was in the making of the santo."

For days after Hipolito and Francisco had left the place they had named Guadalupe, Cristóbal did little more than wander aimlessly. He paced up and down the valley until he had beaten down the high grass and his trails mixed with those of animals. He walked the foothills, stumbling over loose shale and through scrub oak, looking for nothing, but all the time talking incessantly.

He cursed Hipolito and Francisco, and he described aloud how he would shoot them and their livestock and burn their seed and leave their families hopeless. He cursed the junipers along the creek that always watched him and the mountains and hills that crowded closely around the small valley. He even cursed the weather that had remained calm and warm and without a breath of wind and made him feel as if he were in a place where nothing would ever change. And when he wasn't cursing, he would pray. He prayed for the safety of Hipolito and Francisco and that they would shun sleep and food so as to return to him all the more quickly. He prayed that his wife was wise enough to have packed her things and that there would be no early snows to hinder their journey. Even at night while he slept fitfully, he would mumble to himself, and in the morning, he would wake to the sound of his voice. Cristóbal talked so long that eventually he became sick of hearing what he had to say. Then, he began to work like a madman.

He built a small shelter out of mud and sticks on the top of a small hill at the north end of the valley. There, he felt he was far enough from the creek so that the sound of the water and the creaking of the junipers wouldn't disturb him at night. Although the hill was not much higher than anything else in the valley, it was high enough to ease some of the dread of being alone. He dammed one of the creeks with large stones and from it spent days digging a shallow ditch that ran through the grass and along the side of the hill to his shelter.

Each day, Cristóbal told himself that with such good weather, Hipolito and Francisco would reach Las Sombras in no time. After a week, he believed that they and their families and his own must surely have begun the journey back to Gaudalupe. He made plans to winter in the valley. At the first sign of spring, he and his family would return to Las Sombras, where they belonged.

"My family is almost here," Cristóbal would say every night before sleep, as if it were a prayer.

Two weeks after Hipolito and Francisco had left the valley, Cristóbal woke to a day that was like summer. The air was dead and warm and the grass stood tall and frail and thin. The sky was streaked pale white, but above the mountains it was red, the color of fire. By midday, the wind had begun to blow, and Cristóbal could see dark clouds banked over the foothills in the west. Just before dark, it turned cold. By morning, a foot of snow had fallen and the mountains were swallowed in clouds.

Cristóbal ran out of firewood on the second day of the storm. He tied frayed strips of leather around his feet and wrapped his blanket over his shoulders. The wind outside his shelter was howling, and there was so much snow in the air that the junipers along the creek looked like the ghosts of trees. For hours, Cristóbal walked back and forth from the river, hauling branches that the wind had torn loose. He hauled wood until his hands and feet were cracked and numb and his face was blistered from the wind. That night, in a frenzy, Cristóbal began to carve a santo, and although there was always something not at rest in Cristóbal's soul, before then he had not completely lost his mind.

"What happened to the donkey?" Felix asked. The sound of his voice in the kitchen startled Guadalupe and she stopped talking. She looked at Felix as if she had forgotten he was there.

"What happened to the donkey?" he asked again. His feet didn't quite reach the floor and he was swinging his legs slightly.

"I don't know," she said. She had stopped smiling and Flavio thought she had the same look on her face that his father would sometimes get when he'd been drinking heavily and one of his children asked him a question.

"I don't know that part of the story," Guadalupe said.

"Can you find out?"

"No," she said. "There's no one left to ask."

"Maybe he ate it," Flavio said.

"Eee," Felix said loudly, grimacing. "I would never eat a donkey."

"You would if you were hungry," Flavio told him. "And if it was snowing and never stopped."

"I would eat bark first. I would have made that donkey take me to Albuquerque and then if it snowed, so what."

The two boys stared at each other and then Flavio shook his head. "This isn't a story about a donkey," he said.

"Then why is he in it?"

Sometimes Felix would get this way. For the most part, he was a quiet boy who would spend his time using his feet or his hands rather than his mouth. But occasionally, seemingly for no reason, he would grab on to something like a small dog and not let go until he drove Flavio crazy.

"Do you think Cristóbal ate the donkey?" Felix asked Guadalupe.

"I don't know," she told him. "Maybe the burro ran away and became wild. Or maybe he stayed in the valley with Cristóbal and kept him company. I only know what Cristóbal did and on the second night of the storm he began to carve a santo of Our Lady of Guadalupe."

She was carved out of the burned, ragged end of a juniper branch that had been ripped from a tree by the wind. Cristóbal stripped the bark from the wood and worked all night with his knife. By morning, her hands had come out of the wood and the outline of her gown could be seen. The storm continued to rage through the day, and so much snow had drifted around Cristóbal's shelter that all he could hear from outside was the muffled echo of the wind. All day he sat beside the fire, his body rocking gently, while his knife took away one sliver of wood after another. When he was finally finished, it was dark. He stood her next to the fire and looked at her.

Her gown was black from the ashes he had rubbed into the wood. Her body and face were scarred with gashes and stained with blood from where the knife had slipped and cut Cristóbal's hand. Her hands pressed together at her chest, and although she stared forward, her head was bent slightly. Her mouth was severe and coarse, as if she had already seen too much. Cristóbal took her in his arms and then he prayed to her. He asked only one thing of her—that his family be safely delivered to him.

That night, while the storm broke and a bitter cold fell upon the valley, Cristóbal dreamed. In this dream he saw his wife and eight small daughters huddled silently together in the sagebrush. They were without shoes and were clothed in thin garments. Snow was in their hair and in their open eyes. Their faces and hands were frozen white in the image of the santo.

One Christmas Eve, Flavio had stood at his window, his head just above the sill, and he had seen the abuelos coming. There were five of them, and they were dressed in bulky clothes and wide dark hats and their faces were swollen and misshapen. In one hand they each carried willow branches and in the other was a burlap bag. They walked unsteadily, stumbling against one another, and they were singing a song so out of tune and so disjointed that it seemed as if all five were yelling something completely different. Flavio had stood at the window without breathing. As he watched them walk to the house, he remembered everything his sister had told him.

"They will come for you on Christmas Eve," Ramona had said. "They will carry whips and when they're done beating you, they'll stuff you in their bags and take you so far away no one will ever see you again."

Ramona had a way of telling Flavio these things when she was angry, and as far as Flavio could tell, it didn't matter if she was angry at him or at nothing. She would make him sit in the kitchen and then, gleefully, tell him things he would rather not have known. She told him about La Llorona, who walked the ditches and river-banks in search of her dead children. Her voice is like a coyote's, Ramona would say, but you can't hear her until she is behind you, and then it's too late. She'll grab you and hold you under the water until you drown.

Ramona told him that their neighbor, Emilio Silva, an old man who lived alone, was in truth a witch who could change himself into an owl or a feral dog. At night, she told Flavio, he looks in your window while you sleep and tries to pry open the glass with his teeth. And she told him about the abuelos who would come for him on Christmas Eve.

When the abuelos had come close to the house, Flavio's father had gone outside with a bottle of whiskey. Flavio had watched as each abuelo lifted his mask and drank from the bottle. After a while, they had left, shuffling back down the road. Flavio's father had come back inside, carrying cold and the smell of whiskey with him, and stood beside his son. He had placed his hand on Flavio's head and said, "Don't be frightened, hijo. You are a good boy. Nothing bad will ever come to you if you're good." At the end of the drive leading to the Montoyas' house, one of the abuelos had fallen into the snow. The other four helped him to his feet and they had gone off into the night.

The story Guadalupe García was telling made Flavio feel the same way he had on that Christmas Eve, that it was possible his fa-ther had been wrong. Things could happen, good or bad, for no reason at all.

"Were they dead?" Felix asked. His voice trembled slightly and Flavio thought that he was close to tears.

"No," Guadalupe said. "What Cristóbal dreamed wasn't true. His family, at that time, was safe in Santa Madre, not wandering lost in the snow. What the Lady showed him were either things deep in his own mind or it was a trick she played on him."

Felix slapped the table with his hand. "He should have chopped her up and thrown her in the fire."

"He did not have time," Guadalupe said. "Because not only did the Lady steal his family from him, but then she gave them back."

When Cristóbal emerged from his shelter the next morning, he thought his family was dead. His face was black with soot from the fire and his eyes were meshed with blood. His hands were crusted with dirt and covered with gashes from his knife. He was so thin that the bones of his ribs could be seen even through his clothes and his legs were like sticks. It was so cold that his breath made ice in his beard. The snow came to his waist and for a moment, in the sunlight, Cristóbal was blinded.

He closed his eyes and when he opened them, he saw standing together, not far from where he stood, his wife and children. With them were Hipolito and Francisco and their own families and also the three priests who had been murdered by the Indians and others from Las Sombras whom he had known only slightly. For a moment, no one spoke a word. Then, suddenly, everyone spoke at once and the valley filled with noise.

"For two years," Guadalupe said, "Cristóbal lived in this valley surrounded by no one and everyone, and when Hipolito and Francisco finally returned, they found Cristóbal clothed in rags. Throughout the valley were small dwellings made out of mud and sticks."

"Were they ghosts?" Felix asked.

"No," Flavio said sharply and even he was surprised at the anger in his voice. "Don't you listen? He was crazy. He was seeing things that weren't real."

"Was he?" Felix asked Guadalupe.

Guadalupe shrugged. "I don't know," she said. "All I know is that after Hipolito and Francisco returned here, Cristóbal saw two of almost everyone and, worse, he saw the village and the valley not as it was, but as he imagined it to be. He thought he had two wives and his house overflowed with children. Cristóbal saw people wandering everywhere, and if there was a problem in the village, he would deal with it in strange ways that always seemed to make it worse. If you spoke with Cristóbal, which most people stopped doing, he would tell you about things that had happened but hadn't and about villagers you thought you knew but didn't. For the rest of Cristóbal's life not only did he carry confusion with him, but whenever someone died, another of them always remained."

Flavio's mother had spent the last two years of her life secluded in her bedroom. There, she would lie in her bed or sit in a chair by the window and look out on the mountains. Sometimes, Flavio would take her the food Ramona had prepared and she would smile and touch the side of his face and ask him a few questions about his day. Then he would sit beside her while she ate, and the two of them would gaze out the window without talking. When she was done eating, she would say, "Thank you, mi hijo, now leave me for a little while by myself." By the time she died, in her bed while her husband slept beside her, Flavio felt that she had been gone a long time.

Four days after her death, Flavio found himself sitting in his grandmother's kitchen. Before him on the table were a bowl of menudo and a tortilla that he hadn't touched. Rosa was busy at the sink washing the pots, pans, and platters that were stacked high on the counters.

No one else was in the house. Flavio's father, Lito, after days of drinking so much whiskey that his mind had become dull and empty, had returned to work at the mine. Epolito, Flavio's grandfather, had gone to the lumberyard with baby José to buy baling wire, and Ramona was gone. She had left the village earlier that morning to live somewhere else, taking with her only a small brown suitcase that held a few clothes and her brushes and paints. Rosa and Flavio had watched her bus leave the village in a cloud of black exhaust and grinding gears. When it had crested the hill and passed out of their sight, Rosa had lowered her head and grasped her grandson's hand tightly. Then the two of them had walked back home.

Flavio picked up the tortilla. He took a small bite and then laid it back on the table. "Grandmother," he said, "is it true you can die of a sad heart?"

Rosa's hands fell silent in the sink for a few seconds. Then she shook her head slowly and said, "Flavio, where do you hear such things?"

"Ramona told me. She told me we couldn't catch what our mother had because she died of a sad heart."

Rosa dried her hands, walked to the table, and sat down across from her grandson. She let out a long breath of air. "Finish your menudo, hijo," she said. "It's good for you."

"I don't like menudo."

"So you want to hear all the things I do that I don't like? Maybe you think I enjoy washing thousands and thousands of pots? Now eat. I have a gift to give you from your mother and I want you to listen.

"I knew your mother, hijo, her whole life. I remember her as a young girl playing in the irrigation ditches and throwing rocks as if she were a boy and didn't know any better. I watched her grow into a woman, and she had such a soft smile and quiet ways that I was happy my son had found her for himself."

Rosa leaned slightly over the table. "And their wedding, hijo, you should have been there. So many people came that the church couldn't hold them all. And, afterward, there was a party with enough food to feed the village for a year—stacks of enchiladas to the ceiling and soft pork tamales and carne asada and sopapillas with honey and bowls of fresh butter. Your grandfather killed three lambs and dug pits for them and cooked them in cedar all night under the ground. Pablo Mascarenas came down from the north with his two brothers and brought their fiddles and guitars, and your mother danced in her white dress until long into the evening. Her face was shining and laughing, and she danced every dance with your father.

"It was almost dawn by the time everyone had left, except for Alfonso Vigil, who was too drunk to do anything but sleep under the cottonwood by the road. Your grandfather, and you know how he is always so quiet with his words, sat with your mother and he told her that our family would always be hers."

Rosa leaned back in her chair and smiled at Flavio. "I was so proud that day, hijo," she said.

Flavio had stopped eating and was staring at his grandmother. "I remember my mother dancing," he said, though he was almost sure it wasn't true. He had actually never seen his mother dance, let alone dance with his father. His parents had lived in the same house together, and although there was not once a harsh word between them, they had gone about their lives as if they lived a great distance from each other.

"Do you, hijo?" Rosa said. "It makes me happy you have that memory to keep. But I'm not done with this story. Now eat a little more.

"It was not long after the wedding that your sister Ramona was born. Although Ramona was such a beautiful baby, she was also very difficult as an infant. She slept little and never liked to be held closely, as if, even so young, your sister wished to be elsewhere. Your mother had a hard time then, and I think there was also a little sadness in her that she had not had a son. For many years your parents tried to have another child, but there was no luck, and your mother came to believe that, like herself, Ramona would be an only child.

"One day, eight years after Ramona was born, your mother walked alone across the valley to this house. It was a cold cold day with snow frozen on the ground and wood smoke hanging thick in the air. Your mother's hair had turned to frost and her legs were so weak her body trembled. I made her come quickly to the stove, and I rubbed her hands, which were like ice. Over and over I asked her why she had done something so foolish. Finally, when she could speak, she took my hands in hers. She smiled and to this day I still remember each word she said. Would you like to know what that was, mi hijo?"

"Yes," Flavio said.

" 'Rosa,' your mother said, 'I am going to have a baby and this baby will be a son. If anything ever happens to me and I cannot tell him these words myself, I want you to speak them for me so that he'll know. Tell him that now, even before I can see him, he fills my heart with such joy. Tell him that his mother loves him more than anything else in this world and that no matter where I am, I will always be watching over him.' Then, hijo, your mother laughed and cried, and we sat together by the stove, and I listened to all her dreams for you."

Rosa took in a deep breath and let it out softly. "So, Flavio," she said, "that is what your mother said and that is the gift she wished me to give to you."

Flavio was looking down at the bowl of menudo. Grease had cooled on the surface, and he idly moved his spoon through it.

"Look at me, hijo," Rosa said. "Your mother was a good woman, and she tried her best. There was a part of her, though, that could be lonely even in the midst of her family. It was no one's fault, not even her own."

"If she hadn't died," Flavio said, "then everything would still be the same."

Rosa leaned across the table and took her grandson's hand. "Everything is the same, if only you don't forget." She squeezed his hand hard and then patted it. She sat back in her chair. "Now go. Go outside and do something."

Flavio stood up from the table and walked to the doorway. Then he stopped and looked back at Rosa. "Why did Ramona leave, Grandmother?" he asked.

"She left here for a little while, hijo."

"She said she would never come back."

"She will come back someday," Rosa said. "You wait and see."

"I will never leave," Flavio said.

Rosa smiled. "No, mi hijo," she said. "You will always be here with me."

"If I saw two of everyone," Flavio said, "then my mother would still be here." He looked across the table at Guadalupe García and for a second their eyes met. Then she closed hers and leaned back in her chair.

"She wouldn't be real," Felix said. "She'd be a trick."

"She'd be real to me," Flavio said.

"Cristóbal named this place Perdido," Guadalupe said, her eyes still closed, "because he knew that he and everyone else in this valley was lost. You have to be careful what you wish for, Flavio. It's getting late now. Thank you for bringing me the fish. Go home before your families begin to worry."

"Can we come back?" Felix asked.

"Yes," Guadalupe said. "You can always come back."

It was late in the afternoon when Felix and Flavio left the García house. They walked for a while without speaking. Felix was staring down at his feet, and every so often they kicked at the high weeds. Just down the hill, Flavio could see the church. The walls were many feet thick and the corners were rounded and supported by massive buttresses. With the sun setting over the foothills, the mud plaster was bathed in a soft light. Beside the church stood an immense cottonwood, its trunk and branches gnarled and thick with bark. It was early autumn and the leaves, although still green, had faded. A breeze moved through the valley, and even from where Flavio stood, he could hear the sound of the leaves stirring.

"They hung him in the rain," Guadalupe had said. "From the cottonwood that grows beside the church."

5

Flavio was dozing on the sofa, and he didn't wake so much as gradually become aware that his eyes were open and that he was staring blankly out the open door of Ramona's house. He was slouched down on the sofa, his chin on his chest, his legs sticking straight out. Felix sat close beside him, and Flavio could feel the weight and the thin heat of his body. The sun had moved and the light coming in the doorway now fell upon the seven santos. They were spun with cobwebs and coated with years of dust and they stood together as they always had.

For the first time Flavio noticed that most of them must have been carved by the same hand. There was the same softness in the features and almost a shyness in the way each lady held her hands together at her breasts. He wondered how it was possible to bring such things out of a piece of wood and what kind of man would put so much care into the making of one santo after another. And then, to have them end up standing in the dust and shadows of an empty house by themselves. He thought that maybe he should move them— take them to his own house or drive them to Las Sombras where they could be sold to tourists.

In the midst of them was the Lady who was older than the others. She stood no taller than their shoulders. The paint on her gown was faded and flaking and a finger on one hand was broken off. Her features were hard and stern, and her eyes were open wide. She faced slightly away from her companions, and it seemed as if she either was looking for a way out or had spent so much of her life complaining that the others no longer listened.

The one that stood before them all was far younger than the rest. But even she had been carved almost fifty years earlier by Flavio's nephew, Little José. Flavio had never seen José work on it, but he pictured the boy in the kitchen with Ramona. While she painted, he sat with a large piece of wood in his lap.

"It's a miracle you didn't hurt yourself," Flavio muttered. The Lady stood a little lopsided and her features were askew. One eye was lower than the other, and the flames that ringed her body were more like toothpicks. She was smiling broadly and the paint on her gown was garish and smeared where one color ran into the next. She reminded Flavio of Lisa Segura, who was known to drink too much at Tito's Bar and shoot pool and, when it closed, would leave disheveled and laughing with whomever she wanted.

"What shall I do with all of you?" he said. They seemed to stare back at him as if it were he they had been waiting for all these years.

"They're nothing but trouble, Flavio," Felix said. "I would chop them up and throw them in the fire."

In that instant, everything that Flavio had dreamed while dozing rushed back to him, and suddenly, he was wide awake. He pushed himself up straight. "What's happening here?" he said.

Felix was sitting quietly on the sofa beside him. His hands were folded in his lap, and his feet were crossed at the ankles. He was actually beginning to look like the Felix Flavio remembered, or at least the one he thought he remembered.

"What's going on, Felix?" he said again.

Felix shrugged slightly. "I'm feeling a little better, Flavio," he said. "My feet don't hurt so much. While you were sleeping I thought about Pepe's beans and if he still puts in cilantro and garlic like I taught him. I thought maybe we could take a little drive to my café and have him make us a burrito and a sopapilla."

For a moment Flavio didn't say anything. Then he shook his head and said, "That's not what I meant. Whenever I'm not paying attention, you say something about the old García house."

Flavio hadn't been inside the García house in more than seventy years, and whatever it was that had happened to him and Felix that autumn was so distant it might as well have happened to someone else. Although the García house was still standing, it was little more than a ruin and had been for decades. The roof had sunk in and sagged badly over the entire structure. The mud plaster had peeled away and weeds grew out of the eroded adobe. A long time ago, someone had nailed boards over the windows and doors to keep children out, and now the wood was black and warped from the weather. Mounds of dirt lay all about the place where rain had washed away the walls, and half buried in it were rusted beer cans and empty whiskey bottles and shards of glass. It was like any other crumbling adobe or old corral around Guadalupe. There wasn't one reason Flavio could think of for him now to be thinking of the García house, or even of Guadalupe García for that matter.

Felix looked up at Flavio. The skin beneath his eyes sagged and was discolored. There were streaks of dirt on his forehead and down his face where it had run with sweat. "We went to her house when we were little," he said, "and she told us things."

Flavio spit out some air. "So? You think I can remember that? We were just boys then doing stupid things. Besides, that house has been empty so long that no one in the village even remembers who lived in it."

Flavio had once read in a magazine about people who believed that they had led numerous lives and could recall only glimpses of each of them. At the time, he had thought that they were crazy to believe such things. But then it occurred to him that even in his one life he could barely remember what he himself was like ten or fifteen or fifty years earlier and who was he to say what was what? He felt that way now, as if he were talking about another life that he and Felix might have lived.

"I used to think that way, too," Felix said. "Besides, this is all your grandmother's fault. She tells us to take some beans to Guadalupe García's house and now look what happens to us."

"Eee," Flavio said. "I don't even know what you're talking about." He could feel a small knot in the back of his neck. He moved his head from side to side. Then he leaned back against the sofa. "It wasn't beans, either," he went on. "Grandmother sent us over to Guadalupe's with a bag of those little red potatoes."

"No," Felix said. "It was beans. I can still hear the sound they made in the bag. Like a woman's dress." He was quiet for a few seconds and then he said, "At least I think it was beans. I don't know what's wrong with me, Flavio. I only seem to remember these things when I'm remembering."

Flavio stared up at the ceiling and found himself smiling. He was beginning to enjoy this conversation and he had no idea why. "We got old, Felix," he said. "There's too much to forget."

"How do you know?" Felix said.

Flavio grunted and stretched out his legs. "Maybe you're right, Felix," he said. "Maybe we should take a ride to the café and eat a little something." And it was then that they were both startled by the sound of sirens starting up at the village office.

Flavio stepped outside the house, wondering who had wrecked their car on the highway or dropped dead from a bad heart. There was a slight haze in the air, and he realized that, without being aware of it, he had smelled the faint odor of wood smoke from the moment he'd awoken. Across the road and just beyond an empty field was the village office. From where Flavio stood, he could see both the police car and the fire truck pull quickly out of the lot and head south down the highway. He watched as they disappeared down the hill and then, like a blow to the stomach, he saw the thick column of smoke rising from the foothills.

Sometimes, in the spring, when people burned the weeds along the ditches or around their trailers, a wind would blow unexpectedly and the flames would spread to a neighboring field. Seldom did these fires do any damage, and more often than not, they were put out with water hoses and rakes. There had never been a fire in the mountains around or even near the village. But on one ridge, high above the foothills, was a large area where nothing grew but scrub oak. It was rumored that a fire had once raged there and that the ground was so full of the ashes of dead trees that only brush and stunted saplings would grow. But no one in the village remembered that fire or even remembered hearing stories of it. Occasionally, when the rains came in midsummer, lightning would slash the ground and small fires would spring up. But usually the rain that followed would drown them out, and if it didn't, a few men hired by the forest service would hike into the hills with shovels and chain saws and stay until even the embers were dead.

Flavio had never seen a thing like this before in his life. A couple of miles south and a mile west of the village, gray-white smoke poured from just below the rounded top of a foothill. It looked as if there had been an explosion. There was so much smoke that not even flames were visible, only a faint orange hue that churned at the base of the column.

"My God," Flavio said. "The mountain is on fire."

He hurried back to the house, up the porch steps, and rushed into the room. "Felix," he gasped, "there's a fire. The mountains are on fire."

"I told you so," Felix said to him calmly and then lowered his eyes.

Flavio stood breathing heavily just inside the room. He opened his mouth and then closed it. Finally, he said, "How could you know this?"

With some effort, Felix pushed himself up a little straighter on the sofa. One of his hands began to shake and he held it with the other. "Don't blame me, Flavio," he said. "It wasn't my idea."

Flavio stood staring at him. The Felix he remembered was a man who took meticulous care of his café, spent money frugally, and wasted little. He was not a man to go running about the mountains starting fires. "How could you do such a thing?" Flavio stammered out.

"With matches." Felix shrugged. "And a little pile of sticks."

"No, jodido," Flavio said, his voice louder. "I mean how could you do this?" and he raised his arms. "Did you just wake up this morning and think it was a nice day to burn the mountains?"

Felix's head began to jerk again, and he bent forward a little, his back rounded. "Don't ask me so much, Flavio," he said in a way that made Flavio feel as if he were talking to a child.

Flavio walked quickly across the room. He took off his hat, slapped Felix on the shoulder with it, and then shoved it back on. "Vamos," he said. "Let's go see how bad it is." He pulled Felix to his feet and, leaning against each other, the two of them walked out of the house.

Flavio helped Felix take the step up into the cab of his truck. He checked the bed to make sure he had his shovel and then he climbed behind the wheel of the pickup. He switched on the ignition and let the engine idle. He glanced over at Felix, who had begun to breathe hard again and was so hunched over that his head barely cleared the top of the seat.

"I'm sorry I hit you with my hat," Flavio said under his breath. Then, thinking everything had to be one enormous mistake, he shoved the gearshift into reverse and drove off.

Delfino Vigil, a man Flavio's own age, was bent over at the waist beside the stop sign at the end of the road. He had one hand on a knee, the other was grasping onto a shovel, and he was gulping air. He was wearing heavy, oil-stained overalls that were so big for him they dragged on the ground and a baseball cap pulled down low on his forehead. Flavio slowed to a stop and leaned across Felix. "Delfino," he yelled out the open window. "Come on, I'll give you a ride."

Delfino jerked his head sideways and then waved an arm. He hobbled over to the pickup, threw his shovel in the back, and swung open the door. When he climbed into the cab, the air filled with the thick odor of manure and grease. Delfino let out a long ragged sigh. Then he took off his cap and wiped his forehead with his sleeve. His scalp was round and smooth and marked with liver spots and only a few wispy white hairs.

He looked over at Felix sitting beside him. "Flavio," he said, "Felix García is in your truck." His face was bright red as if he'd run the mile from his house to where Flavio had picked him up, and since he'd left his teeth by the sink in his bathroom, his words came out of his mouth slightly mumbled and with a faint echo. He wasn't much taller than Felix, and Flavio suddenly felt as if he were driving a school bus.

"I know Felix is in my truck," Flavio said as he pulled up to the sign and stopped again.

"¿Cómo estás, Felix?" Delfino said, and he reached out and touched the back of Felix's hand. "I haven't seen you in a long time." When Felix didn't answer, Delfino bent forward and looked at Flavio. "Why is Felix in your truck?" he asked.

"I'm taking him back home," Flavio said and tapped the steering wheel with his fingers.

"From where?"

Flavio turned his head. "He's been visiting me at Ramona's," he said. One of Delfino's eyes was the color of milk and the pupil had turned a faded blue. It seemed a little bigger than his other eye and made half his face seem like it belonged to someone else.

"Ramona's dead," Delfino said.

"I know Ramona's dead," Flavio said. He was beginning to feel irritable and wished Delfino would talk about something else. "What happened to your eye?" he asked.

Delfino lifted his hand to his face and then dropped it. "I don't know," he said. "I think it's just tired." One night, Delfino had gone to bed even before the sun had set. His head was aching and outside his bedroom window, he could hear the sound of birds and the voices of the Gallegos children next door, who never seemed to keep quiet. He had slept without dreaming, and when he woke he was in exactly the same position, arms at his sides and legs stuck out stiff, that he had gone to sleep in ten hours earlier. He had slept so soundly that for a second it seemed to him as if he had been somewhere else or had been dead for a little while without knowing it. One of his ears felt like it was full of water and as he walked to his kitchen he slapped the side of his head. When he looked in his little mirror that hung beside his stove, he saw that his eye had turned white in the night. It wasn't until later, when Delfino was cooking his sausages and chile, that he discovered he had also lost his sense of smell.

"I'm a little nervous now when I sleep," Delfino said to Flavio.

Flavio looked out his side window. There was a line of cars driving into town for almost as far as he could see and few of them he recognized. He glanced back at Delfino. "What's it like?" he asked.

"It just looks a little funny," Delfino said. "It still works sometimes."

"No. I mean to not smell."

"You know how many things smell bad? I can stick my head anywhere and it's no problem." He looked out his window at the smoke billowing hundreds of feet into the air. "I never thought I'd live to see something like this happen, Flavio. Look at it. It's burning up our mountains." He turned to Felix. "Don't worry, Felix," he said. "We'll put this fire out. And then we'll shoot the jodido who started it."

Flavio stared out the window at a couple of dogs running along the ditch across the road. One was limping badly, dragging his hind leg, and every so often he'd bite at it as he ran. "Maybe the fire started by itself," he said.

Delfino grunted. "You think two stones rolled together and made a spark? There's nothing up there. I used to hunt all through those hills. There's no roads, not even any trails. Just piñon and brush for the rabbits to hide in." A sudden gust of wind shook the truck and blew dust through the cab. "Pull out, Flavio. Someone will stop for you."

"I've never seen so many cars."

"They're all coming to see the fire." A new pickup passed by with two men in the cab. The driver was bent over the wheel, looking at the foothills. The man in the passenger seat stared at Flavio for a second and then moved his eyes away. "There," Delfino said, and he leaned forward and pointed. "That's Erlinda Gonzales and her Tía Modesta. She'll let you in."

Flavio pulled onto the highway and waved a hand at Erlinda. He could see the fire now framed in the windshield like one of Ramona's paintings. It was bigger at the base than he'd thought, and the wind was beginning to twist the column of smoke so that it leaned slightly. Smoke was trailing away from the top and thinning out over the valley.

"It's too big," Flavio said softly. He glanced at Delfino, who was staring straight ahead. His bad eye was half closed, and he had one arm outstretched, his hand on the dashboard. He shook his head and then looked out his side window.

There were a few old adobes set back off the road, all of them in disrepair and all of them boarded up. The shingled roofs were curled and black, and those with tin had either rusted out or were coated with tar. A few trailers were parked near the houses, the corners shimmed up on cinder blocks, a thin sheathing of plywood around the base to keep out skunks in the summer and cold in the winter. At one time, the Romeros and the Durans had lived along this stretch of road. Their fields had been planted with crested wheat and alfalfa, and their corrals had been crowded with sheep.

Flavio looked back at the road. The sun was angling in his window, and he could feel it sitting hot on his thighs. He took in a deep breath of air and let it out slowly. "What were you doing running to town?" he asked. "That truck of yours finally break down."

"I don't own a truck no more," Delfino said. "The chingaderas took it away from me."

"I didn't hear about this," Flavio said. "Who took it away?"

"How should I know," Delfino said. "I had a little accident, and when I went to get my truck back, they told me it had disappeared. I had that truck thirty-five years, and in all that time it never once disappeared. They must think I'm stupid to believe my truck is hiding from me."

Delfino had driven into the side of Tito's Bar. The collision had smashed the plaster and pushed in a section of the adobe wall on top of Fred Sanchez, who had been drinking beer all morning and complaining bitterly to anyone who would listen about his wife. After Delfino had been helped from the cab of his pickup and after Fred Sanchez had been unburied, Delfino was asked what had happened. It had been, after all, a day in early June and no traffic had been on the road. Delfino had answered that the last thing he remembered was feeding his pigs old potatoes and how should he know what his truck was doing inside Tito's Bar. Then, without another word, he had walked back home by himself.

"That was the last time I saw my truck," Delfino said. "I was a young man when I got that truck. And now, when I'm too old to walk, they take it away from me."

Flavio had not heard this story, and he realized that he couldn't even remember the last time he had seen Delfino. It struck him that somehow, even in such a small village, it was easy to disappear. Like himself, Delfino was getting on in years. It was too bad he had no family to watch out for him.

Flavio slowed down as he came to Felix's Café. The lot in front was empty, and Pepe's car was nowhere to be seen. The lights were out inside and the sign on the door was flipped over to CLOSED. "Where's Pepe?" Flavio asked, and he looked at Felix.

There was moisture at the edges of Felix's eyes from the breeze blowing through the cab and saliva at one corner of his mouth. His head was nodding away, his hands trembling in his lap. Flavio said his name and Felix blinked once and said nothing.

"What is it with you, Felix?" Flavio said. "One minute you can't be quiet and the next you're like a stone."

"Felix can't talk, Flavio," Delfino said. "And he hasn't done a thing in eight years."

"You think so?" Flavio said. "Well, today he's been pretty busy. Tell Delfino, Felix, how you spent your morning."

Delfino put his hand on Felix's arm. "It's okay, Felix," he said. "Flavio's a little upset about this fire." Then he leaned forward and took a better look at Felix's face. "What happened to you, anyway? You been fighting with cats?" He looked at Flavio. "Why is Felix all beat up?"

Flavio shrugged and shook his head. "Don't ask me," he said. "I don't know anything anymore."

They drove past Tito's Bar. Tomás Gallegos, a miner, was standing in the open doorway drinking a beer. He raised the can in a wave as they passed by. The lumberyard was as quiet as the café. The gates were closed leading to the yard, and though the front door was propped open and the lights were on, there didn't seem to be a soul inside. They came to the bottom of the hill, and as the road swung around, the valley opened up before them.

"Eee," Delfino breathed out. "I don't believe my eyes."

Vehicles were parked half on the pavement and half on the shoulder all the way to where the road climbed out of the valley to Las Sombras. People were walking about, visiting or standing in groups. Whole families were sitting in the beds of their pickups, the butt end of the trucks parked so that they faced the fire. The village squad car and a number of state police cars were in the midst of everyone, their lights flashing, their sirens off. It looked like the entire county had come to Guadalupe for a party. Kids were running up and down the highway. Six-packs of beer and soda pop were being passed around. Flavio knew most of the people, but there were others, standing off by themselves, whom he had never seen before. The only traffic moving was in one lane in the center of the road, and even that was almost at a standstill.

Flavio swung his truck off the road and shut off the engine. The fire was not as far into the hills as it had seemed from Ramona's house. In fact, it had started not far above the Guadalupe cemetery, which was on a small knoll halfway up a foothill. Maybe it had once been just a small pile of sticks lit with matches, but now it was hundreds of feet wide and flames rose far above the trees. Worse, it seemed to be moving in all directions at once and was now lapping up against the far edge of the cemetery.

Delfino flung open his door and climbed out of the cab. He grabbed his shovel, then stopped beside Flavio's door. He raised his arm and pointed at the hillside. "I think if I can get up there," he said, "I can make this fire turn to the west. Then, maybe, it will just burn itself out at the river."

"This is a bad idea," Flavio said. He could hear the low rush of noise from the fire, like a high wind blowing. "This is not a fire to fight with a shovel."

The top of Delfino's head rose only a few inches above the bottom of the door window. He turned his head and looked at Flavio. "I brought my shovel," he said, "and my heavy boots. I don't want to stand in the road and drink beer."

Delfino's bad eye looked like clouded glass and as the other moved, it stayed still gazing straight ahead. "But you can't even see," Flavio said to him.

"I know the way well enough for one eye. Besides, sometimes it will fool me and begin to work." What he didn't tell Flavio was that when it did begin to work all he could see out of it was the shadow of things, which made walking about all the more difficult.

The two men looked at each other for a moment and then Flavio said, "I think you should see if anyone else wants to go. Maybe there's a group getting ready and if you go alone you might confuse them." But for all Flavio could tell, nobody was organizing anything. People were either talking together or wandering about aimlessly. There wasn't anyone else with a shovel, and even the fire truck was parked in the ditch on the side of the road.

"Bueno," Delfino said. "That's a good idea." He slapped the side of the truck. "I'll see you, Flavio. Cuidado and take good care of Felix." He turned away and began walking down the highway, his feet stepping on the bottom of his overalls.

"And you, también," Flavio said softly. Then he looked up at the hill. The sage and small piñon bordering the upper edge of the cemetery were smoking. Even from the road, he could see all the white crosses, some of them leaning where the graves beneath them had sunk over the years. Bouquets of plastic flowers were tied to some of them and also onto the rusted wire that ran around the graveyard. My whole family's buried up there, Flavio thought, and he pictured them beneath the ground, startled at the oncoming heat and the roar of the fire.

He turned to Felix. "You had the whole mountain," he yelled. "Why did you have to set the cemetery on fire?"

When Felix had awakened that morning after being asleep for eight years, he was, as usual, sitting alone in the far corner of the café. Although it was not yet dawn, there had been a faint pale rim growing above the mountains in the east. Inside, the room was dark, the only light coming from beneath the door that led to the kitchen. Pepe, after dressing his father and walking him to his table, had left an hour earlier to get kitchen supplies in Santa Madre. He had kissed his father's cheek and told him that he would be gone most of the day and that his good friend Ambrosio would be watching out for him.

Ambrosio Herrera had lived beside the café in a small trailer for twenty-five years. The trailer had only one room. It leaned badly as if hurt, and it shook even in a slight breeze. Ambrosio had first come to Guadalupe from a place far in Mexico, and he had stayed because it carried the same name as his own village. He had found a job at the café where he would sweep the pavement outside and scrub the floors and sometimes help Felix in the kitchen. In return, he was given the small trailer to live in, his food, and a few dollars each week, which he almost always sent to his family. For some time, Ambrosio would only remain in the village during the summer months, returning to Mexico for the winter. But, as the years passed, he grew tired of all the traveling until, eventually, he no longer left at all. Still, he sent his money to his wife and nine children whom no one in Guadalupe truly believed he had and whom he had nearly forgotten. On one day each month, Ambrosio would dress in slick black boots and black pants and a white shirt. He would wear a cowboy hat and then walk to Tito's Bar. There, he would drink whiskey all night and cry bitterly and sing songs about his family that would break only his own heart. Then he would stumble home by himself, back to his trailer, and sleep without dreaming until far into the next day.

The night before going to Santa Madre, Pepe had spoken to Ambrosio, telling him that he would be leaving Felix in his care for the day. He had told Ambrosio he had to do no more than make sure his father's glass of milk was full and to help him to the bathroom if need be. Ambrosio had nodded and looked at the floor. Before Felix's stroke, Ambrosio had treated him only with respect. But since the onset of his illness, he had become increasingly uncomfortable in Felix's presence. He did not like the way Felix stared blankly at nothing or the way his head and hands trembled as if frightened. Sometimes, when Ambrosio would glance at Felix, it would seem as if the old man's eyes were following him. At those times, Ambrosio would cross himself and say a brief prayer to the virgin.

Finally Ambrosio had raised his eyes to Pepe and smiled. He told him not to worry, that he would watch out for Felix like a brother and make sure no harm came to him. Then he had mopped the café floors and wiped the tables and switched off the lights. In his trailer, he opened a small bottle of whiskey and sat on his bed drinking until it was late.

When he awoke the following morning, the sun had already

risen. Ambrosio had hurried from his trailer and into the café. When he swung open the door between the kitchen and the restaurant, he found the room empty, only a glass of milk and a small plate of dry crackers on the table where Felix had sat. At first, Ambrosio stared in disbelief, but then, breathing a sigh of relief, he realized that Pepe must have taken his father with him to Santa Madre. He walked to the front door, opened it, and looked out on the day. Never would he have thought that Felix was wandering about the foothills alone.

Felix wasn't exactly sure just when it was he began to know that he was seeing. He had been gazing in the direction of the plate-glass window in the café when he became aware of the dark shape of the mountains and how they were rimmed in light. He could see a thin jagged line of trees on one high ridge silhouetted by the oncoming dawn. He took in a sharp breath of air, and his hand reached absently for the cigarettes in his shirt pocket that were long gone. He had never seen anything so quiet or so beautiful, and he wondered how he hadn't noticed it before. Then he heard the sound of the front door opening, the brush of wood on the mat just inside the room, and he saw the woman standing in the doorway.

She wasn't much more than a shadow, and she stood motionless, her arms at her sides. Her head was bent slightly and a shawl covered her hair and hung down her back. She was wearing a black dress that fell loosely away from her legs and down to her feet. It was too dark for Felix to see her face, but he thought that she may have nodded at him. As she walked toward him, he could hear the sound of her shoes hard on the tiled floor.

She sat at a table not far from his, and for a while the two of them sat in silence. Outside, the top of the mountains had turned gray and a dull, heavy light was crawling down the slopes. A truck hauling cattle passed by on the highway, its brakes hissing, headlights sweeping the road. When the sound of its shifting gears was gone, the woman turned her head toward Felix. "I told you I would see you again, hijo," she said.

"The next thing I know," Felix said to Flavio, "I'm in the mountains and there's a little fire of sticks at my feet. How was I to know that the cemetery was just below me?"

Someone walked by the truck and slapped the hood, calling out Flavio's name. Flavio raised a hand and didn't even bother to look up. He realized that for all Felix had said, he hadn't said anything at all. He had just made everything even more confusing. "So who was this woman?" Flavio asked. "Did she tell you her name?"

"I think it was the virgin," Felix said softly

"The Mother of God came to your café?" Flavio said. "And then she made you start a fire in the hills?"

"Well," Felix said.

"How did you get from the cemetery all the way to Ramona's house?"

"I don't remember that part," Felix said and leaned back on the seat. His head had stopped shaking, and he folded his hands in his lap. Flavio wondered if Felix was truly suffering from small seizures or if they just came and went when he wished. "It was good to see Delfino again," Felix went on. "I was never too fond of him, though. He always thought he knew everything. Maybe because he never married, no one taught him when it was better to keep quiet. You know what I think, Flavio?"

"No," Flavio said, raising a hand. "I don't want to know what you think, anymore." He pulled up the handle on the door and swung it open. "I'm going to see what's going on. If anyone asks you how you've been, maybe you should follow your own advice." Flavio climbed out of the truck and slammed the door behind him.

The fire had jumped the fence at the west edge of the cemetery, and the graves of the Cordova and the Trujillo and the Valdéz families were beneath flames. The white crosses near the heat were blistering and turning black, and the plastic flowers were melting. At the bottom of the road leading up to the cemetery, Sippy and a group of his friends and relatives were standing about the hearse that still carried his Tío Petrolino. A state police car was parked just beyond them, and the officer was in the midst of them. His hat was off and he was shaking his head.

Flavio walked slowly down the highway, keeping an eye out for Delfino and trying to stay out of the way of children who were darting about everywhere. He nodded to people as he passed by. Some said his name back in greeting, but others stared, and when he met their eyes, they looked away as if they hadn't seen him. He stopped beside a large group of men, most of whom were the eight brothers who ran the lumberyard. All were drinking beer, and they quieted as he neared. Flavio asked if anyone had seen Delfino.

"He came by here a little while ago, Flavio," Joe said. He was the oldest of the brothers and had taken over managing the place when their father had retired. "He was dragging a shovel and looking for someone to go up there with him."

"I think he was going to talk to Sippy," Lawrence said, and he brought his beer to his mouth. "Maybe you could ask Sippy." A few of the men laughed, and then they turned away, talking in low voices among themselves.

Joe walked over beside Flavio and put his hand on his shoulder. "Don't worry about Delfino," he said. "They're not letting anyone go up there. They got a plane that drops water coming from Santa Madre, and two crews of firefighters are being bused up from Las Sombras. That should handle it pretty easy, unless this wind keeps up."

The cemetery was half in flames now, and the rest of it was covered with a shroud of smoke. The Montoyas were all buried close to the east fence line, and for a second Flavio could see Martha lying in her white dress. He shook his head. "My whole family's up there," he said.

"And mine, también," Joe said. "Petrolino is the only one who got away. Who knows where he'll end up now."

"I better go," Flavio said, and he began to turn away.

"Wait a second, Flavio." Joe reached out and touched Flavio's arm. "What's this I hear about you starting this fire?"

"What?" Flavio said. "What did you say?"

"Sippy's been telling everyone that you knew there was a fire even before it started. Then I heard that a state cop was looking to talk to you. I'm not saying anything, Flavio. I'm just telling you what I heard."

Flavio felt light-headed and he took a step to balance himself. He opened his mouth and took in some air. "You think I could do something like this?" he asked, and even to himself his voice sounded shrill and weak.

"No," Joe said. "But I don't know why Sippy does. You should stay away from him right now. Maybe go home and let things quiet down."

As Flavio walked back to his pickup, he looked only at the pavement and tried to shut out the voices around him. When he reached his truck, he took one more look at the foothills, and at the base of the hill he saw Delfino. He was all by himself and using his shovel to help him make it up the slope. The fire was a few hundred yards south of him and so large that it made Delfino look like nothing.

Flavio opened his mouth to yell Delfino's name, but then he closed it. A wave of exhaustion passed through him, and he knew that no matter how loud he yelled, Delfino would not hear him over the noise of the fire. Besides, he thought, I have enough trou-ble as it is.

He pulled open the driver's door and climbed into the cab be-side Felix. "They think I started this fire," he said.

"You think I could do such a thing without you?" Felix answered.

6

When Guadalupe García was a young girl," Rosa Montoya said to her grandson, "she saw this village on fire.

"No one had any idea how long she had watched Guadalupe burning until her father, Moises was his name, finally went to the priest for help. For all people knew, she had seen smoke and flames forever as the Garcías kept to themselves and what went on in that house was anyone's guess. She was a small girl then, hijo, no more than four or five years old, and I can remember her so well at that time. Her hair was long and black, and I would see her every Sunday on my way to mass playing between the sagebrush in the grass. When I would wave at her, she would raise her own hand shyly and then turn away and look at the ground. There was something sad about her in her faded dresses and dolls made of old cloth, but even so, no one ever went near that house, and Guadalupe was always alone.

"This is a small village, hijo, and once the priest found out what Guadalupe was seeing, it was not long before everyone else knew, también. Horacio Medina tried to start trouble one day in church. At the end of mass, he stood and said loudly that if this girl could see such things in her mind, how long would it be before it actually happened? He shook his head and said that he had no wish to see his alfalfa burned or his neighbor's field and that it would be better for everyone if Guadalupe were sent away. He said that it was the duty of the priest to take her from her house and send her to a parish where she would do no harm. There was no place here, Horacio went on, for someone who saw the things she did.

"No one said anything for a little while after Horacio spoke, and I watched the priest standing on the altar. His name was Father Joseph. He was a large man of German descent and was priest here for so long that few could remember when he wasn't. Through the years, he had kept the village records and did his best to keep peace between families. I knew that he was troubled by what Guadalupe was seeing, but I also knew that he was not a man who could easily do what Horacio had asked.

"Finally, Toribio Vigil, who always sat in the back row and who came to church only to sleep, rose to his feet. He was dressed in the same clothes he had worn the day before and carried the odor of whiskey and stale tobacco. He said that he had seven grand-daughters, many the same age as Guadalupe García, and if anyone tried to send them away, he would, himself, burn down Horacio's alfalfa fields and Horacio's house and all of his corrals. Besides, he went on in a voice like gravel, if anyone should be sent to a parish far away, it should be Horacio, who had not only cheated his brother out of four cows years before, but was always happy to take a great deal from the people of this village and give little in return. No one else spoke after that, and when everyone had left the church, Father Joseph stood outside alone looking up the hill at the García house.

"For seven days, hijo, all Guadalupe García saw was fire. Each morning when she woke, she would see smoke pouring from the church windows. The roof would begin to smolder, and then the old wood shingles would burst into flames. The fire would spread from there like water and sweep through the valley, burning alfalfa and cattle and all of the houses. She would hear the sound of cows screaming and children choking on smoke. Late in the day, when the fire was finally approaching her own house, Guadalupe's skin would flush, her eyes would roll back in her head, and she would fall into a faint that would last until the following morning, when it would begin all over again.

"I think that Father Joseph grew old in that week. Each morning at dawn, he would walk up the hill, his shoulders bent, his feet moving as if he carried too heavy a weight. He would sit alone beside Guadalupe somewhere deep in that house, cooling her face with water and telling her stories of rain and great snowfalls. Although it was true that Toribio Vigil's words that day in church put a stop to sending Guadalupe away, it was also true that the village seemed to fall under the spell of what Guadalupe was seeing. People began to believe that they could smell the odor of smoke in the air. The cows stopped grazing and stood close together along the creek. The dogs in the village began to run wild, howling all night at nothing, and for all that Father Joseph did, not one thing changed.

"On the seventh day, Guadalupe woke whimpering. She was such a little girl, hijo, so small for her age, and she lay on the bed in just her nightgown. Her arms and legs had grown thin. Her dark face was as pale as ashes. For all the time Father Joseph had been in that house, he had seen no one but Guadalupe. Moises would let the priest into the house each morning. Then he would step outside and not return until nightfall. Guadalupe's mother, a hard and bitter woman who seemed to live only in that, would remain in her room until Father Joseph was gone. The only other person in the house was Percides García, Guadalupe's great-grandmother, but she, too, was nowhere to be seen.

"One afternoon, Guadalupe's skin began to blister. Father Joseph, who had been dozing, heard her moan. When he saw what was happening, he rose to his feet in shock. He called out for more water, but the thick walls of that house seemed to drown his voice. He stood beside her bed, staring down at her. Her skin was too hot to touch, and he could smell the odor of burning hair.

"Although Father Joseph stayed in the house all that night, I think a part of him had left. He prayed for Guadalupe and her family and the whole village, but in his heart he had given up. He had no belief in himself or anything else in that house. When Guadalupe finally awoke the next morning, her eyes were clear and her skin was cool and she remembered nothing of that week. And then the village, too, forgot, as if we had all been lost somewhere for a little while."

Flavio and Felix were sitting on the ground listening while Rosa spoke. She was bent over pulling weeds from among her hollyhocks outside her kitchen window. It was late in the afternoon, when the sun was not so hot. Rosa's hair was tied back and covered by a black scarf. Her fingers dug in the dirt, loosing the roots from the earth. Epolito had left earlier that day for Las Sombras to buy seed and flour and beans, and baby José was asleep inside the house on Rosa and Epolito's bed.

When she was done, Rosa stood up slowly. She put her hands on her hips and arched backward. "This is work for strong young boys," she said, "not old women like me." Beside her, though, was a large pile of weeds, and the ground between the hollyhocks was clean and smooth. She looked at the two boys. Then she squatted back down.

Felix's eyes were open a little too wide, and there was a smear of moisture just below his nostrils. Flavio was idly pulling out strands of grass from the ground. Rosa picked up a small stone and tossed it awkwardly into his lap.

"Where did Delfino go?" she asked.

"I don't know," Flavio said, without looking up.

The three boys, Flavio and Felix and Delfino, had spent the day together at Delfino's house pulling rotted, warped boards off an outbuilding and then nailing them onto a cottonwood tree. They had spiked steps thirty feet off the ground when Delfino's father had limped from out of the house, his bad leg trailing as if it belonged to someone else, and yelled at them to quit wasting nails and to get out of the tree before they fell and broke something.

They had left, wandering the irrigation ditches for a while, until they ended up at Rosa's house. They had watched her pulling weeds and then, without thinking, Flavio had asked his grandmother why Guadalupe García was the way she was.

"She's lived all her life in that house, hijo," Rosa had said, yanking out a weed that was nearly as tall as she. "And for most of it, she's been alone. Even when she wasn't, she might as well have been. Her mother was named Maria Velásquez, and she came from a large family that had a poor ranch a few miles north of here. Her own mother was a beaten, tired woman. Her father had such a fondness for whiskey that he passed it on to all of his sons. What he gave to his daughters no one knew and no one asked. They have all moved from here now, drifting away as if they had no roots. Maria was the only one who remained, and what she needed from her husband or the García house or even Guadalupe for that matter, she never received. So she, too, became lost in that house. How she and Moises came to have children at all is a mystery to me.

"Guadalupe's father did what he could with her to keep peace in that house, but after a while a deadness came to his heart and he became like a man who had drowned in himself. He began leaving the house each day long before dawn and not returning until late at night. He never spoke of where he went or what he was doing, but by then there was no one in that house who cared.

"It was rumored that years before Guadalupe was born, Maria gave birth to another daughter. The baby was a sad, weak creature and when Maria saw it, she told her husband to take it away from her, that she had no wish to be a mother to anything. The midwife, Magdalena Varela, an old woman with a humped back and twisted hands, went to the priest, Father Joseph. She told him that a baby had been born in the García house. And she told him that for three days the infant had not eaten and was held only by her father. Magdalena Varela said that if something was not done, the baby would die.

"That afternoon, the priest walked up the hill, and Moises met him at the door. His face was haggard from no sleep and his eyes were red as if they had bled. For a while, the two men only stared at each other. Then Moises told Father Joseph that his help was not needed, that the Garcías had always taken care of their own. From inside the house, all the priest could hear was silence.

"No one ever knew what truth there was in what Magdalena Varela had said. Maybe Moises had hid the infant somewhere in that house or maybe he gave it to the Indians who sometimes passed by the village. As far as anyone knows, Guadalupe is the last of the Garcías and she carries in herself all that they have ever been. No one in this valley ever wanted to have anything to do with her or her family. Father Joseph, at times, did what he could, but there are some things nobody can change. I'll tell you three boys something that happened to her when she was little," and then Rosa had gone on to tell them the story of when Guadalupe García saw the village on fire.

Again, Rosa tossed a small stone at her grandson. "Did Delfino just disappear?" she asked.

"I think he went home," Felix said.

Halfway through Rosa's story, at the part where cows were screaming and children were choking on smoke, Delfino had stood up quickly. Then he had backed away and run all the way to his house, his short legs pumping like crazy. Flavio and Felix had remained behind, listening to Rosa as if they had become accustomed to hearing stories such as these, which, in truth, they had.

"That was a sad story, Mrs. Montoya," Felix said.

"Thank you, Felix," Rosa said.

"So you know any more?"

"I know a whole bunch of them." Rosa smiled and looked back at Flavio. "And what's wrong with you, hijo?"

"He gets this way sometimes," Felix said, leaning back on his elbows and crossing his legs at the ankles. "Whenever he asks a question, he ends up hearing too much. But it doesn't bother me."

It had begun to seem to Flavio as if Guadalupe García was all around him. While that was partly his own fault, it was also true that whenever he asked a question, the depth of the answer never failed to startle him. On top of that, every time he now left his grandmother's house, his eyes were drawn to the García house and to the cottonwood tree shadowing the church. At night, just before sleep, he would picture Guadalupe García wandering through the empty rooms in her house. He would see her stumbling across things she had never seen before: a small nicho hidden in a dark corner holding a faded image of a saint, a fragile piece of paper in the dust beneath a bed, a small gold ring hung on a nail. He would lie in his bed and think that Guadalupe lived in a graveyard where not only did the dead still breathe, but they also left their things lying about.

One afternoon, he and Felix had even hunted among the junipers along the creek for the blackened end of the branch that Cristóbal had cut to make his santo. But, it was one thing to daydream about such things or hear Guadalupe tell her stories, and another to listen to his grandmother. What he had thought while Rosa was speaking was that she could just as easily have been Guadalupe García.

Flavio raised his head and looked at Rosa. There was dirt on her face, and the scarf tied around her forehead was damp with sweat. She was still smiling, and for a second, with her gray hair covered and her skin pulled smooth, she seemed like a younger woman, as if beneath the life he had known her to lead was another far richer. From inside the house came the sound of his brother crying and then he fell still.

Rosa reached out and touched Flavio's hand. "Guadalupe García's life," she said, "is not yours, hijo." And with her words, she became who she always had been.

"Eee," Felix said. "I would never want to have her life and live in that house. The walls are made of bones."

"Just in one room," Flavio said.

"That's what she says. Maybe her whole family is buried in there. Maybe the little baby is there. I would never want to be buried in a wall and stay standing forever and not be able to sit down."

"You would be dead," Flavio said. "It wouldn't matter."

"How do you know? If I was dead, I would want to lie down like everyone else. You can stay standing and see what happens." He pushed off his elbows and sat up. "But, I would sure like to see those bones."

Flavio picked up the small stone in his lap and flicked it off the side of Felix's head. "I'm never going back there," he said.

"That's what you always say," Felix said. "And stop throwing stones at me."

"Did she tell you whose bones they were?" Rosa said.

Both boys fell quiet for a few seconds, and then Felix said, "She told us they were some bandit's bones. But she didn't say why he was in a wall."

"Emilio García, the bandit," Rosa said.

"Grandmother," Flavio said, "is it true that they used to hang people at the church?"

"Many things have happened at the church," Rosa said slowly, which wasn't quite the answer either Flavio or Felix had expected to hear. "And so many priests have lived there, if only for a little while. Who's to say what has happened there? But of all the priests that have been here, it was Father Joseph who tried to make this place his own. He was here in the years the church forgot about us and left us to ourselves. He was here so long that when he died, he was almost like one of us."

One day, near the end of Father Joseph's life, he stood before a tall, narrow window inside the empty church. The only sound in the room, other than the sound of his own breathing, which had become slow and heavy with age, was the occasional creaking of the vigas high overhead. It had finally grown light outside and the sky was the flat color of ashes. He could see the foothills to the east, hazed slightly from the soft rain that had fallen in the night. And just up the slope from where the church had been built nearly two hundred years before, he could see the García house.

Each morning, Father Joseph would rise while the day was still dark. He would dress slowly, feeling the stiffness in his joints. Then, he would start a small fire in his cookstove to boil water. He'd make himself a cup of coffee that was always too strong and burned. Then he'd go into the church and stand quietly before the same window, staring out at the darkness and waiting for daylight. As had been the case for almost as long as he could remember, when morning came he would see Guadalupe García step outside her door.

In the last few years, she had worn the same nightgown each morning. It hung loosely against her body and came to just below her knees. Her black hair was knotted from sleep and fell far down her back. The priest would watch as she moved her hair from her face and looked out at the village along with him. In the winter it was no different, and he would wonder how it was she did not fall ill. Then he would realize that if she did there were few who would know and fewer yet who would care.

Father Joseph took a sip of coffee and watched as Guadalupe wrapped her bare arms tight across her chest. Smoke drifted from a few stovepipes and hung low over the valley, seeming more like mist than anything having to do with the village itself. The priest wondered what both he and Guadalupe looked for, staring out at the village each morning. He took in a deep breath and thought that later in the day, Telesfor Ruiz would be coming to the church to help him do repairs on the roof. Even the thought made his bones ache.

"I remember you when you were a little girl," Father Joseph said aloud, his words dying in the empty room. "And then, too, we would stand here together."

When Guadalupe was small, she would sometimes step outside with her mother, Maria. Guadalupe would wander a few paces away from her mother and crouch down to study something on the ground or play in the sage with what she had left out the evening before. Her hair was long then, too, and it would hide her face from the priest. Maria would watch her daughter for a little while, and then she would cross her arms around her chest and stand stiffly, staring out at other things.

"Your mother was a hard woman, hija," Father Joseph said. "And I'm sorry for that. You deserved better." He watched as Guadalupe raised her arms and ran her hands through her hair. She was a woman now, almost twenty years old, and though the priest couldn't see her body, nor did he wish to, he could almost feel it beneath her nightgown. She dropped her arms and then turned and looked down the hill at the church. For a second, Father Joseph felt as though she could actually see him standing behind the glass. Then she turned and walked back inside the house, leaving the door open behind her, as she always did.

He had been inside the García house only three times in all his years as priest in Guadalupe, and each time had been a disaster. It seemed to him now as if his whole life in the valley had somehow been separated into stages that ended or began with a visit inside that house. The first time had been when he was a young man, full of his own pride, and looked upon the village as something shared between himself and God. He had walked to the García house after being told about a sick infant. There, after one look at Moises García's face, he knew that whatever he had come to stop had already happened. The second time had been when Guadalupe had seen the village on fire.

He brought his cup to his mouth and drank. The coffee had grown cold, and his fingers were numb and cramped from holding the cup. He bent over and set it down on the wide sill. The sky outside was now tinged red, and the color fell onto the foothills. The priest folded his hands together before him. His eyes were heavy and his heart felt knotted in his chest. The vigas overhead creaked gently as if from the weight of footsteps. The priest closed his eyes, and he remembered the last time he had been inside that house. For all the good he had done in this valley, it was possible that it had come to nothing.

"That house," Father Joseph said softly, "has been only bad luck for me."

"Murderer," was what Percides García had said to the priest on the night she died.

Father Joseph had smiled in confusion and thought that whatever it was Percides had just uttered couldn't have been what he thought he had heard. Then she said it again. This time, though her voice was little more than a harsh whisper, the force of her words startled the priest.

"Murderer," she said. "With your empty robes and your prayers you are no more than a thief."

Moises García had come for Father Joseph in the middle of the night with word that his grandmother was dying and that before she did, she wished to see him. The priest had been awakened from a deep sleep, and at first he had no idea who this man was standing in the darkness outside his door. Moises had aged severely in the years since Father Joseph had last seen him. His hair was long and knotted and had turned white, and his face was drawn and seamed deep with creases. An odor of dust and grease came from his clothes.

"My grandmother is Percides García," Moises said.

The priest shook his head to clear it of sleep. "Moises," he said. "Give me one moment." While he dressed, he realized that he could not even remember the last time he had seen Percides García, and that for all he knew, she had been dead for years. A vague misgiving came over him, but he shook it away as if it had more to do with fatigue than anything else. As he walked up the hill in the darkness behind Moises, he found some comfort in the thought that even Percides could, at the time of her death, seek some understanding of her life.

If Father Joseph had not known the woman on the bed was Percides García, he would never have recognized her. She lay as still as stone, and though the heavy blanket that covered her came to just below her breasts, the priest could see that she had shrunk with age and seemed not much larger than a child. There were no pillows under her head, and her hair, white and sparse, fanned out about her face. Her skin was thin and fragile and as delicate as parchment, and she stared up at the ceiling, her eyes wide open, as if she wished to see whatever was to come. The taste in the air was brittle and dry and stale.

A kerosene lamp was lit on a small table beside the bed. Next to it stood a carved santo. It was only a foot high and so old that it had faded to a dull black. Gashes from a knife covered the Lady's body, and the wood on her face was rubbed smooth from being touched over so many years. Father Joseph sat on a chair beside the bed and then looked across the room at Guadalupe, who was lying on a narrow banco built out from the wall.

When the priest had first entered the room, he had thought that Guadalupe was asleep. But in the brief time he had been there, she would sometimes move her legs up to her chest or drop her hand to the floor, her fingers drawing on the hard-packed mud.

"In the cold you hung him," Percides said.

"With rain in his eyes," Guadalupe suddenly chimed in, looking up at the priest.

"Hush, Guadalupe," Father Joseph said. "You should be with your mother. This is no place for you to be."

"My mother's asleep."

Moises had led Father Joseph to this room and then, without a word, had turned and left him. There had been no sign of Maria. Percides García has been dying for years, he thought, and it was possible everyone had grown tired with a such a long death. But still, this house should be full of the odor of food cooking and the sound of hushed voices instead of silence.

"If you are to remain here," he said to Guadalupe, "then lie down and close your eyes. This is a time to be quiet."

"Murderer," Percides hissed.

"Be still, Percides," Father Joseph said softly, "and think of other things." He reached out and lay his hand on the bed. "No one has been murdered."

"My great-grandfather was," Guadalupe said, and she raised her head again and looked at the priest. "You hung him from a rope un-til he was dead."

Not for the first time Father Joseph thought that something was drastically wrong in this house. He had no idea what it was— something so large that he couldn't comprehend it, or a thing so small that it was just beyond his grasp. He felt as if everything here was one heartbeat off from the rest of the world.

"Your great-grandfather," he said, "was a gentle man who died in an accident long before you were born."

"No," Guadalupe said, shaking her head. "That was someone else. My great-grandfather was Emilio García, the bandit."

"Who has told you these things, hija?"

"My grandmother," Guadalupe said.

One day, when Guadalupe was six years old, her great-grandmother, Percides García, began talking, and she didn't stop until her death five years later. It had begun on a summer morn-ing that was gray and damp and too cold for the season. Guadalupe and her grandmother had been alone together in the kitchen. Guadalupe's mother had left the house earlier in a black anger, and her father was, as usual, gone doing the things he never spoke of.

The door to the kitchen was closed that day, and the room was lit only by the dull light that came through the small window and a lamp that was burning too high, staining the chimney black. Guadalupe sat beside her grandmother printing words in a tablet that looked not like words, but like strange drawings of trees. At times, she would move her arm to show Percides what she had written. But her grandmother would stare straight ahead and nod and say nothing.

It began to rain outside, and when Guadalupe looked up from her tablet all she could see was mud and water running down the glass of the window. She wondered if her mother was still out walking by herself in such a downpour. Then she thought that she would try to print the word *porcupine*. It was at that moment that her grandmother placed her hand over the paper and said, "Hija, the only man I truly loved was Emilio García. He was my first cousin and they hung him on a day like this from the tree beside the church. With rain in his eyes and his clothes wet and cold."

From that moment on, Percides García never stopped talking. She talked while cutting garlic and mixing flour for tortillas. She talked while sweeping the dirt floors and cleaning the counters of the dust that always fell from the ceiling. She talked to the back of Guadalupe's head in a low, calm voice while she brushed her great-granddaughter's hair. Even in her sleep, she would mumble, and finally her voice became only a harsh whisper, a sound that, after a while, seemed to come not from her but from the house itself. She told of Emilio García and of her family and of thoughts that would come into her head and then vanish. She spoke in a monologue that lasted five years. Even after her death, it seemed to Guadalupe that still she could hear the sound of her great-grandmother's voice.

Finally, Guadalupe's mother, who barely spoke at all and had little patience for anything, moved Percides to a room far from the center of the house. There, she would sit by herself, and Guadalupe would bring her food and the things she needed.

"Emilio García," Percides would say to Guadalupe or to no one at all, "was lost from my life . . ."

". . . and he was the only man I ever loved," she now said to the priest. "He was hung at the church by the priest and the people of this village. And on that same day, you also took from me my grandfather, Cristóbal García."

"I don't know these people you speak of," Father Joseph said, confused. "The church would never harm anyone. Nor would it steal grandfathers."

The only husband Percides ever had died years and years before, just after Father Joseph had arrived in Guadalupe. The priest realized that he could not even remember the man's name. He had been a small, reserved man who had gone alone to mass every Sunday and who seldom spoke to anyone. He had cared for his cows and irrigated his fields and had even done repairs on the García house. One day, while cutting juniper posts not far from the village, he had fallen into an arroyo, breaking both his legs. He was not found for a number of days, and when he was no one was sure if he had died from his injuries or if he had lain among the rocks, his legs twisted beneath him, staring at the sky until his breath stopped. I can remember this man's death, the priest thought, but not his name.

"Please rest now, Percides," Father Joseph said, and his hand patted the bed gently. "Soon this night will be over."

Percides turned her head slowly. She looked at the priest. "I've waited all my life to say these things to you," she said. "Why else do you think you're here?" In her eyes, Father Joseph could see a clarity so hardened that he knew for all the reasons he had come to this house, none was why he had been called.

"There is a mistake here," he said. "Never have I harmed anyone."

"Even now," Percides went on, as if the priest had said nothing, "when I look down the hill I can see the rain in sheets and I see him with his head bowed and his clothes wet and his hands tied behind his back. And in my own mouth is the taste of mud. The whole village was there that day, huddled together like cowards beneath the cottonwood tree. And by then, my grandfather was already lost somewhere inside the church. The priest said a prayer, and then he led the horse slowly forward. Emilio fell back like a child falling, and his face looked up to the sky in confusion and rain fell in his eyes." Percides stopped talking and closed her eyes. When she opened them again, she said, "I curse you for this. And I curse this village for what it did."

"Percides," Father Joseph said, and even he could hear the trembling in his voice. "I have never heard of such a thing happening." The wick in the kerosene lamp flickered, and when Father Joseph glanced at it, his eyes fell upon the santo. The Lady stared back at him, her hands together at her breasts, and suddenly he knew that what was true and what wasn't did not matter in this house.

"Hija," Percides said, "tell the priest." Then she turned her head so that she was once again staring up at the ceiling.

"My great-grandfather was Emilio García," Guadalupe said. The girl was lying on her stomach now, her fingers tracing the small cracks in the adobe floor. "He was the son of Pilar García and the grandson of Cristóbal García, who was the first person ever to come to this valley, and he was hung from the branches of the cottonwood that stands beside the church. It was raining, too."

"That's good, mi hija," Percides said. "Now tell this man to leave us."

"Leave," Guadalupe said, and she looked up at Father Joseph and smiled.

7

Flavio sat motionless in his pickup in the parking lot outside Felix's Café. The engine was running and he was leaning back against the seat, his hands still on the steering wheel, looking out at the plate-glass windows of the café. Behind him on the highway, traffic was still moving, but this time northward, away from the fire. Half of the sky, just to the left of the café, was a vast, black cloud of smoke.

"I told you," Felix said. "Pepe went to Santa Madre. He won't be back until late." He was sitting in the middle of the seat and, like Flavio, was gazing straight ahead out the windshield. "Besides," he went on, "I don't think I want to stay here anymore."

Flavio stirred on the seat and pulled himself up a little straighter. "I don't care," he said, which were the first words he'd spoken to Felix since driving from the fire. "We're not leaving un-

til Pepe gets back. Or Ambrosio. Or someone. And move over a little. It's too hot to have you sitting so close to me."

After pulling off the road, Flavio had jumped out of the cab and
tried the front door of the café. It was locked. When he cupped his
hands and peered through the glass, not only had he seen no sign of
life inside the place, but it looked as though the café hadn't even
been opened for business that morning. The chairs were still stacked
on the tables, and the tile floor shone from being mopped the night
before.

"What's happening here?" Flavio had mumbled to himself.
"Where's Ambrosio?" Then he had walked quickly around to the
back of the building. There, he had found the door to the kitchen
locked as well. He had called out Ambrosio's name, but there was
no answer. He went over to Ambrosio's small trailer and cracked
open the door. In one glance, he could see that the trailer, too, was
empty. Dirty dishes were piled in the sink, and the bed against the
far wall was unmade. On the table in the middle of the room was
an empty whiskey bottle, a deck of cards, and a few coins. The air
inside the trailer was stifling and smelled like that of a man living
alone for too long. Flavio had closed the door and then, moving
slower, had gone back to his truck.

"This is where you live, Felix," Flavio said, without turning his
head. "This is where you've always lived."

"I might get sick again if I go back in there."

"Ambrosio will be back soon. He's probably at the store getting
a few things. He can watch out for you until Pepe gets back."

"Oh, sí, Ambrosio. I bet you he's at Tito's singing his songs," Felix said, which was exactly where Ambrosio was.

After finding Felix gone earlier that morning, Ambrosio had
walked back through the café and out the kitchen door to his
trailer. He had sat at his table for a while playing cards and sipping
a little whiskey. The breeze had picked up by then, and it blew the

thin, warped door to the trailer back and forth. He thought that he should be in the kitchen heating up the beans and making coffee, and then he wondered what his children were doing in Mexico and if their day was as hot and dry as it was in this valley. He took one long drink of whiskey, draining the bottle. Then he stood up, wobbling a little bit, and said out loud, "To hell with the damn beans. My name is Ambrosio Herrera and I am more than a heater of beans." Then, he pulled on his black boots and his cowboy hat and walked down the road to Tito's Bar. At that moment, he was drinking his fourth beer with Fred Sanchez, and both were talking excitedly at the same time about different things.

Felix reached out and touched Flavio's arm. "I'm sorry, Flavio," he said, "if I upset you when I said that you helped start the fire."

Flavio pulled his arm away. "Things like this don't happen to me," he said.

"Maybe they have always happened and you just got used to them."

Flavio grunted and looked over at Felix. "I would remember burning down the mountains," he said. "How could I forget a thing like that?"

"I forgot eight years." Felix shrugged. "My son became a man and one by one my old friends died, and I didn't notice anything."

"I was in Ramona's field irrigating her alfalfa," Flavio said slowly, "and you came walking out of the hills like a ghost." He could see himself standing by the ditch with his shovel, the day still cool and gray with no sun. He remembered seeing a shadow moving between the piñons and thinking it was a deer.

"Who knows," he said softly. "Maybe I saw the Lady, too, and I didn't know it." Flavio rubbed his eyes with his fingers. They felt hot and scratchy, and he realized that it wasn't just from being tired, but from the smoke in the air. He let his hand drop to his lap. "What a mess. I don't even want to think about what will happen if someone's house burns down."

Felix patted Flavio's arm. "It's not our fault, Flavio," he said. "We didn't ask for this. Besides, things could be worse."

"Oh, sí?" Flavio said. "You tell me how," and it was then that the two police cars pulled up close behind Flavio's truck, blocking him in.

One of the vehicles was the beat-up green jeep that the village sometimes used when there was a reason to go into the mountains. Its body was rusted out along the frame, and the passenger door was dented in from sliding off the highway years before and slamming into a post. It was a vehicle, though, that always kept running and when shoved into first gear would crawl its way up anything. The other car was from the state and, other than a faint layer of dust that dulled the color, there wasn't a mark on it. Both doors swung open, and the two officers climbed out. They glanced at each other, and then each walked up to one side of Flavio's truck.

The state cop stopped a few feet away from the side of the pickup. Then he stooped down and looked in the cab window.

"Are you Flavio Montoya?" he asked, speaking Flavio's name flat and empty, without even a hint of an accent. He was of medium height and too thin. His uniform was wrinkled and carried the stale odor of tobacco. His face was burned brown from the sun, and a web of fine lines stretched down from the corners of both eyes. He pressed one hand flat on his thigh; the other rested loosely on his revolver. The name tag on his shirt read N. OLIVER.

Flavio stared at him for a few seconds and then leaned forward and looked out the other window at Donald Lucero. Donald was one of the two Guadalupe police officers and had been for the past ten years. He was a big man who was known to have little sense of humor and to see only what was in front of him. He was not someone to whom Flavio had ever given much thought, but Flavio knew his father and all of his uncles.

"¿Cómo estás, Donald?" Flavio said. "I haven't seen you in a long time. How is your family?"

Oliver let out a long breath of air. "Sir," he said. "I asked you a question." He had been a police officer in northern New Mexico for twenty-five years and lived with his second wife, who was too young for his age, and two small daughters in a house outside Las Sombras. He spent his days smoking cigarettes and driving the highways and back roads in the northern part of the state, and he had never had much luck in the small villages.

"You are too white and too blond," his wife would tell him. "And worse, you are from somewhere else." These were all things Oliver knew, but the older he got the more difficult it had become for him to make sense of them. He had grown tired of the wrecks on empty stretches of highway and the mangled carcasses of deer he would find on the side of the road. When he passed through the small villages, he could glimpse the guarded look in the people's eyes, and he realized that like them, he only wished to drive through their lives. He would light yet another cigarette and look out his window at the sagebrush. From time to time, he would say to his wife that once there had been a reason he had chosen this job but that now he had forgotten what it was. Then, his wife, who had lost much of her happiness in the last few years, would close her eyes and let her mind fill with other things.

"Sir," Oliver said again, and he suddenly felt a chill as if something had passed before the sun.

Flavio turned his head and looked up at Oliver. "Yes," he said. "I am Flavio Montoya."

"I have a few questions I'd like to ask you, if I may," Oliver said. Whatever had been cold in the air left, and he was once more standing in the heat beside an old truck. "Can you please shut off your vehicle for me."

"Oh, sí," Flavio said, and he reached out, his hands shaking slightly, and switched off the ignition. A wave of heat rose from the hood of the truck, and Donald Lucero turned his body away.

"Can you tell me who your passenger is?" Oliver asked.

"My passenger?"

"The man sitting beside you."

For a moment the two men just stared at each other. Then Flavio moved his eyes slowly past Oliver and looked at the sky. If he hadn't known any better, the smoke could be no more than one of the thunderstorms that came to the valley every summer—clouds so black they were almost blue. Wind would sweep over the hills, and sometimes the storm would catch Flavio in his fields. When he would return home, wet and muddy and cold, Martha would be waiting anxiously by the door, afraid in her heart that her husband had been hit by the lightning that slashed from the clouds and never cared what it struck. She would be waiting with a towel and would help Flavio with his boots. The house would be lit well and would smell of things baking. They would sit together in the kitchen, and Flavio would drink hot coffee and Martha would watch the dark day and how the rain fell on the apple trees.

"Mr. Montoya," Oliver said sharply. "There is a fire burning in this village. Can you help me out and tell me who your passenger is?"

Flavio moved his eyes back to the police officer. Oliver's eyes were bloodshot, and there was a haggard look to his face. He looked like a man who didn't sleep well and when he woke was always tired. "Who are you?" Flavio said. "I've never seen you before."

"My name is Nick Oliver," he said. "I'm out of Las Sombras. Can you tell me who's sitting beside you?"

"Felix," Flavio said, "this man is asking you a question." When there was no response, Flavio turned his head. Felix was lying back against the seat. His eyes were closed and his head was twisted at an awkward angle. His mouth hung wide open and he was snoring lightly. Flavio shook his shoulder, which only seemed to make Felix snore louder. "Eee," Flavio breathed out, "why are you doing this to me, Felix?"

"The viejo's name is Felix García," Donald said over the cab of the pickup. "He owns this café. I don't know what he's doing out here. He had a stroke a long time ago and hasn't gotten around much since then."

"His son went to Santa Madre," Flavio said, looking back at Oliver, "and I've been watching out for him. We were sitting here waiting for Pepe to show up."

"You might be waiting a long time," Oliver said. "The highway south to Las Sombras was closed thirty minutes ago. It's only open to emergency crews. The only way into this valley right now is from the north." Oliver stood up straight. He let his hands drop to his sides and looked over the cab at Donald. "You sure we haven't made a mistake?" he said. "These guys aren't exactly kids messing around."

"This is the only Montoya who lives in the village," Donald said. "And I didn't hear wrong."

The two men stared at each other and then Oliver dropped his eyes. He reached in his shirt pocket and dragged out a cigarette. He cupped his hands away from the wind and lit it. When he glanced back up, he looked at Flavio. "Can you please get out of your vehicle, Mr. Montoya," he said. Then he took hold of the handle on the truck door and pulled it open.

Flavio stood with his back to his truck. Oliver and Donald Lucero were standing together a few feet in front of him. The wind was blowing dust on the opposite side of the highway, and every so often it swept through the parking lot, sending up swirls of dirt and empty cigarette packs. The air was hazy from smoke, and in it was the taste of trees burning. One car after another was driving by the café, and as they passed, they slowed down and stared.

Oliver dropped his cigarette butt and stepped on it. Then he took off his hat and wiped his forehead with his sleeve. His hair was a dull brown and damp with sweat. "It's too damn hot," he said to no one. "And this wind just makes it hotter." He put his hat back on and looked at Flavio. "Can you tell me where you were this morning, Mr. Montoya?"

"What's all this about?" Flavio said. "Why are you asking me these things?"

"This is about you telling him where you were," Lucero said. "You see these cars? The whole west side of the valley is being evacuated and if the fire jumps the highway, everyone will leave." He was taller than Oliver and thicker in the body, and he stood half facing the road, watching the traffic. He shifted his eyes to Flavio. "People are saying that you started this fire, Flavio. If it's true and if this fire gets any worse, I wouldn't want to be you. This is our village, jodido, and it's burning down. So if I were you, I'd answer the man's questions."

For a moment, no one spoke. Then Flavio said, his voice trembling, "I've lived here all my life." But even he knew that what he had said meant nothing.

"Can you tell me where you were this morning?" Oliver said, and he spoke softly, as if embarrassed.

"I was in my field," Flavio said. "I was irrigating like I do every morning."

"What time did you start irrigating?"

"Before it was light."

"Did anyone else see you?"

"How should I know?" Flavio said, lifting his arms and then dropping them. "I was in my field."

"Can you tell me exactly what time it was when you picked up Mr. García?"

Flavio fell quiet. Then he took a step backward and leaned against the side of his truck. He could feel his heart beating too fast in his chest, and he realized that he was frightened. He had no idea what to say to this Anglo whom he didn't know. And worse, he could see each question leading to another until he would become so mired in his own answers that not even he would know what he was talking about. Behind him, in the cab, he could hear the rough sound of Felix snoring. Flavio shut his eyes and took a few deep breaths until his mind went away and he remembered the time he had killed his grandmother's favorite rooster by mistake.

This rooster was so old that his feathers were falling out and those that were left were black and grew only in clumps. It was small, with swollen purple feet, and Ramona had once told him that when this rooster was young, it had been known to kill small dogs. It was the oldest rooster among his grandmother's chickens, and he and Flavio had never gotten along well.

It was Flavio's chore each day during the summer to feed the chickens. When he would go to their coop to toss them handfuls of chipped corn and seed, the rooster would skulk around the perimeter of the fence until Flavio's back was turned. Then, it would fly at him in a rush, its mouth open, its wings flapping in a flurry of madness. Flavio would scream and flap his own arms, and then, with chickens all about his feet as if nothing were happening, he would flee the coop for safety.

One afternoon, when Flavio was returning home from Felix's house, he saw his grandmother's rooster perched on a low branch in the cottonwood that grew near the ditch. It was squatting down as if either nesting or hiding, and even from where Flavio stood, he could see that the rooster was watching him as he walked to the house. Flavio stopped dead in his tracks, and then he waved his arms and yelled for it to get back where it belonged. He grabbed a handful of small stones and flung them into the tree but the rooster didn't even stir. Flavio suddenly pictured himself running down the road with his grandmother's rooster chasing him. If that happened, it would be seen by, or at least told to, half the village. He bent over and picked up a large rock. After a quick glance toward the house, Flavio let the stone fly, and at that second, the rooster stood up on the branch as if to crow. The rock struck it full in the head, and Flavio watched horrified as his grandmother's favorite rooster fell dead into the irrigation ditch.

At dinner that evening, Rosa said that her rooster had escaped from the chicken coop and that with so many coyotes and savage dogs roaming about, she feared the worst. Flavio lowered his head and looked at the tortilla folded on the edge of his plate. Then, Ramona, with a faint smile for her brother and a lilt in her voice, said that she had watched Flavio kill it with a rock and that it now lay thrown in the weeds behind the shed.

For a moment no one spoke, and then Epolito said sharply, "Why would you do such a thing?"

"It was an accident," Flavio mumbled, his eyes still facing down.

"How do you kill a rooster with a rock by accident?" Epolito said.

"The rooster was in a tree, and it jumped in front of my rock."

"The rooster killed itself on purpose?" Epolito said, and then while Flavio sat thinking that some things were impossible to explain and that Ramona had always been her grandfather's favorite, he leaned across the table and slapped his grandson on the side of the head.

That night, just before sleep, Rosa had come to Flavio's bedroom. She sat on the side of the bed and touched his hair.

"That rooster was always mean, hijo," she said softly. The room was dark and warm air drifted in the open window. "Hijo," she said.

"Ramona said it would kill dogs," Flavio said.

"I think your sister likes to frighten you, hijo," she said, and her hand brushed where Flavio had been slapped by Epolito. "Your grandfather gets angry sometimes, Flavio, but in his heart he loves you so much. Never forget that."

"I didn't mean to kill it," Flavio said, although he wasn't sure if that was true.

"I know, mi hijo. Now sleep and dream sweet things."

In the parking lot outside Felix's Café, Flavio opened his eyes to wind and smoke and to the two police officers standing a few feet in front of him.

"Are you all right, Mr. Montoya?" Oliver asked, and his hand reached out, not quite touching Flavio's arm. Although Flavio had only closed his eyes for a few seconds, there had been a sudden slackness in his face that made it seem to Oliver as if Flavio were suffering from a stroke, not Felix García.

"Yes," Flavio said and pushed himself off the side of the truck. He could see a concern in Oliver's face that embarrassed him. "I'm fine. But I should tell you that I didn't pick Felix up this morning. He came walking out of the foothills and into my field by himself."

Donald grunted and spit out a stream of air. "Felix García doesn't walk anywhere," he said to Oliver. "And he hasn't for years. Everyone in the village knows that."

Oliver looked past Flavio at the old man asleep on the seat of the pickup. There were scratches on his face that could have come from piñon branches and his trousers were torn at the knees. But he didn't look strong enough to climb out of the truck by himself. Suddenly all Oliver wanted to do was get back in his squad car and start driving. He would light up a cigarette and crack open the window and switch off the radio that only brought him news he didn't want to hear. He would drive over roads and look at the mountains and not think about anything—not his wife or his daughters, who were only happy when he was gone, and not this village where everything was slightly askew and made less and less sense by the second. He reached in his shirt pocket and then dropped his hand.

"When did this happen, Mr. Montoya?" he asked.

"Just before the sun came to the valley," Flavio said. "I could hardly believe my eyes. Then later, after Felix had rested, he told me that he had awoken from his sickness before dawn and that he and a woman who might have been the Virgin walked out of the café and into the hills. There, they made a little pile of sticks and started it on fire."

Donald took a step forward. "What the hell's wrong with you?" he said. "Are you trying to make us look stupid? You know what happened down there today? I watched as this fire swept over Delfino Vigil. I saw it with my own eyes. One gust of wind and he was buried in fire, and you stand here making jokes."

For a second, no one spoke, and Flavio saw Delfino struggling up the foothill with his shovel. Not far from him was a fire that was much too big.

"I told him to wait," Flavio said in a whisper. Then, for some reason, he wondered who would feed Delfino's pigs and what they would think when they heard the news. He raised his eyes to Donald and said, "I went to school with your grandfather. And when your mother died, my wife, Martha, brought enchiladas and posole—to your house. I am too old for you to talk to me like this."

A caravan of cars and pickups swung off the highway and stopped at the edge of the parking lot. In the lead vehicle were Sippy Valdéz and two of his brothers. Their mother was in a car just behind them with relatives Flavio had never seen before. The other vehicles were full of people from the village, and pulling up behind all of them was the hearse carrying Petrolino.

"Hey, Flavio," Sippy called out, half leaning out the open window. "I hope they lock you up and throw away the damn key." He raised a beer to his mouth and took a long drink. The birthmark on his face was flared a dark red.

Oliver took a few steps toward the cars and stopped. He shrugged his shoulders and raised both his hands. "Why don't you guys keep moving," he said. "There's nothing to see here."

"Fuck you, jodido," Sippy said, and his brothers both laughed. "I don't even know who you are. Hey, Donald, what am I supposed to do with my tío? Park him in my driveway?"

A couple more vehicles pulled up behind those already stopped. A few truck doors swung open, and men stepped out of the cabs. One of them called out, "Why did you do this, Flavio?"

"See what you started," Donald said, his voice a harsh whisper. "You Montoyas always thought you were better than everyone else. You think I don't remember your sister? And the stories how she would drown little children and how she would call them into her house?"

"No," Flavio said. "Those things never happened."

"Hey, Flavio," Sippy yelled out. "You killed Delfino. You know that?"

A few more car doors swung open and Oliver turned back. "Donald," he said, "I could use some help here."

"No one here forgets," Donald said, "even if they don't remember." Then he walked away. He brushed past Oliver and went up to the side of Sippy's truck. He stooped down a little, and although Flavio couldn't hear what was being said, he could hear the rise and fall of Sippy's voice. After a few minutes, he straightened up and slapped his hand on the hood of the truck. "Bueno," he said. "I'll come by later."

Sippy looked once more at Flavio, and then he pushed the vehicle into gear and drove off slowly. One by one, the other cars followed behind him.

Donald watched them drive up the hill, and then he folded his arms and turned to look at Oliver.

"I want you to go home, Mr. Montoya," Oliver said. Sweat was running down the side of his face and his skin was ashen. "I want you to stay there. I'll come by when I can, and we can straighten this out." Then he turned away and walked over to Donald. They spoke for a few seconds and then climbed into their cars. Oliver flicked on his lights, and they both drove back down the hill.

Flavio drove without seeing back to Ramona's house. He parked in the shade beneath the cottonwoods and switched off the engine. He could hear the sound of ditch water running. The windows in the house shimmered black, and he could see the wavering reflection of the trees and his truck. Overhead came the drone of an airplane, and he watched as it passed low over the foothills. As it neared the fire, its belly slid open and a cloud of red, like dirt and dust, washed into the smoke. Then the plane veered sharply west and disappeared over the hills.

The sky is bleeding on Delfino, Flavio thought, and he let out a long, tired breath of air. Felix stirred on the seat and Flavio looked at him. "This has been a hard day, Felix," he said softly. He reached out and brushed dirt from the side of Felix's face. Felix's eyes fluttered open and Flavio leaned closer to him. "Delfino is dead," he said. Felix stared back at him blankly and then closed his eyes again.

"Why did you do this, Felix?" Flavio asked, and for the first time, he truly believed that his old friend had actually set the mountains on fire. And worse, he knew that he had played a part in it, but for the life of him, he didn't know what it was.

Not long after Flavio's brother had died in a car accident, Ramona had begun working on a series of paintings. Each painting had been of the Guadalupe cemetery, and in each one the cemetery was on fire.

"Cemeteries don't burn," Flavio had said to her one afternoon.

"This one does," Ramona had answered him. She was standing before a large canvas on which she had painted charred sagebrush and melted flowers and burned grass. Only the crosses remained, and they stood untouched and as white as snow. Hanging on all the walls of the kitchen was the cemetery in various stages of being consumed by fire. In some, there was only smoke among the crosses. In others, the graveyard was washed in flames. Ramona had placed her brush down on a flat plate smeared with paints and looked at her brother.

"I can do anything I want in my paintings," she had said. "It's where I go when I want to be gone." Then she had smiled. "It's like standing in a field with a shovel. Where are you then, Flavio?"

Flavio had not known how to answer his sister. He had only grunted and then looked at the walls of her kitchen covered in fire and smoke.

Now Flavio wondered where all of Ramona's paintings had gone to. Sometimes she would wrap what she had painted in thick cardboard and then send them to a city where Flavio pictured them hanging, with their alfalfa fields and dry arroyos and tired adobes, in a world of glass and rusted steel. But these of the cemetery, she had told him, were meant for this village and would always remain here. He knew that some of her paintings were packed away in the small shed where his grandmother had once kept her chickens. The building now sat overgrown in weeds and shadows beneath the cottonwoods. The thin pane of glass in the one window had broken long ago, and nests of wasps and swallows coated the overhangs. Most of the shingles on the roof had blown off, and the exposed rough lumber was stained black from the weather. Whatever was stored inside was now rotting in dampness. Flavio thought that he had not been able to keep safe even the things his sister valued the most.

One morning, Flavio had gone to Ramona's house, and just as he had found Martha, he had found Ramona. She was sitting in her kitchen facing the small window over the sink. A slight breeze pulled at the curtains. On the table beside her were a cup of coffee, a pad of paper, and a few scattered pencils. Her hands were folded in her lap and her eyes were open. For a moment, Flavio talked to her as if it were any other morning. When she didn't answer, he put his hand on her shoulder and said her name. And in that instant, he remembered his grandmother dying so gently it seemed to him that wherever it was she had gone, she had taken him with her. He had touched his grandmother's hand and said softly, "Grandmother," as if she might turn her head and say to him, "I'm here, hijo. I will always be here with you."

Ramona and Rosa and everyone else Flavio had ever known were all buried in the small cemetery that was now only ashes. It occurred to Flavio that he had been surrounded by fire his whole life and had been too blind to see it. He wondered why he was suddenly being flooded with memories that were so distant to him that they had nearly been forgotten. He took in a deep breath and pushed himself up on the truck seat. He shook his head and then rubbed at his eyes. He looked again at Felix asleep on the seat and thought it possible that this day, too, was just a memory.

Six deer came walking out from behind Ramona's house and stepped their way through the yard. They stopped by the irrigation ditch, close enough to the truck that Flavio could hear the rough sound of their breath and the dry grass beneath their feet. He cracked open the truck door, and all six froze. Then they ran scattered across the road and into the field on the other side. They made their way through the debris near the old, abandoned village office and then crossed the highway, making for the mountains to the east. If it had been any other day, Flavio thought, all six would be hanging by their feet in someone's garage.

Flavio left Felix sleeping in the pickup and walked up the path to the house. He took the steps up to the porch and swung open the front door. Sunlight swept across the floor to the opposite wall. Flavio leaned against the door frame and gazed inside.

"What am I doing here?" he muttered. He suddenly pictured Oliver and Donald Lucero driving to his house and finding him gone and then who knew what would happen. "Who cares, anyway?" Flavio said to the empty room. "I've spent the whole day doing nothing and look at the trouble I'm in. How can it matter what house I sit in?" Then he pushed himself up and walked into the room.

He sat down on the sofa, picked up the glass of water from the floor, and took a drink. Then he leaned back and stretched out his legs, holding the glass on his belly. He could see his truck out the open door and thought that if Felix were to wake, he would be able to see movement inside the cab and hopefully get to the pickup before Felix tried to drive away, which, Flavio thought, might not be the worst thing to have happen. He took another sip of water, and his eyes fell upon the painting of the two men and the small boy on the wall across from him.

The men wore caps and while one of them worked his shovel, the other watched, his hands shoved deep in his pockets. The boy was crouched down peering at something on the ground. His skinny knees jutted out, and his own shovel was lying thrown in the alfalfa. The sky above was streaked a blood red and sat low over the field.

"I know who those people are," Flavio said out loud. "The two men are me and my grandfather. And the boy is my nephew, Little

José." Flavio brought the glass to his mouth and drank again. "I don't know why Ramona painted the three of us together. It was something that never happened."

He looked at the two men in the painting, and although there was a difference in age, he could see how closely they resembled each other. They were solid men of the same height, and they stood somewhat flat-footed, leaning slightly forward. They even wore their hats the same, the brims pulled down low on their foreheads.

"Ramona was always my grandfather's favorite," Flavio said. "With me he was always a hard man. Even when he said my name it made me feel as if something was about to fall on my head. But with Ramona, it was different." Flavio shook his head. He had always thought that the older one grew, the more one would leave behind. But here he was, the same age his grandfather had been when he died, feeling as if he were still someone's grandson.

Resting his head back against the sofa, Flavio looked at the boy in the painting and, for a second, felt as if he had fallen into the field. He could hear the water running fast in the ditch and feel the air cool on his face. His grandfather grunted as his shovel slid into the wet ground, and Little José was mumbling softly to himself and tossing clumps of mud into the ditch. Suddenly Flavio's throat felt tight and swollen and his eyes burned.

"Little José," he said, "was such a good boy. Some things should never happen."

Flavio's brother and his brother's wife, Loretta, were killed on a warm August morning in a car accident. They had been on their way to shop in Las Sombras when they topped the first hill and ran into a cow that was standing in the center of the road, as if it were waiting just for them. José and Loretta had left their son by himself that morning and after the burial it was decided that Little José should remain with his Tía Ramona. At first, it had bothered Flavio that his sister, who had always lived alone and had had little to do with her family or anyone else for that matter, would take on the responsibility of a small boy. But, in truth, though Flavio and Martha had tried so hard and for so long to conceive a child, Flavio had actually become so accustomed to being alone with his wife that the thought of anyone else in his house made him uncomfortable. Little José moved into Ramona's, and after a while it was as if he had always been there.

Flavio, Ramona, and their brother, José, had always been distant with each other, but it grew worse after the deaths of Rosa and Epolito. Flavio had lived quietly with his wife, irrigating and tending to his own cows, in the house that had once been his parents'. José, who often drank too much and preferred the company of his friends over that of his own family, lived in a trailer on a barren piece of land. His house was always full of angry voices and Loretta's tears, which never changed a thing. And Ramona, who had returned to Guadalupe after being gone for years, lived her life as if she were truly from somewhere else. The three of them lived in the village of Guadalupe as if all they shared was their name. It was the deaths of José and Loretta that changed everything.

"My whole family had to die before I remembered I had one," Flavio said to Martha one morning. He was sitting in the kitchen watching Martha prepare a large platter of enchiladas to take to Ramona's. They were going to have an early dinner and then drive into the mountains and fish one of the small creeks.

"Don't worry yourself, Flavio," Martha said. She finished wrapping the enchiladas and went to the cupboard for another platter.

Flavio shook his head. "But everything is so different now," he said.

"I am bringing sopapillas with honey," Martha said, smiling. "And biscochitos for Little José."

Almost every day now, Flavio would stop by Ramona's house. He would go there early with his shovel and walk to the field. The house would still be dark, and the light in the air would be gray. Before the sun had crested the mountains, Little José would come running from the house, dragging his shovel behind him. Ramona would stand in the doorway for a few minutes. Then she would wave to her brother and go back inside. Flavio and his nephew would irrigate the field together, and Flavio would show him how to twist the water to where you wanted it to flow.

Afterward, Flavio would have a cup of coffee with Ramona while she prepared eggs and chile for breakfast. Sometimes Martha would join them, and she would sit quietly, listening to her husband and her sister-in-law talk. She would watch José eat, and her heart would be so full she thought it might break.

Sometimes, late in the day, when Flavio was done with his own chores, he would drive to Ramona's and work a little on her house. He and José would fix the roof leaks around the stovepipes and replace the rotten boards on the porch. They cleared the weeds from around the shed and even swept out the inside so Ramona would have a clean place to store her paintings.

The house where Flavio and Ramona had spent much of their childhood began to feel like what it once was. While it was true that occasionally there was still an awkwardness between them, it was also true that it seemed to matter little to either of them. A softness had come to Ramona along with Little José, and in it Flavio had found a place that he only vaguely remembered.

It lasted for a full year, and then Ramona lost Little José at the river.

During the year José lived with Ramona, the two of them would sometimes walk high into the foothills. They would pack a small lunch of tortillas and meat and hunt for arrowheads and pot shards that had been left behind long before there had ever been a village in the valley below. Sometimes they would come across markings on rocks of stick men and small deer and of women, their bellies full and rounded with child. Ramona would tell José that once Indians had lived in these hills and now all that was left of them were fragments of their lives mixed with dirt and stone. When he asked what had happened to them, Ramona would answer that she didn't know. Maybe they became us, she would say. Or maybe they were here for so long that they grew tired and weak and were scattered as if blown by a great wind. They would spend the day walking, and when they returned home late in the afternoon, José's pockets would be stuffed with broken bits of clay and pieces of obsidian.

Sometimes Ramona and José would walk to the river. It ran deep in a gorge a few miles west of the village. And like the foothills, it was a place few people went. The river ran fast through boulders, and even when it flowed smooth, the currents twisted and churned just beneath the surface. Ancient junipers grew along the bank and along the hard-packed trail leading down. Their trunks were thick and weathered, and their sparse limbs were gnarled from feeding too long on rock and wind. Ramona would sit and watch the river while José would throw stones at the swollen fish that swam in the pools near the bank.

The day Ramona lost José, she had seen a shadow out of the corner of her eye and felt the fine hairs on her neck rise. José was lying on a boulder not far away, a pile of stones on his stomach. A hawk soared high above at the rim of the gorge, and Ramona thought it must have been his shadow she had seen. A few minutes later when she looked back, José was gone.

For days, Flavio and many from the village scoured the rocks and the waters for José. Some thought he had fallen into one of the crevices that were everywhere and that his body lay broken who knew how many feet beneath the ground. Others thought that the river had grabbed him when Ramona wasn't looking and filled his mouth with water so that he could not even call out. But what everybody agreed upon was that Ramona was to blame.

"She should have known better," they said. "To take a child to such a place." They would say these things to Flavio, and then they would shake their heads. "But your sister was always like this. Even when she was young, she thought she knew better, and never did she think she was part of this village. She shouldn't have been allowed to keep José in the first place."

Flavio didn't know what to think, and when he heard what people were saying, he chose to say nothing. He, too, knew that the river was not the place for a small boy, but to have him vanish like smoke was something he couldn't comprehend. The first day of José's disappearance, he asked his sister where along the river she would search.

"I looked away only for a moment, Flavio," Ramona said and shut her eyes. "Only a few seconds."

"Maybe you fell asleep, Ramona. Maybe the sound of the river confused you."

"No," Ramona said sharply, and she opened her eyes and looked at her brother. "There is nowhere to look. If there was I would know it. He is not in the rocks, Flavio. And he is not in the river."

"But where can he be?" Flavio cried out. "He cannot be nowhere." Ramona lowered her head and wouldn't answer.

For seven days, long after everyone else from the village had given up, Flavio walked the bottom of the gorge. He would yell Little José's name into the small holes between the rocks and hear only his own voice echo back at him. He would stand on the bank of the river for hours staring at the water for a glimpse of José's hand or the sleeve of his shirt or his hair that was too long. At night, he slept uneasily wrapped in a blanket beside the river. He thought that at least his presence would be a comfort for Little José.

Finally, it was Ramona who returned to the river and told Flavio that it was time for him to come home.

"He's gone, Flavio," Ramona said, and she took his hands in her own. "Come home now. Your wife misses you."

"I'm his tío, Ramona," Flavio said. "How can I leave him here by himself?"

"He's gone, Flavio," Ramona said again. "And it was me who lost him in this place. Not you. And I know in my heart he is not here to find." She pulled gently at his hands. "So please come."

"But, Ramona, small boys don't just disappear."

"He didn't just disappear. La Llorona took him, Flavio. She was here and I saw her and didn't even know what I was seeing." She dropped her hands and began to weep.

For a few seconds, Flavio didn't speak. Then he said, "That's a story for children, Ramona. There is no such thing. It was the river," and then his own voice caught in his throat. "You should never have brought him here."

"Then it was the river," Ramona said, and again she took her brother's hands. "Come, Flavio. Please, it's all I ask of you. Let José be still. You must come home or we'll never leave this place."

Slowly, Flavio followed Ramona up the same trail she and José had walked down seven days before. At the rim, he stopped and looked back down at the river. From there, it seemed to flow slow and easy and the noise of the water could not be heard. It was early evening and the gorge was all in shadow. Swallows were swooping in the air beneath his feet. He took in a deep breath and let it out. When he turned to Ramona, she was already walking away. Her arms were wrapped around her belly and her face was looking at the ground.

Ramona changed after Little José disappeared into the river or into the rocks, or into the arms of La Llorona. It was not a change so big that anyone in Guadalupe, other than Flavio, noticed. To them, she was as she always had been. The day after she brought Flavio home from the river, she packed all of José's things in cardboard boxes. Then she took them to the church and left them sitting on the ground outside the closed doors. When she returned home, she scrubbed and cleaned each room in her house until even the wood floors were rubbed dull. Then she began to paint. To see her go about her life as if nothing had happened caused even more talk in the village than José's disappearance.

"The woman's heart is like a stone," people said. "Her nephew isn't gone a week and she empties her house of him. And what does she do then? She sits and draws her pictures."

"Worse," they would go on, "she paints this village as if it were hers, which it isn't." Ramona stayed in her house, and from early in the morning until dusk, she painted the village. Whatever people said about her were not things she heard or even cared about.

For a while, Flavio stayed away from his sister. He, too, went about his life in much the same way as before. He would rise each morning from a fitful sleep and go to his fields. He would feed his cows and fix his fences. At night, he would lie awake beside Martha. He would stare at the ceiling and wonder how things could change so drastically and seemingly not at all.

One afternoon, Martha prepared a small platter of tamales and warm tortillas and wrapped it in foil. She gave it to Flavio and told him to take it to Ramona.

Flavio took the platter of food. Then he opened his mouth, but before he could utter a word, Martha said, "I know what you are going to say, Flavio. But I want you to be quiet and take this food to your sister."

At Ramona's house, Flavio stood awkwardly outside her door. He could smell the sweet scent of corn and pork from the tamales, and it occurred to him that whenever his wife handed him a platter of food, a request often went along with it. When Ramona finally came to the door, she looked at him for a long time without speaking. Then she took Martha's gift and smiled and told him that the small window over the sink had swelled and wouldn't close. And if there was a breeze, she said, it would swing open and pull the screws from the hinges.

Until Ramona's death, Flavio would visit her a few times each week. They would drink a cup of coffee quietly together, and then he would do small chores around her house or work on her truck if it was running poorly. For some time after José disappeared, Flavio would return home from Ramona's and tell his wife that something had changed in his sister.

"It's as if," he would say, "she has become more of what she was and less at the same time." Although he was confused by his own words, Martha grasped the meaning of what he said.

"You are her brother," Martha would tell him. "For you to visit her and help her with things is more than you'll ever know." Then she would pat his hand, "So don't worry yourself, Flavio."

What he didn't tell Martha was that even Ramona's paintings were different. Maybe it was true she painted the same old adobes and empty arroyos, but now there were shadows in them. Shadows in open sunlight and moving about inside abandoned vehicles. Sometimes the shadows were so subtle he could only glimpse them out of the corner of his eye. Then he would think that it was the light from outside moving on the canvas or that it was possible his eyes were getting old and he was seeing what wasn't there. For the rest of her life, Ramona sat in her kitchen with her brushes and sought La Llorona. But not once did she ever see her again.

Ramona's house was now full of paintings covered with dust, and the air in the room where Flavio sat was still and thick with the odor of smoke. Out the open door, he could see smoke beginning to settle over the mountains in the east. He moved his eyes to the santos standing in the far corner, and all of them, even the one he had earlier thought was looking away, stared back at him.

"And where were all of you?" he said. "You were in this house when Little José was lost. Your job was to protect him from harm. He was just a little boy and he deserved better. I don't know why Ramona didn't throw all of you in her stove."

Flavio looked at the one standing before the others, at her lop-sided features, at the grin on her face. "You are the one he made with his hands, and in return you left him by the river by himself. You should be ashamed." Flavio took off his hat and flung it across the room. It toppled over three of the Ladies, but the rest still stood staring back at him.

8

The cottonwood tree stood almost as tall as the church, and it leaned in toward the structure so close that the branches of its upper limbs reached down to trail on the old wood-shingled roof. At the base, the tree was many feet in diameter and the bark was thick and coarse. Low to the ground, where the trunk split and became two, it was stained dark with dampness.

"It's blood," Ramona had told Flavio one day after mass. They had been standing together in the shade beneath the tree, and Flavio had been young enough then still to hold her hand. "At night, some of them bleed and no one knows why. I think they were hurt a long time ago and their blood comes from a wound deep inside them that never heals."

Flavio had stared at the patch of moisture without speaking. It was so dense that the bark had turned black and the dirt just below it was wet.

"You have to remember, Flavio," Ramona said, "to not climb cottonwoods. If you do and if you touch their blood, you'll carry it with you forever. And then, who knows what will happen to you?" She had smiled slightly and then, as they often did, her eyes grew distant and she looked out over the valley.

One late afternoon Flavio and Felix stood on the loose dirt beneath the tree. They were both gazing up into the branches, and their mouths hung half open. The limb that Emilio García must have been hanged from grew out of the trunk of the cottonwood about twenty feet above their heads. It was some two feet thick and ran parallel to the ground before its own weight bowed it low toward the earth. It was mid-September, and though the leaves had not yet begun to fall, they had yellowed and were as thin as paper.

"I would never want to be hanged," Felix said softly. "With your hands tied behind your back and everybody watching."

A slight breeze rustled the leaves, and the fragile sound they made was like voices to Flavio. Shadows moved about him and he thought that he would not want to be standing in this place once it grew dark, even if it was next to the church.

"We should cut that limb off," Felix said, his voice a little stronger, "and drag it away where it won't bother anyone."

"Maybe it was just a story she was telling us," Flavio said slowly. "A priest would never hang anyone. Especially so close to the church. All they do is stay inside and say mass and pray for everyone."

"Oh sí?" Felix said. "What about your grandmother? She said there was a priest here who used to whip himself naked and hang goat's feet full of blood on all the branches. I bet you he didn't pray so much. I bet you if we climbed up on that branch we'd find a burn mark on it from the rope. There's probably old rotting goat heads buried in the dirt and gold coins that fell out of Emilio's pockets when they hung him." Felix kicked at the ground and then bent over and picked up a small piece of wood he had uncovered. It was smooth and burned. He rubbed his fingers over it, and they came away smudged black. "See," he breathed out and held it up.

"Eee," Flavio said, looking at it. "It's just a piece of wood from a stove."

"That's what you say," Felix said. "I think Emilio was holding it for good luck just before they hung him." He clenched it so tight that his hand shook slightly and his knuckles whitened. "It's still almost warm," he said, and then he shoved it deep in his pocket. He looked back up at the branch above him. "I would like to be a bandit," he said softly. "They would never catch me."

Flavio grunted. "There's nothing to steal here," he said, and he, too, raised his face.

"Then what did Emilio steal?"

"Who knows," Flavio said, shrugging slightly. "Maybe he stole sheep from the ranchitos. Or maybe he stole somebody's horse."

"A horse? You must be crazy. Nobody would steal a horse. Where would he ride it? Back to his house? I think he stole gold and silver and if we cut off that limb then they won't be able to hang us if they catch us."

Flavio looked over at him. "Us?" he said. "I don't want to be a bandit. I want to grow alfalfa and have so many cows that my fields will be bursting. No one likes bandits and they always sleep outside." He also thought that if he even considered being a bandit, his grandfather would beat him with a stick. "Besides," he went on, "if we cut that branch, Father Frank would find out."

Father Frank had been priest in Guadalupe for the past year. He was a small, round man who had planted irises and tulips and climbing roses in narrow beds all around the church. During mass, he would often use his flowers and the cottonwood tree as examples of rebirth and hope and enduring beauty. Flavio had a feeling that the moment their saw sliced into the bark, Father Frank would come rushing from the church yelling, his arms waving frantically in the air.

"We could do it at night," Felix said, "when it's dark. And wear bandannas. Then he wouldn't see our faces."

"I'm never coming here at night," Flavio said. Even the thought made him uneasy. "Besides, my sister told me not to mess around with cottonwood trees because they bleed."

"What are you talking about?" Felix said, shaking his head. "You believe everything. Trees don't bleed." He pointed to the base of the tree. "That's just sweat. My father told me that trees sweat when it gets too hot."

"How can a tree get too hot?" Flavio said. "All it does is stand around in the shade."

Suddenly, from the other side of the church, came the flat sound of breaking glass. At first, neither boy knew where it had come from. They stared at each other, vaguely frightened, as if they had somehow been responsible.

"I didn't do anything," Felix said quickly, hunching his shoulders so much that he looked years younger and smaller than he was. "You're older than me, Flavio," he said. "You should tell Father Frank that we didn't break anything."

"Come on," Flavio said. "We didn't do anything wrong. Let's go see what happened." He grabbed hold of Felix's sleeve and pulled him over to the corner of the building.

The church had been built on the side of the hill almost two hundred years before. Below it, the hillside sloped gradually down to the base of the valley where alfalfa and crested wheat grew. Irrigation ditches, overgrown with weeds and white clover, wove along fence lines. Branching off of them like tendrils were the smaller ditches that fed the fields. It was already late in the season, and the alfalfa and wheat had been cut for the last time. The fields were only sharp stubble, and when the cows straggled down out of the mountains after the first snow, it was there they would be wintered.

Above the church, the hillside was covered with patches of sparse grass that had yellowed and gone to seed. As the hill rose, the grass grew smaller until it finally gave way to tall spindly sagebrush whose branches reached as high as a man's chest. In the midst of that brush sat the García house, and standing in the sage, not far from one wall, was a young girl.

She was facing away from Flavio and Felix, and they watched as she stooped over and picked up a large stone. She held it up to her face as if talking to it and then cocked her arm and let it fly at the small window on the side of the house. It smashed through the thin wood slats and billowed out the cloth hanging inside. Again, the boys heard the sound of breaking glass.

"Mira, Flavio," Felix said hoarsely. "That's Victoria Medina. Look what she's doing." The girl stood still for a moment, her arms hanging slack at her sides and her legs slightly apart. Then she shook her head gently and bent over again. This time the stone she threw struck the wall so hard it chipped loose a chunk of adobe from beside the window.

"Did you see that?" Felix said. "She even throws like a boy."

Victoria Medina lived a few miles south of the García house where her father operated a small gravel pit on his land. He sold piles of small stones and fine sand to the county and hauled it in trucks that bled oil and grease and groaned like animals too old even to walk. Victoria was an only child, and she lived so close to the gravel pit that she carried with her the sweet scent of gasoline and exhaust. In her hair, close to her scalp, were tiny grains of sand. Like her father, her face was dark and a sullenness often shadowed her features. When she spoke, her words were sharp. She was a year older than Flavio and a classmate of his and Felix's. She was not someone either of them was fond of. At school, she sat far apart from everyone else, and when Flavio's eyes would sometimes wander toward her, she would stare back at him blankly until his face grew red and he lowered his eyes. What she was doing so far from her home and why she was throwing rocks at Guadalupe's house, Flavio had no idea.

He remembered his mother had told him that children were known to throw stones at the old García house. At the time, he had given it little thought for the simple reason that it was not a thing he had ever been inclined to do. But now, as he stood beside Felix, he found himself flinching each time a rock struck the wall, as if each one were being thrown at Guadalupe herself. He pictured her sitting at the table in her kitchen, her hands flat on her thighs, and, like him, without the slightest idea of what to do.

"Guadalupe should come out and yell at her," Felix said.

"She would never do that," Flavio said, and though what he said was true, he didn't know why. "Maybe she'll just go away." His voice, like Felix's, had dropped to a whisper.

Felix grunted. "I know that Victoria," he said, looking at Flavio. "She won't ever go away."

On the last day of school the year before, Victoria had slapped Felix on the side of the head so hard that he had cried. It had happened outside the school, and there had been no one about to do anything. Flavio had been standing nearby, and when Felix had begun crying, he had looked off somewhere else. Victoria had let out a soft laugh and then told Felix that it had been a gift she had given him. When she saw him again, she said, she would give him another.

"Maybe you should go there and tell her to leave," Felix said.

"Me?" Flavio had little desire to go to the García house when just Guadalupe was there, let alone Victoria Medina.

"Maybe she'll listen to you," Felix said. "It's not right what she's doing. I could get help if she doesn't stop."

The sun had fallen below the horizon, and shadows now stretched from the foothills to the east end of the valley. There, the mountains were still washed in sunlight and the slight breeze that had blown earlier was still. From far off came the low bellow of a cow, sharp and clear in the air.

"But I don't want to go up there by myself," Flavio said. Felix's hands were in his pockets, and he moved his foot around on the ground without answering. Flavio stared at him for a few seconds and then looked back up the hill. He could see that Victoria was still standing in the sage and that she was once again bending over to pick up another rock. Then, his eyes passed by her and fell on the figure standing at the edge of the road above the house.

At first, Flavio had no idea who it was. She was dressed in black and a shawl covered her head and fell far down her back. Her arms were wrapped around her body, and she stood motionless gazing down the hill. She was too far away for Flavio to see her face clearly. As he looked at her, she lifted her hand out from under her shawl and raised it as if greeting him.

"Grandmother," Flavio said beneath his breath. She stood in the darkness that lay beneath the cottonwood trees that grew near the road.

"What are you talking about?" Felix said, glancing up.

"My grandmother's here," Flavio said, and without looking at Felix, he took a step away from the church.

"Wait, Flavio," Felix said. "Don't leave me here by myself."

"Come on, Felix," Flavio said, and he took another step and then another.

"I can't," Felix called out to him. "I'll come in a little while, Flavio. I promise you."

Flavio was almost to the García house when he stumbled over a small sagebrush. He tripped forward a few steps, and when he looked back up, his grandmother had vanished, leaving behind only a patch of wavering shadows beneath the cottonwoods. Victoria was no longer throwing stones but was standing still staring at him. She was wearing the same clothes she always wore, a worn sweater buttoned up to her neck and a dress that fell between her ankles and her knees. There was a beaten path through the sage where nothing grew, and Flavio could see that the calves of her legs were dark and hard and as thin as sticks.

"What do you want?" Victoria said.

She was less than twenty yards away, and Flavio thought that if he were smart he would either turn around and go back to the church or walk right by the García house and go home. Instead, he shrugged and said, "Nothing," and then, as if his feet were thinking for him, he walked through the sage and stopped a few feet from Victoria.

"Where's your stupid friend?" Victoria asked. She was holding a rock, and her hands and the skin around her wrist were stained with dry dirt.

Flavio shrugged again. "I don't know," he said.

"Eee, you're such a liar," she said. "I saw you two hiding behind the church spying on me." The hair around Victoria's face was damp with sweat, and she was breathing a little too fast. There was a small knot of saliva at one corner of her mouth.

"We weren't spying," Flavio said. "We were just looking." He wondered all of a sudden how he had come to be by himself out-side the García house with Victoria Medina. He felt the same way he sometimes did when he dozed off during the day and awoke un-sure of where he was or where he'd been. He glanced back up the hill and saw only the empty road.

"Felix went home," he said. "And my grandmother was calling for me."

For a second Victoria was quiet. Then she said, "You can stay here with me if you want to. You can help me throw stones."

Flavio watched a beetle make its way over the dirt near his feet, leaving a light trail in the dust. He moved his foot and flicked it into the sage. "I don't want to throw a stone," he said. "My mother told me it's bad luck to throw stones at this house."

"You don't have a mother. Remember?" Victoria said. Her face suddenly fell flat and expressionless, as it often did at school when she would catch Flavio looking at her. She stretched out her hand. "Go on. It's just an old house that everybody's forgotten. It won't hurt nothing."

Flavio stared at the rock in her hand. Her fingernails were uneven and torn down to the skin, and there were rings of black dirt deep beneath her nails. Suddenly, all he wanted to do was grab the rock from her hand and throw it blindly at the García house. Then he could go home.

"I bet you can't get it through the window," Victoria said. "If you do, I swear I'll be nice to you at school."

Flavio raised his eyes. The panes in the window had all been broken, and the wood slats between them were dangling from bent nails. The cloth hanging inside was almost torn down, and beyond it, in the darkness of the room, he thought he saw a flicker of movement. In his mind, Flavio could see Guadalupe García inside looking out at him, and he knew if he threw a stone she would see it come toward her. And that would be difficult to forget. On top of this, it occurred to him that the bones of Emilio García were buried in a wall and it would be just his luck if his stone struck against those.

"People shouldn't mess around with this place," he said. "My grandmother told me anything can happen here."

Victoria jerked her head back slightly. "You're crazy," she said. "Your grandmother just says that to scare you." Then she gestured with her hand. "Throw the stone, Flavio. If you don't, I'll tell everyone that you did."

"What if it hits someone?" Flavio asked, and even he could hear the whine in his words.

"No one lives here, stupid," Victoria said. "Everyone knows that. My papa told me that all these Garcías were sick in the head and when they died it only made people happy. He says this house should be torn down so that it's just dirt and all the wood should be burned." She fell quiet for a few seconds. Then she smiled and said quickly, "Here, I'll get you your own rock and we can throw them together."

Where the two children stood, the sagebrush was thick and tall, the top branches thin and knotted and dry. Willowed reeds of grass and pale wildflowers grew in the loose dirt between the sage. Scattered throughout were heaps of stone that had sunk at odd angles back into the earth. Dirt crusted between them like mud plaster, and it all lay beneath a layer of fine dust and small yellow leaves. Where Victoria reached for a stone lay a child's shoe, the brown leather split and curled from many years of weather and the eyelets rotted out. It seemed small enough to fit in the palm of Flavio's hand. Hanging in the air just above it, a cross was snagged in the brush. It must have been pulled out of the ground as the sage had grown.

It's a grave, Flavio realized. It's a grave where a little baby's buried.

Suddenly, wherever he looked, he saw piles of stones half buried in the ground. Near some of them were wooden crosses, blackened from the weather, their arms bound together with rusted wire or nailed with spikes. The words that had been carved into them were almost completely worn back to wood, but on one, not far from his foot, Flavio could make out the inscription, "Manuelito García, 1802–1806, mi hijo, I give you back to God." And on the top of the rocks and embedded in the dirt were small colored stones like marbles. But on the others, there was nothing, as if even they had forgotten who they were.

"This is a graveyard," Flavio said with panic in his voice. "We shouldn't be here."

It was nearly dusk now, and the mountains were cast in shadow. The sky was streaked a pale red and seemed to hang just above the mountains. A flock of ravens picked up out of the foothills slow and heavy, and other than the whoosh of their wings against air, there wasn't a sound to be heard in the village.

Victoria was still stooped down. She let the stone drop from her hand. Then she rubbed a palm hard on her dress and stood up. "You don't know that," she said. "These rocks came from when they built this house."

"It's a cemetery," Flavio said, and he felt as if not only was the house full of ghosts, but so was all of the ground about it. Emilio and Cristóbal and Percides and every other García he'd been told about all lay about him under a thin layer of dirt and stone.

Victoria rubbed her hand against her sweater, and Flavio caught the stale odor of gasoline. "You're crazy," she said. "People don't get buried in sagebrush. No one does that." Then she froze at the sudden noise of footsteps behind her and the sound of Guadalupe García's voice.

"Flavio's right," Guadalupe said. Her voice was thin and wavered like heat in autumn. "All of my family is buried out here."

She was standing at the corner of the house so still that Flavio had not seen her. He wondered if maybe she'd been there all the time. She moved a strand of hair from her face and smiled at him. She looked smaller to Flavio and out of place, as if she didn't belong where there was so much space about her.

"I would play here as a small girl, and my great-grandmother would sit in the shade against the house and tell me who was out here with me." She closed her eyes and her face suddenly seemed younger than it was. "'Lucía García, daughter of Soveida and Roberto García. Born October 2, 1839. Died February 29, 1842. Our hearts will remember. We give you back to God and keep you here with us.' She was born with soft blond hair like silk and some people made trouble about that. But my grandmother told me that there are people who have nothing better to do. 'Rosita García, daughter of Evita and Carlos García. Born August 17, 1801. Died January 4, 1816, when I was not watching. Your mother loves you.'" Guadalupe opened her eyes. "I don't know them all, and sometimes I think it makes them sad that there is no one to remember." She raised her hand and pointed to an area not far from the house where the sagebrush was not so high. "My great-grandmother, Percides García, is buried there. I helped my father dig with a small shovel, and my mother watched from inside the house. She wished for no marker for her grave because she wanted to forget."

"Where is Cristóbal buried?" Flavio croaked out, surprising even himself.

"Cristóbal isn't here," Guadalupe said. "He was lost to us. My grandmother told me that at one time there were some who knew what had happened to him, but it was a thing no one ever dared talk about. Especially to us. If my grandmother was here now, she would tell you to ask your friend. She's a Medina, she should know."

While Guadalupe had been talking, Victoria's shoulders had been hunched up around her neck and her eyes had been darting back and forth. At the mention of her name, her body jerked and her eyes met Flavio's. "I didn't mean what I did," she said. "I didn't know they were graves. Tell her we're friends, Flavio. Tell her I don't even know any Cristóbal and that I swear he's not at my house." Then, without even a glance behind her, she walked past him stiffly, down the hill. For a brief second Flavio wondered what

Felix would do when he saw Victoria walking toward him. I hope she slaps him a good one, he thought. Then his mind filled with other things when he realized that he was alone with Guadalupe García.

"I'm so glad you came to see me again, Flavio," Guadalupe said.

Flavio stood in the sagebrush. It wasn't yet dark, but there was no color in the sky, and all he could see clearly of Guadalupe was her hair and the nightgown she always seemed to wear. He was beginning to feel as if he would never get home and would end up standing in the cemetery outside the García house until the moon rose and set and until the sun came up the next morning. He wondered what would happen to him then. Children will come and throw stones at me, he thought. Then he realized that Guadalupe was talking and that possibly, if he listened to her, he could run home when she finished and never again ever even wander close to this house.

"Did you know, Flavio, that the first Montoya ever to set foot in this valley was your great-great-great-great-grandfather and his name was Tomás Montoya? He came alone out of the north where there is only the valley that stretches flat and empty forever, and no one ever knew where he came from or what had become of it. For five days and five nights before walking down into this village he stayed in the foothills. At night, people would see his fire, and they thought that it came from a band of roving Indians who only meant them harm. He came in the early spring, just after the first winter that Hipolito and Francisco and a few others had spent here. There was little to see then, only a few poor mud dwellings, and life had not been easy.

"Only one room of this house stood, and in it were Cristóbal and his wife, Ignacia, and their eight daughters. Hipolito and Francisco had settled near the creek, and Francisco had lost his eldest son to a blizzard. The boy had been hunting deer by himself, and when the clouds fell with snow, he lost his way. Where he thought his home lay was only a small basin high in the mountains surrounded by ridges that he could not even see. The others who came here with Hipolito and Francisco were scattered throughout the valley. All of them were ragged and hungry, and their houses did little more than block the harsh winds. What dreams Hipolito had once had for this place were only remnants of thoughts that he could barely remember. Many wished to leave that winter, and there were bitter arguments and hands were raised in anger. Some blamed Hipolito for bringing them so far from anything. Others blamed Cristóbal, as if he and the santo he carried with him everywhere had cursed this place with their presence.

"Your great-great-great-great-grandfather was a tall, gaunt man who was no longer young. I think the reason he stayed in the hills for so long was that he knew if he entered this valley he would never leave. When finally he walked out of the foothills, those here were so relieved he was like them and not what they feared, that they greeted him openly. And for a little while the village became a thing that even Cristóbal would have wished it to be.

"The stone foundation for the church was laid by your grandfather's hands. He built the heavy doors that hang on the church even today, and he forged the hinges out of iron. He built the altar out of red spruce, and the stairway behind it that leads to nowhere. He, along with Hipolito, dug the ditches that Cristóbal had begun so that water flowed from the creeks to every field.

"When he first came into this valley, he lived in this house and he married the oldest daughter of Cristóbal and Ignacia. Her name was Pilar and she died giving birth to their first son, Emilio. Soon after her death, Tomás built a small house near the foothills, not far from your own, and seldom did he come here. My grandmother told me that he married again, but who she was, she didn't know.

All she knew was that Emilio remained here in this house and, in name, he was a García."

It was now nearly dark, and still, among so many graves, Flavio stood in the sagebrush. His body was relaxed and his mouth was open and his eyes were half closed. In his mind, he saw the village full of sun and the sky such a deep blue that it almost swallowed him. He could see a figure walking out of the foothills, and it wasn't Tomás Montoya, but himself. His pants were dirty and torn and his cap was pulled down low. His face was smeared with dirt and soot from five nights of fire. Although he was tired and his legs and arms ached from carrying all of his tools, he was whistling softly under his breath. He thought that the valley he was walking into was the most beautiful thing he had ever seen. He watched the villagers come toward him, and he tried not to stare at Cristóbal's daughter—who vaguely resembled Victoria Medina but softer and fuller—as she glanced at him shyly with a half smile. Cristóbal and Hipolito and Francisco came up to him together. Before they could speak, he said, "I am Flavio Montoya and I'll never leave here."

"Are you dreaming, Flavio?" Guadalupe asked.

"Yes," he answered.

"You would have to be so strong. Like your grandfather."

"I will be," Flavio said. "What happened to my grandfather?"

"He died," Guadalupe said. "What else could have happened? When he did, this village fell back to what it once had been. And later, after Cristóbal was lost at the church and Emilio was hung, whatever reason this place had even to exist was gone."

For a moment Guadalupe fell quiet. Then she said, "There was a santero here not so long ago, and what his knife carved in the wood brought some peace to the valley. He was named Antonio Montoya and he lived alone in the house Tomás built at the base of the foothills. I don't know what became of him, but I do know that the priest gathered all the santos this man had given to the people of Guadalupe and burned them beneath the cottonwood beside the church. From my house I saw the smoke rising black above the roof of the church, and if I had closed my eyes I think I would have heard the Ladies screaming."

"I would have stopped him," Flavio said. "I would have taken them away from the priest." He could see himself walking up the hill from the church. Behind him, gathered together and walking on such small feet, came a number of santos, all of them smiling but their heads bowed.

The moon had risen above the mountains by now, and the valley was so bright it seemed to be covered with snow.

"I know you would have," Guadalupe said. "Someday you will. Someday you will be a hero, Flavio," and she turned and walked away so quietly that he never heard her leave.

9

From another room and through his sleep, Flavio heard the
kitchen door in Ramona's house creak open and then, after a few
seconds, it slammed shut. He heard the sound of footsteps shuffling across the floor. A part of him thought that this might be
something that should be of concern to him. But at that moment,
most of him didn't seem to care much about anything. In fact, he
had no idea how long he'd been sitting slouched on Ramona's sofa
or whether he'd actually been dozing or just staring straight ahead
in a trance. Whoever had entered the house was moving slowly and
breathing with difficulty. He heard a muffled cough followed by a
low groan and then the room flooded with the odors of burned
meat and of old, rotted wood left out in the rain. Flavio pushed
himself up on the couch and glanced over his shoulder. Standing in
the doorway between the two rooms was Delfino.

"Eee," Flavio said softly. "What now?" He was still groggy from sleep and he knew what he was seeing couldn't be.

"Flavio," Delfino croaked out. His overalls were charred so badly that the cloth on one side was leeched of color and splitting apart. There were ragged burn holes through his shirt where embers had fallen on him, and his boots were warped and cracked from too much heat. He had lost his baseball cap, and his bald head was streaked with soot and filth and clumps of something that looked like red paste. His bad eye was wide open and bulging and as white as marble. Below it, Flavio could see a trail of clean skin as if Delfino had been weeping.

"Flavio," Delfino said again. He took a few steps forward and then fell to his knees.

"Delfino?" Flavio said, suddenly wide awake. He swiveled off the sofa and knelt beside Delfino. Delfino's hands were flat on the floor and his head hung down. Beneath the dirt on his scalp were large flat blisters. Some of them had broken, and clear fluid ran down one side of Delfino's face. A smell rose from his body that nearly made Flavio gag. "Delfino," he said again. "What in God's name has happened to you?" He could feel a wave of panic start up in his belly and begin to flutter up into his chest.

"Water," Delfino gasped. "I need a little water, Flavio." He lowered himself onto his elbows and rested his forehead on the floor. Flavio realized that if Delfino were to lie down, he might never get him up.

"Let me help you." Flavio took hold of his arm gently. "You can sit here on the sofa and I'll get some water."

"Maybe if I rest a little," Delfino said.

"Come, Delfino," Flavio said as he slid his arms around Delfino's waist. "Let's sit you up." Lifting him was like lifting air. As soon as he had Delfino on the sofa, Flavio ran into the kitchen and turned on the tap. While the glass filled, he glanced out the window. The fire had moved so far north now that it was just a mile from Ramona's alfalfa field. Smoke rolled in waves ahead of it, and for a second it seemed to Flavio as if it had actually followed Delfino across the foothills. The air outside was dusty and gray and the sky was orange. There was a drone of planes from overhead and a low, muted sound of sirens. The thought that this was not just some little fire went through Flavio's mind, and then he let it go, turned off the faucet, and hurried back into the other room.

Delfino was sitting back against the sofa, his eyes half closed, his arms flung out to the sides. Flavio sat down beside him. "I've brought you some water, Delfino," he said. There were tiny blisters on Delfino's lips, and his breath was thin and shallow.

"I breathed fire, Flavio," Delfino said. "I tried not to. I tried to hold my breath and breathe into my hat, but my hands hurt so bad that I dropped it, and then I couldn't find it with all the smoke. It was so hot, Flavio, that the air was on fire and I breathed it."

"Don't talk so much, Delfino," Flavio said. "Drink a little water." He brought the glass to Delfino's mouth and held it there while he drank. After a few small sips, Delfino leaned his head back.

"That's a little better," he said, though his voice was still harsh and each word he spoke sounded like he was spitting dirt. "I lost my teeth, también, Flavio. One minute they were in my mouth and the next thing I know, they're gone. I had those teeth a long time."

"You weren't wearing your teeth, Delfino," Flavio said.

Delfino turned his head. "No?" he said.

"No. When I saw you earlier, you didn't have your teeth."

"That's good. I tell you, my teeth were lucky they stayed home." For a moment, Delfino sat without speaking, staring blankly out the open door across the room from him. A slight wheeze was coming from his chest, and there was a glazed look in his good eye. Flavio felt his stomach knot up again, and he realized he had no idea how badly Delfino was hurt. The last thing they should be doing was sitting in Ramona's house. Then he suddenly remembered that he had left Felix alone in his pickup.

"Eee," Flavio said, and he stood up. "Felix is in my truck."

"I was wondering where he had gone," Delfino said. "But then I thought he was like my teeth."

Flavio walked across the room and looked out the door. He could see Felix's head bumping up and down just above the dashboard. "Felix," he called out, "I'll get you in a minute." Inside the truck Felix lifted his head a little higher and said something that Flavio couldn't make out. "I can't hear you," Flavio yelled back.

"Flavio," Delfino said. "You were right, Felix can talk."

"I know he can talk," Flavio said.

"It's like a miracle," Delfino said. And then he began to cough, a wet, grating sound. His body shook and he held a hand to his mouth as if to stop himself. It reminded Flavio of the noises his father had made just before he died. It had been one of the few times that Flavio and his brother, José, and Ramona had all been together. As always, they had had little to say to each other. At the news of her father's illness, Ramona had returned to Guadalupe from the city in which she lived. Flavio remembered her cooking alone in the kitchen or sitting beside their father's bed and gazing out the window at the same mountains their mother had once looked at. José had paced the house nervously, and whenever their father's coughing had become too severe, he would go outside and sit by the woodpile, his shoulders hunched and rounded, and smoke by himself. Flavio had only sat across from Ramona with his head lowered and his eyes closed tightly, trying to shut out the sound of his father's death. When he and Ramona had spoken, which had been seldom, it had been about nothing that mattered to either one of them.

As quickly as the spasm had come upon Delfino, it left. And when Delfino dropped his hand there was a smear of blood across his face. "I don't feel so good, Flavio," he said.

"We should go, Delfino," Flavio said, "and get some help for you. We can take my truck."

"Go?" Delfino said. His voice broke and for the first time the dazed look in his eye left and he looked frightened. "I don't want to go anywhere. Who'll feed my pigs? Besides, I saw this fire jump the highway. There isn't even a road now."

"But we can't just sit here."

"Do you think driving around on bumpy roads will help me? I tell you what. You go get Felix and we can all have a little talk. Then we'll see."

Flavio stepped outside and went down the porch steps slowly. The sky was flat and white with smoke, and the air beneath it was thick with haze. There was no sign of Felix in the cab of the truck, and Flavio thought that he must have lain down on the front seat to rest. The fire, as Delfino had said, had jumped the highway leading south out of the valley, and Flavio realized that it had nearly made a half circle around the village. The wind had died down, but flames and smoke were slowly eating their way down the slopes. He watched a plane dip low, empty itself of water, and then fly south, probably to refill at the small airport in Las Sombras. A squad car drove past on the highway, and Flavio recognized N. Oliver. Oliver glanced out his window as he drove by and, though he looked again when he saw Flavio, he kept on driving.

When Flavio came to the irrigation ditch, he stopped walking. It was cool beneath the cottonwoods, and there was the gentle sound of water running in the ditch. For a second, Flavio thought it was possible that everything that was happening around him was not real. He had gotten out of bed that morning, just like any other morning, and, with his shovel, had driven to Ramona's to irrigate. There had still been stars in the sky as he drove across the village, and he had slowed once so as not to hit Alfred Trujillo's dog, which always slept on the warm pavement. He had parked where his truck now sat and walked out into the field. The day had promised what it always had, and not once in his life had Flavio ever asked for more. Who was he to say that he still wasn't standing in his sister's field, leaning on his shovel, and dreaming a dream of fire?

"I'm frightened, Flavio," Ramona had said to him, and then she reached across the table and placed her hand on his.

It was exactly a year before Flavio would find her dead in her kitchen. The two of them were sitting at the table in the same room. It was late spring and outside there was rain and mud and a chill in the air that was too late for the season. Ramona had made a pot of coffee, and then she had filled two cups and sat down across from her brother. Near the window, just in front of the sink, was a canvas that Ramona had been working on. It seemed to Flavio to be only a painting of color. The surface was a dark, burned red. The paint was applied so thickly that it seemed aged and cracked. Beneath the surface were faint drawings as if of things moving about. Flavio wondered why anyone would go to the trouble of drawing a picture and then cover it up with so much paint. He had no idea of the meaning of Ramona's painting or even if it had any. The thought went through his mind that if he were to spend his time doing such things, he would draw pictures of sunsets and snow-crested mountains and alfalfa fields in bloom. Never would he paint something that seemed to ask more than he was willing to give. He glanced at the painting once more and then moved his chair slightly so that it wouldn't bother him.

"I've been waking up in the middle of the night," Ramona said, and she leaned a little toward her brother. "I'm frightened, and I don't know of what. I feel as if there are always things around me in this house and I don't know what they are."

Flavio, who never woke in the middle of the night—and if he

had would have thought about his cows—patted his sister's hand awkwardly and said, "It's probably those stupid santos. They would be enough to frighten anyone." Flavio hadn't seen the santos in years, but he knew his sister well enough to know that they were lurking somewhere about the house.

Ramona pulled her hand away and leaned back in her chair. "No," she said, "it's not the stupid santos, Flavio. If anything, they give me a bit of peace. It's something else. I feel as if there was something in my life that happened and didn't. Or else something that happened and shouldn't have. At night, when I wake, I can feel the answer just within my grasp, and then, like smoke, it's gone."

Flavio had absolutely no idea what his sister was talking about. He wished Martha were with him. While it was true she didn't understand Ramona any better than he did, at least Ramona never grew irritated in her presence.

"These things happen, Ramona," he said, waving his hand.

For a few seconds Ramona just stared at him. Then she said, "What things, Flavio?"

"Well," Flavio said, and then he stared down at the top of the table. There were faded smears of paint on the wood and bits of dirt that filtered down from the ceiling whenever the wind blew too hard. He could hear the dim sound of rain beating down on the old metal roof and, beneath it, the steady sound of Ramona's breath. He raised his eyes and looked back at his sister.

She was eleven years older than Flavio. Her face was deeply lined, and her hair was gray, though there were still streaks of black running through it. While age had brought a thinness to Ramona that bordered on frailty, her eyes had remained dark and clear and her hands were smooth and steady. Sometimes, when she brushed her hair back, Flavio would glimpse her as she had once been, and he would realize that not so long ago each of them had been young and that even after so many years little had changed between them.

Now, there was a tautness in Ramona's face, and she sat looking at him as if he had something she wanted.

Flavio took in a deep breath and let it out slowly. "We're growing old, Ramona," he said to her.

Ramona sat staring at him and then her face relaxed and she leaned again across the table. "He was going to be a great santero, Flavio," she said. "I could see it in him even though his hands were too small to hold the knife. Even though he often preferred to be outside doing the stupid things boys always do. He was given a gift, Flavio. I know that in my heart. Something went wrong and I don't know what. For years I searched for him in my paintings, in the santo he carved for so long. I would stand outside just before dark and listen for his voice. In the mornings, when I would wake, I would lie in bed and wait to hear his footsteps. I would even study your face, Flavio, just to catch a glimpse of him. I knew he was lost, but I could feel that he was still here with me, just beyond my sight. Nothing else made any sense to me."

"What are you talking about, Ramona?" Flavio said. "It's been almost forty years. Little José drowned. He was lost at the river. You told me yourself."

"Flavio," Ramona said and took his hand again. "He was taken from us and I don't know why."

"But you were alone with him, Ramona. There was no one else there to take him."

"It was not La Llorona, Flavio," Ramona whispered. "It was Grandmother."

What Ramona had said shocked Flavio so much that he didn't say a word. He moved his eyes past her to the small window over the sink. Rain was running down the glass, and through it, Flavio could see the blur of the field. It was now nearly all mud, but he knew that after so much rain slender shoots of alfalfa would begin to grow. "I taught José how to use his shovel," he said to himself, "and he would use it to beat prairie dogs on the head." He smiled and looked at Ramona's painting, at the shadows beneath the surface. He realized that what was buried under so many layers of paint wasn't really so difficult to see. If he closed his eyes, he would be able to see it even better.

There was the smell of enchiladas layered with cilantro and garlic and hot green chiles cooking in the oven, and Flavio could almost feel the heat from the stove washing against his face. He could hear the rustle of his grandmother's apron and her footsteps sharp and clean on the kitchen floor. In the other room, his grandfather was sitting in his chair, and every so often he would clear his throat roughly and scold José for never being still. Flavio opened his eyes slowly, and sitting across from him was his young sister. She was rolling out tortillas, and her hands and her bare arms were dusted with flour. She was gazing past him, a distant look on her face, and even Flavio could see that wherever Ramona was, it wasn't here with her family. Their grandmother paused by the stove, and Flavio heard clearly each word she spoke.

"Be careful, Ramona," she said. "You know how your grandfather likes his tortillas. And you, Flavio, make yourself useful and wake up your sister if you see her dreaming."

In a daze, Flavio realized that he had heard his name being called for some time. "Flavio," Felix yelled again, "I could drink a little water."

Felix was leaning his head out the driver's window of the truck. The two men looked at each other for a few seconds before Flavio shook his head and then stepped over the irrigation ditch. He hurried over to the side of the pickup and pulled open the door.

"Help me out of the truck, Flavio," Felix said; his lips were parched and his legs were shaking badly. "I have to take a piss."

Flavio stood with his arm around Felix's waist. Felix fumbled with the buttons on his pants and, after what seemed like a long time, urine began to dribble half on the ground and half on the legs of Felix's trousers. "Eee," he breathed out. "I thought you forgot about me, Flavio."

"No," Flavio said. "You were sleeping. And then Delfino came."

"Delfino?"

"Sí. He's in Ramona's house. He was burned by the fire. When he coughs, blood comes from his mouth."

Felix looked down at the ground. He shook himself off and buttoned up his pants. "I don't understand," he said. "The fire is in the mountains."

"So was Delfino," Flavio said. "Don't you remember? He went up into the hills with a shovel."

Felix sagged slightly and leaned against Flavio. "I should have stayed asleep," he said. "I should have stayed asleep and never woken up."

"Come, Felix," Flavio said, and keeping his arm around Felix's waist, he walked the two of them slowly back to the house.

"Felix," Delfino said, and he raised his hand and smiled. Flavio and Felix stood in the doorway together and looked inside the house. Light from outside ran across the floor to the sofa and up Delfino's outstretched legs. In his lap was a santo and he held it cradled in one hand. The Lady's face was smudged with soot and blood, and she stared back at Flavio and Felix. "I borrowed her, Flavio," Delfino said.

"You shouldn't have moved, Delfino," Flavio said as he took a step inside the room.

Delfino gave a slight shrug. "I saw her looking at me." He dropped his hand and rested it on the Lady. "She didn't want to be on the floor."

For a moment no one spoke, and then Delfino said, "You don't look so good, Felix."

Felix raised his eyes. They were red and bleary, moisture gathered in the corners. "You don't look so good either, my friend," he said.

"I was doing pretty good for a little while," Delfino said. Felix was sitting close beside him on the sofa. His hands were in his lap and his neck was so bent that he stared down at the Lady in Delfino's lap. Flavio had dragged a chair out from the kitchen and sat leaning forward just a few feet away. "And then," Delfino went on, "a wind came and, I tell you, everything went to hell."

By the time Delfino had stumbled his way up to the top of the foothill, his bad eye had begun to throb and his vision was wavering so badly that it seemed as if the juniper and piñon were walking along with him. Below him, in the valley, vehicles were beginning to drive away, and he realized that if he were to wait for help, he would be waiting a long time. Off to the south he could see that the fire was rounding back toward the highway. At the top of the hill, the road was blocked with police cars. Not far from him was a wall of smoke that towered hundreds of feet high and, buried in it, Delfino could hear the rush of flames. For a moment, Delfino stood leaning against his shovel, catching his breath. On a rock near his feet were two small lizards. "This is a bad fire, no?" he asked them and watched as they darted down the side of the rock and disappeared beneath it. Then, for some reason, Delfino thought of his pigs and how, at this moment, they would be smelling smoke and staring through the twisted wire of their pen, wondering what had become of him. He had named all of his pigs, and though their fate was to end up, one by one, in his freezer, he was always careful never to mention this to them. They, like himself, had done nothing to deserve such a thing as this fire. He pushed off of his shovel and looked at the wall of smoke.

"I used to hunt rabbits in these hills," he yelled, "and cut fence posts, and my pigs are all alone because of you, you jodido.

"Then I started to shovel," Delfino said, looking at Flavio. "Whenever a little fire would start on the ground near me, I would beat it to death with my shovel. I thought to myself that if I could turn the fire west it would burn itself out at the river."

Delfino didn't see the fire engulf him so much as hear it. One moment he was madly throwing dirt over embers, and the next there was a great roaring noise all about him and all he could see was smoke. The sparse weeds and scrub oak ignited and flames crawled up the legs of his overalls. He covered his face with his hat, and the few hairs on his head singed down to nothing. He stumbled about blindly and when the heat scorched the back of his hands, he dropped his hat and fell to his knees.

"I breathed fire," Delfino said. "At first it tasted cold, like my lungs had swallowed ice. The kind of ice that smokes. It was like being born and in the first breath you take you know things will never be the same." Delfino paused for a second and wiped at his mouth with the back of his hand. "And then that chingadera plane came."

As Delfino knelt on the loose rock, his hands covering his mouth, he suddenly found himself in a cloud of red dust. It fell from the sky like a dense rain. It put out the fire burning his legs and soothed the blisters on his scalp and on the back of his hands. And for a moment, it caused the fire to pause, as if it, too, was startled by what it had inhaled.

"I started to run," Delfino said. "I ran like crazy. It was just my good luck that I ran the right way. When I could finally see clearly again, I was north of the fire and I could see your field, Flavio, and Ramona's little house."

Delfino stopped talking and though he hadn't moved, his body sagged farther into the sofa. He coughed gently and then swallowed what had been in his mouth.

Flavio had no idea how someone in Delfino's condition had managed to come so far. He sat looking at Felix and Delfino sitting side by side, and he thought that somehow these two viejos had, on the same day, done the exact opposite thing in the same place. Just hours after Felix had started a small fire out of grass and sticks, Delfino had walked up there with his shovel and tried to put it out. Then they had both come to Ramona's house. Flavio rubbed his face hard with his hands. "How could this happen?" he muttered.

"I ran fast," Delfino said. "That's how."

Felix stirred and raised his eyes. "It was the Lady," he said. "I think she helped you."

"Qué lady?" Delfino said. "There was nobody up there but me." Then he reached out and touched Felix's leg. "Felix," he said. "It's so good to hear your voice. What, all these years you didn't have nothing to say?" Then he smiled at his joke and brought his hand back to the santo. His thumb moved gently against the side of her face.

"You just didn't see her, Delfino," Felix said. "She was probably standing behind you all that time."

Delfino moved his eyes away from Felix. "What's he talking, Flavio? Why would there have been a woman wandering about the foothills?"

"He's still a little confused, Delfino," Flavio said. "After all, he was sick for so long." Flavio knew exactly what Felix was talking about, and he had no desire for the conversation to go where Felix was taking it. "We should talk about getting some help for you."

"She was wearing a black dress that fell to her feet," Felix said softly, "and her head was covered with a shawl. At first, I thought she was the Virgin, but now I don't know." He was looking down at the santo in Delfino's lap, and she looked back at him, a slight smile on her face. "I didn't see her face so good, but I think she was some-one I once knew. I don't know from where. She came to the café before it was light and sat with me. We watched dawn come to the village, and then I followed her into the foothills. How could I have said no to her when she told me what to do?"

The day before Flavio's grandmother died, Flavio had walked quietly into her bedroom and found his grandfather sitting beside the bed. Rosa had been talking to him in a whisper, and Epolito's head was bent low. He held his wife's hand in his own. Rosa's eyes had moved to her grandson and she had smiled weakly and said, "Leave us for a little, hijo." The curtain over the window was drawn open, and sunlight was lying upon both his grandparents. Epolito had turned his head to look at Flavio, and on his face was the same expression Delfino now had.

For a little while, Delfino stared at Felix. Then the muscles in his face grew slack and he closed his eye. He drew the santo tight against his chest and held her there. "I don't want to hear no more," he said. "I should have stayed home with my pigs."

Nick Oliver swung his squad car off the road and parked beside Felix's truck in front of Ramona's house. He switched off the igni-tion and sat for a moment listening to the clicking of the engine. The radio started up again, and he leaned forward and switched it off. "Talk to someone else," he said. "I've got enough problems." He reached in his shirt pocket, pulled out a cigarette and lit it. The smoke was clean and sharp in his lungs. He leaned his head against the top edge of the seat and looked at the Montoya house. The plas-ter on the walls was cracked and mottled where it had been patched over the years, and the tin roof was rusted and coated with tar. One side of the house sagged and the porch was cocked at an odd angle with the ground. The front door of the place was wide open, but all he could see inside was darkness. It looked like every other old adobe Oliver had ever seen, tired and sad and used up.

"Maybe no one's home," he said out loud. He brought the cigarette to his mouth and blew the smoke out slowly. Once again he was tempted to start the car back up and drive north out of the valley. He could drive with the windows open until the smell of wood smoke was gone and the sun set and it grew dark. He could stop in a town far from New Mexico and change out of his uniform and into the dress clothes he kept in a bag in the trunk of the car. Then he could take a bus to a place where no one knew him and no one would think twice when they saw him—a place where cows don't stumble out of the mountains on fire making noises cows aren't supposed to make and where old men don't start fires for no reason.

He took another drag off his cigarette and glanced out his side window. The entire south side of the valley was cloaked in smoke, and the fire had burned so low that four houses and a couple of trailers had already been lost. Flames were beginning to lick up against alfalfa fields. Sheep and cattle that had been corralled were now roaming loose, and Oliver had watched a flock of chickens run scattered and mistakenly up into the hills, their wings flapping, the hard claws of their feet clicking on rocks.

He had spent the last two hours driving from house to house on the entire south side of the valley with Donald Lucero. Most of the places they had stopped were already empty, and the vehicles that had once been there were gone. At each place, they would pound on the door and, after waiting a moment, would push it open and go quickly from room to room making sure that no infant had been left in a crib and that no one was sleeping off a hangover. Then, they would go out the back and check the outbuildings for livestock.

At one house that sat amid huge cottonwoods and willows, they had found an old woman sweeping red ants out from the hard-packed dirt beneath her portal. The fire was just a hundred yards behind her property. The plumes of smoke had dwarfed her home and reminded Oliver of pictures he had seen as a child, paintings of the apocalypse. She was sweeping with a broom that was only bristles, and every so often she would curse and bend over and brush an ant off the side of her bare leg. Her thin gray hair was tied with a bandanna, and her legs were heavy and veined and mottled with red welts. They were standing in the shade, but Oliver could feel the heat of the fire on his face, and his shirt, damp with sweat, was warm against his back.

"Venga, Mrs. Flores," Donald had said. At each place they had stopped, Oliver had hung back a few feet behind Lucero. He had lived long enough in northern New Mexico to know that, along with his name, his presence could sometimes make things difficult. He had let the Guadalupe police officer do the talking. Even then, as Lucero had told them that they must leave their homes until it was safe, Oliver could feel their eyes on him as if it were he who had brought this calamity to the village.

"Cuándo mi hijo venga aquí," Mrs. Flores said, without looking up, "yo voy." Her voice was deep and the words came out of her mouth mumbled. Ants were swarming over her feet, and she swept at them with her broom. "I have enough trouble here as it is," she said.

"The fire is getting too close," Donald said. "Everybody must leave. It's no longer safe here. Tomorrow you can come back and sweep ants."

"The fire won't bother me," she said, glancing up. Her face was flushed and when she spoke only one side of her mouth moved. "The ditch will stop the fire."

Donald took off his hat and wiped his forehead with his sleeve. He fanned his face and took a step closer to the house. "Then there's nothing for you to worry about," he said. "Come. I'll give you a ride to your son's house."

"I don't know," Mrs. Flores said, and she moved her eyes to Oliver. "Who is that man?"

"He's nobody," Lucero said. "He's here because of the fire. We should hurry. I still have your neighbors to see."

"I don't want to leave my house," she said, and her voice suddenly broke. "My husband's clothes are here. And his shoes. All those little stones he liked to carry in his pocket for good luck."

"I'll try to send someone back to get them," Donald said, and he lowered his head and stepped beneath the portal. He stooped down beside Mrs. Flores and brushed her legs gently with his hat. "If you stay here," he said, "the ants will eat you." He stood up and took the broom from her and leaned it against the wall of the house. Then he took her arm. "Come, Ascensia, your son will be happy to know you're safe." He tugged her arm slightly and the two of them came out from under the portal.

"It's bad, no?" Mrs. Flores said. "This fire."

"Yes," Donald answered her. "It's pretty bad. But men are coming to put it out and there are planes dropping water."

"I saw it when it was just a little fire," the old woman said, "and I thought it was nothing. Someone burning grass by the cemetery or boys doing something foolish."

They passed by Oliver without so much as a glance, but he nodded to them absently and then stood for a moment staring at the house. It wasn't much, he thought. Maybe four or five run-down rooms that would smell of mildew and age. The old wood floors would be covered with linoleum and would be warped and cracked and faded away. The roof of the portal was layered with old roofing paper, and it sagged badly from years of snow loads. The viga ends were rotted and crumbling. Weeds had grown high about the place and dried out. The only green he could see, besides the cottonwoods and willows, was behind the house where the ditch ran. He gazed up at the fire burning high on the hillside and then took one last look at the house. A couple of straight-backed chairs were set beneath the portal. Between them and at eye level, a nicho was carved into the wall. Even from where he stood, he could see the painted picture of a saint inside it. He grunted softly and reached for a cigarette. "Good luck," he said to her and struck a match.

When he turned around, Mrs. Flores was already sitting in the front seat of Lucero's vehicle. Lucero was leaning against the door and shaking his head. A couple of miles away, in the middle of the valley, smoke was billowing up into the air.

"Jesus Christ," Oliver breathed out. For the first time it struck him that not only were the mountains around Guadalupe about to burn, but so was the village itself. "That's a house, isn't it?" he said to Lucero.

Lucero turned his head and looked back. "It's Flavio Montoya's house," he said and turned his head away.

Oliver walked up to the car and stopped a few feet from Lucero. "You better get somebody over there," he said. "Before it gets out of hand."

"It's already out of hand," Lucero said. The skin beneath his eyes was dark and his face was heavy and drawn. He pushed off of the car. "Well, either Flavio's decided to burn everything up or Sippy and his brothers are out to get even. I tell you what. I'll get the fire department over there, and then me and Mrs. Flores will go talk to the neighbors. You can do me a favor. You know Flavio's truck. Go by his sister's old house north of town. If you find him, get him and Felix the hell out of here before someone shoots them."

On the drive across the village, Oliver was told that the first fire crews had arrived, but instead of coming into the valley they had been dispersed into the hills south of the fire.

"They want to keep the fire away from all those big houses," the dispatcher had said, his voice coming like tin through the speaker.

"We're about to lose some houses here," Oliver had radioed back.

"Don't blame me," the dispatcher said. "I'll see what I can find out, but there's more money in one of those houses than in that entire village. So you go figure."

Nick Oliver took one last hit off his cigarette and let the butt drop out his open window. In the ten minutes he'd been sitting in his squad car beside Flavio's pickup, he hadn't heard a sound come from the house. His throat felt tight and his eyes were beginning to burn. He pushed himself up on the seat and rubbed his face hard with his hands. He'd been in this village for only a few hours, and it was beginning to feel as if he'd been here forever.

When Oliver stepped through the doorway of Ramona's house, the first thing that struck him was the smell. Although it was the same smell of smoke as outside, here it was heavier and thicker and carried something beneath it, as if the adobe walls themselves were smoldering. He breathed through his mouth and then stood still just inside the room, letting his eyes grow accustomed to the light.

Gradually, he could make out the three old men sitting motionless in the shadows across the room. Two of them were staring back at him. The third had his head turned away and in his arms he was clasping something that looked like a small doll. On the floor near Oliver's feet were small carved figures. Some were standing; others were strewn about. And one of them stared up at him. Her eyes were open and she was smiling slightly. Her face and gown had been painted, but the colors had dimmed from cobwebs and so much dust. Outside, the wind suddenly picked up, and a screen door in an adjoining room creaked open and then slammed shut. A feeling of unease passed through Oliver, and he fought off an impulse to turn around and walk out of the house.

On the opposite wall were two large paintings. In one, a thin, muddy creek lined with bleached stones ran through a steep arroyo. Stunted sagebrush grew out of the steep sides and the roots of a dead juniper hung bare. And where the arroyo curved out of sight were the shadows of things Oliver couldn't quite see. In the other, three horses stood still in the rain. Breath came from their nostrils and the mountains behind them were draped in clouds. Oliver moved his foot slightly, and one of the santos spun a slow half circle on the floor. Where am I? he wondered. The room breathed with things he had only glimpsed in the years of driving through the villages of northern New Mexico. He felt that if he were to go close to the paintings, he would feel heat on his face from the bleached rocks or hear the sound of rain and the heavy breath of horses. Even the three old men sitting across from him seemed more like figures from a long time ago than anything else. He stared at the paintings for a few more seconds and then lowered his eyes.

"Mr. Montoya," he said. "I'm afraid I have some bad news for you."

Flavio had heard the squad car pull up to the house, and when he had seen Oliver walking up the path, he had actually said a small prayer of thanks that someone was coming to take care of this mess in his sister's house. At the mention of bad news, Flavio rose slowly from his chair and stood before the sofa. He took off his hat and held it in front of him with both hands. He thought that with no family left and what friends he had either dead or in this room, there was little news anymore that he could actually consider bad.

"I have to ask you and Mr. García to come with me," Oliver said.

For a moment, no one said anything and then Flavio felt Felix's hand brush the back of his leg. Flavio raised his face and gazed back at the police officer. "This is my house," he said.

"No," Oliver said. "This is your sister's house. Someone has set fire to your house. It's burning now. For your own safety, I'm asking you to come with me."

At first, Flavio couldn't even grasp what Oliver had told him. He stared blankly at the police officer and then moved his eyes away and looked out the open door. Outside, all he could see was the thick haze of smoke. My house is on fire, he thought. He had been born there, as had his sister and his little brother. As a young man, his father had built the place solidly out of adobe and stone, and then he had plastered the walls with mud and laid the thick planks for the floor. In that house, Flavio's father had drunk whiskey by himself late into the night. He and his wife had died years apart in their small bedroom where, later, Flavio and Martha would make love so often and so well that Flavio would occasionally think of himself as someone else. The letters Martha had written him were on the table by the side of his bed, and there were photographs in all the rooms.

Flavio felt his knees weaken, and he sat heavily back down in his chair. "My house is on fire," he said.

As soon as Flavio fell back into his chair, Oliver, for the first time, looked closely at the two men on the sofa. One was the old man he had met earlier at the café, but the other, he had never seen before. The man's legs were stretched out almost rigid, and he was breathing harshly. His clothes were torn and frayed, and what looked like blood was smeared across the lower part of his face. Oliver inhaled sharply and then took the few steps across the room. When he stopped beside Flavio, he knew what the odor was in the air and where it was coming from.

"What happened to this man?" he asked sharply. He stooped down and touched Delfino's knee. Delfino's hands tightened around the santo and he let out a low groan. Oliver could see the flat blisters on his scalp and that beneath the soot and blood on his face the skin was burned white. He, too, let out a soft moan and then straightened up. He looked down at Flavio. "Who is this?" he asked.

"His name's Delfino Vigil," Flavio mumbled, without even looking at Oliver. Then he turned to Felix. "My house is burning down. This is your fault, también. Now I have no house. Not even any place to put my things."

Felix was leaning forward, his head nodding, his eyes staring straight ahead. His hands were clasped in his lap and he was rocking a little back and forth. "Felix," Flavio said loudly. "Did you hear me? My house is burning down."

Oliver had no idea what was going on in the room. While one man sat charred on the sofa, the other one was yelling at a stroke victim who was brain dead. On top of that, Oliver realized that Delfino was the old man supposedly lost in the fire, and here he was in the Montoya house. "What's happening here?" he said to Flavio. "I was told this man died in the fire. How did he get here?"

Delfino grunted and then looked at Oliver. "I don't know you," he said. "You're not from this village."

"I'm a police officer," Oliver said. "We're going to get you some help."

"I don't need no help," Delfino said. "I need a little rest and then I'll go home." He looked at Felix, who was rocking a little faster now. "To my pigs. Wait until they hear what you did."

Oliver walked out of the room. He glanced in the kitchen and then went into a side bedroom. He pulled the blanket off the bed and then hurried back into the living room. He draped it over Delfino and tucked in the sides tight around his body. "I'm going to lift you up now," he said, "and get you to a doctor." Then he bent down and lifted Delfino in his arms. Delfino kicked his feet weakly. His head rolled from side to side.

"Flavio," he called out, and then he began to cough. "I don't want to go."

Flavio stood and put his hand on Delfino. He could feel the hard wood of the santo beneath the blanket. "It's just for a little while, Delfino," he said. "Me and Felix will come and see you."

"Where?" Delfino said, and then Oliver carried him past Flavio, across the room, and out the door.

Flavio followed them and stopped in the doorway. "I'll watch out for your pigs," he yelled. All he could see of Delfino was the top of his head sticking out past Oliver's shoulder as they walked to the squad car. Oliver pulled open the back door and laid Delfino on the seat. Then he hurried around to the driver's side and climbed in. He started the car and, with the lights on, backed out of Ramona's drive. Out in the middle of the valley a thick plume of smoke hung in the sky. Flavio leaned against the door frame. I had a house once, he thought. And in it was my whole life.

10

The room where the santo stood was small and bare and without a window. The ceiling was cobwebbed and danced with shadows from the kerosene lamp that Guadalupe García held. The vigas
overhead were so bowed from the weight of the roof that Flavio
thought they might snap at any moment and bury Guadalupe
and Felix and himself under so much dirt that no one would ever
find them. The walls were a rough mud plaster, and the floor, like
every other floor in the García house, sloped with the ground and
was dirt.

In the center of the room was a narrow bed, the steel frame
pocked and rusted. The blanket that covered the mattress was thin
and tucked in tightly on all sides, the surface gray and covered with
dirt. Beside the bed was a small table, and on it stood the santo. She
was the first thing Flavio saw when he entered the room, and the

sight of her startled him. When he inhaled sharply, Guadalupe placed her hand on his shoulder.

"Pay her no attention, Flavio," she had said. "If you do that, she won't bother you."

"Is she the one Cristóbal made when the storm came?" Felix asked. His voice was hushed and thin, and Flavio could tell that Felix, like himself, was uneasy being so deep inside this house.

"Yes," Guadalupe said. "She has stayed in this room since my great-grandmother Percides died years ago. I don't think about her often, but when I do, I think that it's better if she stays here. Maybe then she won't cause trouble."

"How would she cause trouble?" Felix asked. His voice was a little stronger now.

Flavio glanced again at the santo. "She keeps looking at me," he said.

"She's looking at me, too," Felix said.

Guadalupe walked over to the table. She put the lantern down and then turned the santo so that it faced the wall. "There," she said, smiling slightly. "Now she will look at no one. Besides, we didn't come here to visit her. We came to see the place where Emilio García is buried." She raised the lamp and held it close to the wall. "Do you see?" she asked.

Flavio and Felix crowded closer and stood beside Guadalupe. At first, neither boy could make out anything, but as their eyes adjusted to the light, they could see that just above the bed a section of the wall was sunk in a few inches, as if the space behind the mud was hollow.

"I see them," Felix said in a whisper, and he glanced at Flavio. "Eee, you're looking too high. Down lower."

They didn't look like bones to Flavio. They looked like small sticks, stripped of bark, that someone had stuck in the wall. A number of them were scattered about and, against the dark plaster and in the light from the lamp, they stood out smooth and stark and white. Felix reached out and ran his finger over one.

"This one," he said, "must have been his little finger, since it's so small." He pulled his hand back. "Touch it, Flavio. It feels just like a bone."

Flavio didn't have the slightest inclination to touch whatever was buried in the wall. The only thing he could think was that if they were truly bones from Emilio García's hand, why were they strewn about and not all in one place? For them to be like this, Emilio would have had to be placed in the wall in pieces. Flavio shoved his hands in his pockets and chased the thought away.

"They're sticks from an aspen," he said. "They just look like bones."

"They are bones," Guadalupe said, and she sat down on the edge of the bed and looked at both boys. Light moved on her face, and her skin seemed dark and heavy. "Maybe behind the plaster," she said, "there are more. Or maybe there's nothing but adobe bricks. No one ever told me how they came to be here, so I don't know. I found them by accident, and my story is that they are the bones of Emilio García. He was carried up the hill in the rain and placed here where my grandmother could watch over him—where no one would hurt him again."

Felix traced a bone with his fingernail. A small piece of mud chipped away, and Flavio could make out a slight swell in the bone like the beginning of a joint. "Look at this, Flavio," Felix said. "Sticks don't do this."

"No," Flavio said, and he lowered his head. The floor had once been mudded, and deep cracks now spread through it as if there'd been a drought in the house. "I don't want to look at it."

It had been Flavio's idea to come to the García house. He had filled a burlap bag with loose beans, a little flour, and a jar of lard and told Felix that his grandmother wished them to bring these things to Guadalupe García. He had walked in front of Felix and, until they reached the García house, the only thought in his head was about his own heroism and what it might turn out to be.

When Guadalupe had opened her door, she had stared at the two boys and then taken the bag from Flavio without a word. Her hair hung flat against her scalp, and its color had faded to that of paper left lying in the sun. There were dark rings beneath her eyes and lines that ran from the corners of her mouth down her face. She stood a little stooped, and what Flavio had been thinking on the walk over left him.

"What do you boys want?" Guadalupe asked, passing a hand over her eyes as if the sun were too bright.

"We came to see the bones of Emilio García," Felix said suddenly, his voice shrill even to Flavio.

Guadalupe lowered her hand slowly, and after a moment she said, "Are you sure?"

Before Flavio could say no, Felix stepped beside him. He stuck his hand in his pocket and brought out the burned piece of wood he had found beneath the cottonwood tree the day before. "We found this," he said.

Guadalupe squinted down at the thing in Felix's hand. Flavio could see that Felix had washed it and then rubbed it hard with a cloth. Soot was still seeped into the grains of wood, but even he could see that it had once been worked with a knife.

"It's Emilio's," Felix said. "I brought it to give it back."

Guadalupe looked at it for a little longer and then she reached out and took it. When she looked back at the boys, she said, her voice low and tired, "Come, then."

Flavio and Felix had followed closely behind Guadalupe as they walked through the house. There were rooms off to each side of the narrow hallway, and every so often, by the light of the lamp,

Flavio would glimpse a bed up against a wall or a small trastero, cloth hung over the shelves. Some of the rooms had windows, the glass broken or cracked, the panes streaked with mud and dust. In these, he could see blankets nailed to the walls, and in the nichos were the stems of dead flowers or wood boxes coated with dirt. In one room, he saw a doll lying on the bed looking out at him, her hair braided, her legs long and thin, and beside her was the figure of a carved horse. By the time Guadalupe had led them into the room where Emilio García was buried, all Flavio wished to do was leave. He felt that he had wandered too far inside something that he shouldn't have, and he told himself that soon he would be out-side where the sun was high in the sky and the breeze carried the scent of apples and bitter cherries.

"You're just scared," Felix said. "Look," and he placed his hand flat on the wall where the bones were buried. "They won't hurt you."

"I don't want to touch any bones," Flavio said, and he lifted his face and looked at Guadalupe. "It's not right." She was still seated on the edge of the bed. Her legs were slightly apart and her night-gown rose to just above her knees. A strand of hair had wandered in front of her face and she moved it aside.

"One night," she said, "when I was a small girl, my father taught me to dance." Guadalupe closed her eyes and stretched out her arms. She began to sway just a little back and forth. "It was late that night and my mother had gone to bed hours before. I had fallen asleep at the kitchen table. When I woke, I saw my father standing in the doorway. His hair was long and knotted, and his beard was heavy with gray. My father was a thin man. I can remember how his hands stuck out from the sleeves of his shirt as he stood there star-ing at me. Then he walked into the house to where I was sitting. He took my hands and pulled me from my chair, and he showed me how to dance. 'Move one foot,' he whispered, and I could smell his breath, 'and then the other. Lift your arms higher, Guadalupe,' he said to me. We danced in small circles about the kitchen, and all the while my hands were wet with sweat and my heart beat so quickly I could hear it pounding in my ears. The next night, though I waited in the kitchen, my father did not return home. The following night was no different. And all those after."

Guadalupe's mother said that her husband had forgotten he had such a thing as a family and had chosen to become lost in the mountains. There was no bitterness in her voice, but only a satisfaction that what she had always thought was true.

"Soon after," Guadalupe went on, "my mother fell ill. She stopped eating and grew so thin that her face was like bone and rock. She moved about the house without seeing. Her body became rigid and would not bend. One day she did not come from her room, and when I found her, her eyes were open and her face was restful as if whatever had been inside my mother had finally left."

Flavio and Felix watched Guadalupe swaying on the edge of the bed. Felix had taken a few steps back into the middle of the room, and his mouth was hanging open. Flavio could hear how fast he was breathing. It struck Flavio that he was deep inside the García house with a woman who was now dancing. If the kerosene ran out in the lamp, the light would be gone. Then the three of them would be in the dark where bones were buried and a santo stood facing the wall. If he hadn't feared he would lose his way in the house, he would have fled—even if it meant leaving Felix behind.

"I've frightened you, haven't I, Flavio?" Guadalupe said. She had stopped moving and her hands were folded in her lap.

"No," Flavio lied.

"I remember things," she said. "But none of them can hurt you. Your grandfather, Tomás Montoya, would not have been frightened. He helped build some of the rooms in this house. He carved the trastero that still stands beside the bed where Cristóbal García slept. And later, after the death of his wife, he left his young son here to be raised by my family."

Flavio could feel Felix staring at the side of his face. "Eee," Felix breathed out, "Emilio García is like your tío, Flavio. If Emilio was my tío I wouldn't be scared of nothing. I would be proud to have a bandit as my tío. Tío Emilio I would call him."

"They said he was a bandit," Guadalupe said, "so that they could hang him without guilt. This village is full of so many lies that no one any longer knows the truth. Emilio and Percides were raised together, and they were born just weeks apart. And when he was hung, he was only a few years older than you two. The people of this village did this because his grandfather was Cristóbal García. My grandmother always said that the moment the rope was put around his neck, this valley truly died.

"'I can see him as a boy even now,' she would say to me. 'I see him crawling on his hands and knees across the floors of this house, the soles of his small feet black and caked with dirt. I watched him stumble as he learned to walk, and the first word he uttered was my name, Percides.' And later, when the two of them were more than children, she saw him in other ways. 'All my life,' my grandmother would say, 'I watched him until I was no longer sure where I ended and he began.'"

"I don't want Emilio to die," Felix said suddenly. The flame in the lantern flickered, and the walls and ceiling moved with shadows and light. Flavio could smell the faint odor of apricots and then only the damp inside the house.

"You don't have to listen, Felix," Guadalupe said softly, and Flavio realized that everything she had said or would ever say had been meant for him alone.

"Don't worry, Felix," he said, reaching out and touching Felix's arm. "It's just a story. Besides, it happened a long time ago."

"Oh sí?" Felix said. "That's what you always say. If it was just a story, why are there bones in the wall and why is that santo looking at the wall?"

"Hush, hijos," Guadalupe said, startling both boys. "I am not feeling so well today, so if you wish to hear anything, you must be quiet."

"One night in early spring," Guadalupe said, "when there were still crusts of snow in the shadows and the fields were yet half frozen, Hipolito Trujillo and Francisco Ramírez came to this house. So many years had now passed when this happened that both were old men. Hipolito walked slowly with the help of a heavy stick. Francisco's back was weak and bowed, and the bones in his hands had grown together and were swollen and misshapen.

"They came to this house holding each other's arms and asked to speak with Cristóbal," Guadalupe went on.

By this time, the village of Guadalupe had grown. The church stood young and strong. Its walls were thick adobe, and the plaster was smooth and dark. The roof was layered with rough wood shingles, and when it rained or there was snow, the church filled with the sharp odor of cedar. Small houses, their roofs flat and sagging, were huddled about the church and scattered along the ditches that ran throughout the valley. A few cows were now pastured in alfalfa fields along with sheep and many goats. Wild apricot and apple trees had taken root near the creeks, and in the autumn the fruit they bore was dried and stored for the winter.

When Hipolito and Francisco had returned to the valley after leaving Cristóbal alone for so long, two other families had come with them. Manuel Ruiz and his wife, Isabella, were from a small ranchito near Santa Madre. He was a small, thin man of middle age who spoke seldom and had one eye that sat fixed in its socket without moving. He was a weaver of wool and spun blankets and cloaks. His wife was little more than a child, still too young to conceive. Miguel Esquival was Francisco's second cousin. He and his wife, Dolores, and their children had joined the small caravan in Las Sombras. As an infant, Dolores had been taken from a pueblo by a priest, and her blood and skin were Indian. Her eyes were sometimes too black to gaze into, and she came to Guadalupe frightened and weeping at leaving everything behind. They built their house close to where the church would one day stand. Three of their four children were sickly that first winter and would not live to see spring.

Over the years, others had followed. They would appear in the foothills carrying their few possessions on their backs or in small wagons pulled by burros. They would wind their way slowly through the loose rock and piñon down to the valley. Then they would settle without trouble. After a while, it was as if they had always been there.

Fifty years had passed since Hipolito and Francisco and Cristóbal had stood together on a ridge and gazed down upon the valley for the first time. And throughout all those years, what Hipolito had said had proved to be true. Always enough snow fell in winter in the high mountains to swell the creeks and ditches so that the fields were wet each summer. Game, turkey, deer, and bear remained plentiful, and crops grew well wherever the earth was dug. And if the Indians passed nearby, no one saw them. They left the village to itself.

"The only weight on this place," Guadalupe said, "came from within this house. From my grandfather, Cristóbal García."

"He saw two of everything," Felix said, nodding. While Guadalupe had been talking, Felix had inched across the floor and was now sitting on the bed so close to Guadalupe that his arm brushed against hers. "I wouldn't want to see two of everyone," he went on. "Then there would be two Victoria Medinas, and both of them wouldn't like me. I wonder if Cristóbal saw two of the burro? That way he could have kept one when the other one left. I would like to have a burro. I wonder what happened to that burro."

"Why do you keep talking about the stupid burro?" Flavio said. He was sitting on the banco across the room, and all the while Guadalupe had been talking, he had stared at the santo. He could see that her gown was black from ashes and soot, except in places where it had been rubbed smooth. There were streaks of rust throughout that he thought must have come from Cristóbal's blood. Sometimes when the flame in the lantern wavered it seemed to him as if she had moved slightly. He was still staring at her because he felt that if he looked away she might do something too quickly. All the things Felix had said just meant that Flavio would have to remain uncomfortable even longer. "Can't you be quiet and listen?" he said.

"What?" Felix said and shrugged his shoulders. "I didn't do nothing."

"The Lady won't hurt you, Flavio," Guadalupe said. Her voice was low and so heavy that both boys fell quiet. "She listens," she went on, "and never does she forget. She was here even before Cristóbal took her from the wood. She will still be here after all of us are gone. I think she is waiting."

"What's she waiting for?" Flavio asked, moving his eyes carefully to Guadalupe.

"I think she's waiting for the bus," Felix said. "Then she could go to Albuquerque."

For a moment no one said anything, and then Guadalupe looked down at Felix beside her. "Cristóbal did not see two burros," she said softly. "He saw two of everyone in this village. And he saw them so clearly that each was like the other, even of those who had died. But he did not see two burros."

On the night after Cristóbal's wife was buried in the sagebrush outside the García house, Cristóbal watched her walk into their bedroom. She paused in the doorway for a moment, as if lost, and then she smiled, said her husband's name, and lay on the bed beside him. Cristóbal could feel her weight on the mattress, and he smelled the odor of mint and sage. He groaned softly and closed his eyes as she told him about their children and their children's children and how the last few days had been especially difficult for her. Then, as she always had before sleep, she touched the side of his face and said that she still remembered him as he once was, even if no one else did. In the morning, she rose early and, still in her nightclothes, went to prepare breakfast. Cristóbal listened to the sounds of her leaving. Then he turned his head and stared at the santo. For a long time he said nothing, and then, in a harsh whisper, he told her that his life and the life of his family had become like air.

When Cristóbal went out in the village, which was not often, he would speak to people with words that carried only confusion. After a while, those who lived in Guadalupe would look at the ground when he approached or turn away. No one listened to his mumbling, so that he and what he saw became a curse, and, as the years passed, the village grew more and more uneasy with itself. Some went so far as to say that as long as Cristóbal lived, the village of Guadalupe had no future, but only a past that no one understood. Even at mass, prayers were silently uttered that Cristóbal would breathe his last and leave the valley in peace.

Other than Pilar, Cristóbal's daughters had married into the families of Hipolito Trujillo and Francisco Ramírez and Miguel Esquival and all of the others who had come to the valley. And each of them, with their husbands, had remained in the García house. Flat adobe bricks mixed with rocks and sticks were formed by hand. Heavy vigas and white aspen latillas were brought from the mountains, and rooms were built off of rooms. The house smelled of wet mud and green wood. Women cooked and talked in the kitchen, and there was always the noise of children underfoot. Chickens and small turkeys nested in the sagebrush and wandered about the house for scraps of food. Goats slept on the roof, and corrals were built for when the sheep lambed in the spring.

"If you walked through these rooms at night," Guadalupe said, "you would hear the hushed voices of mothers whispering to their babies and the muffled sounds that men and women sometimes make. This house was like a village within a village."

When Hipolito and Francisco came to the García house, it was late afternoon and Cristóbal was lying in bed. His eyes were half closed, and his breath was shallow and ragged. Minute pieces of dust and dirt from the ceiling had settled on his face and chest. Recently, he had lost all track of time. He wasn't sure if it was early spring or late autumn, but he was content that it mattered nothing to him. Other than his granddaughter, Percides, and occasionally his grandson, Emilio, few came to Cristóbal's room. At those times, Percides would bring him a bowl of food and then sit on the bed and help him eat. She would make Emilio sit close enough beside her that her leg rested against his, and as she fed Cristóbal beans and small pieces of meat, her arm, bare and warm, would slide along her cousin's.

Percides was fourteen years old. Her hair was long and black and braided, with thin white cloth. There was always a slight smile on her lips, and her eyes were wide and startled. Emilio would sit beside her and, as she fed Cristóbal, his breath would deepen. He would think that his cousin's eyes seemed somehow to know that anything could happen at any time and that her mouth hoped that it would.

"Stop looking at me, Emilio," Percides had told him one day, "and talk to Grandfather." Then she had leaned her face close to Cristóbal, her breast grazing Emilio's arm, and gently wiped her grandfather's face, saying, "Grandfather, Emilio is here with me."

By this time, both of Cristóbal's eyes had turned to the color of old snow. His body was thin and hard and stiff, and on his head were only a few wisps of long, white hair. He was no taller than his grandson, and looking at him lying there, Emilio had thought that his grandfather resembled something carved out of wood.

"Grandfather," Emilio had said then, his voice so hoarse that Cristóbal's head jerked and his arms flailed to the side.

"Hija," Cristóbal had spit out, almost in a panic. "I don't want him to feed me. I remember when he was little. He was always falling off his feet and sticking things where they didn't belong."

"He's not little anymore, Grandfather," Percides said, smiling. "Like me, he has grown up." Then her voice dropped to a whisper. "And he is the only one I will ever love." A braid fell on Cristóbal's chest, and Percides laughed softly.

"Don't say such things to me, Percides," Cristóbal had muttered, and then his mind drifted to his life with Ignacia before they had children. Emilio sat awkwardly beside the two of them and though his face was hot and his breath still ragged, the room had suddenly felt too small for him.

The afternoon Hipolito and Francisco came to the García house, it was raining outside and Cristóbal's room was gray and smelled of damp. Water mixed with mud streaked the one small window, and the wall beneath it was wet with moisture. By the time Percides brought the two men to see her grandfather, Emilio was already lying dazed and bloodied on the floor of the church.

"Grandfather," Percides said. "Hipolito Trujillo and Francisco Ramírez have come to talk with you." She helped the two old men sit in straight-backed chairs close to the bed. Then she walked back to the door and pulled it shut. She leaned back against the rough wood and folded her arms across her chest. She looked out the window at the rain and wondered what Emilio could be doing out in such weather. For a brief second, a shadow passed through her heart. She shook her head sharply to chase it away, and then she smiled and half closed her eyes.

Cristóbal's head and shoulders were propped up on folded blankets. His feet were bare and the bottoms of them were white and wrinkled. His eyes were open and he stared blankly straight ahead. He had paid little attention when Percides had entered the room with the two men; already, he had forgotten who she had said they were. But he could dimly see their shadows and hear the rasp of Francisco's breathing. He hoped they would tell him what they had to say as quickly as possible and then leave him in peace.

"Buenas tardes, Cristóbal," Hipolito said. "We have come to see you."

At the sound of Hipolito's voice, Cristóbal reached out a hand and let his fingers rest on the trastero beside his bed. The bottom drawers were full of things that had once belonged to his wife. Her wedding dress was there, and when a certain draft sometimes entered the room, Cristóbal could still smell the faded scent of roses. There were clippings of each of her children's hair wrapped in soft paper and a book of prayers that her father had given her, saying that they would always keep her safe. On the top shelf of the trastero was the santo, and she gazed into the room.

Hipolito had first seen that Lady on the day he had walked back into the valley. She had been cradled in Cristóbal's arms like an infant, and at the sight of the two of them Hipolito knew that something had happened during those two years that he would never understand. Now, more to himself than to anyone, he said, "You still have the santo."

Cristóbal turned his head in the direction the words had come from. "Yes," he said. "Where would she go? Besides, she and I have an understanding. It's just my bad luck that I don't know what it is."

Francisco grunted and, with some difficulty, shook his head. "I told you," he said to Hipolito. "I told you he would be no different."

It had been Hipolito's idea to come to the García house. He had gone to Francisco and told him that what was about to happen in the village was not a thing they would be able to live with easily afterward. He had listened patiently to Francisco's complaints and then, in a low, hard voice, had told his cousin to be still. He told him that there was little left of their life and if anything they had ever done was to have meaning, then they should take one last walk together and talk to Cristóbal.

Hipolito moved his eyes away from the santo and let out a long breath of air. "It's been a long time, my friend," he said. "We've come to speak with you about some trouble in this village."

"Qué village?" Cristóbal said. "I don't know any village. I don't even know you," which wasn't completely true. Both voices were vaguely familiar, but other than their sound making him feel slightly irritable, he didn't much care who they were.

"Grandfather," Percides said. "You remember. It's Hipolito Trujillo and Francisco Ramírez." She had followed the conversation closely and was beginning to feel as if she were in a room with three men who knew each other not at all. She had heard of no trouble in Guadalupe, and although she loved her grandfather, she wished he would be quiet for once and let Hipolito tell his story.

"I don't know these men," Cristóbal muttered. "I've never known those names."

"I knew you would be like this," Francisco said, his voice sounding years younger. "How could you not know us?" He was sitting humped over in his chair. His twisted hands were lying open on his thighs, and one leg had begun to tremble so badly that his heel tapped against the floor. "My wife," he went on, "and yours were like sisters. My youngest son, whose mind was dull and never listened to a thing I said, married your daughter Marcella. We share grandchildren, you and I. And you say you don't know us? It was Hipolito and myself who half carried you, crying and complaining, all the way from Las Sombras."

Cristóbal turned toward Francisco, squinting his eyes as if that would make him see clearly. "Las Sombras," he said. "I once lived in such a place. There was a small plaza, shaded by large cottonwoods, where you could meet with friends. The cows were always fat and gave milk rich with cream. In Las Sombras the alfalfa grew as tall as my head and there were fields stretching to each horizon. Not like in Perdido, where the breath catches in your chest because there isn't enough air and the cows grow like goats and where what is real isn't. I lie in this room and dream of Las Sombras."

"It was not like that, Cristóbal," Hipolito said. "I, too, remember. Las Sombras was a hard place that we all wished to leave."

"I left you my burro," Francisco blurted out.

"And just like you," Cristóbal suddenly yelled back at him, "your stupid burro ran off into the mountains and left me alone."

For a few seconds, no one said a thing. Even Percides was startled. She had never heard her grandfather speak with such vehemence to anyone. She took a step away from the door. "Grandfather," she said.

"I know who you are," Cristóbal said. He had propped himself up on his elbows, and the top half of his body arched forward at each word he spoke. "You are traitors, and now when I've finally found a little peace at the end of my life, you've come back to torment me."

Francisco glanced at his cousin. "Didn't I tell you so? We will waste our time, I said. All the talk in the village about Cristóbal García who talks to the dead. About this house being a place no one ever leaves. About a santo that is more than wood; the truth is that this is the same Cristóbal García who whined and complained all the way from Las Sombras."

"Any man would complain when he's forced away from his family and dragged off into the wilderness."

"And whose idea was it to leave?"

"Stop this," Percides yelled. She walked to the bed and eased her grandfather back against the blankets. She wiped the saliva from his chin and the corners of his mouth with her fingers. "Quítate, Grandfather," she said softly. "I will tell them to leave." She put her hand flat on Cristóbal's chest and could feel the thinness of his ribs and, beneath that, how fast his heart was beating. Then she looked at Hipolito. "Leave," she said.

Hipolito shook his head slowly and then closed his eyes. In his darkness, he saw the valley. He saw it empty as he had when he and Francisco and Cristóbal had first stood on the foothill. Tall grass swayed in the breeze, and the creeks flowed slow and heavy through the junipers. The valley to him then had been like a first breath. All his life, he had cared for one thing, and only now, so near his own death, did he truly realize that it had never even existed. He wondered what had gone wrong.

He opened his eyes and looked across the room at Cristóbal. "This valley was like a gift to us," he said.

Cristóbal grunted. "It was never that to me," he said. "The first time I saw this place, I only wished never to see it again."

"Maybe that's another wish the santo gave you," Francisco said.

196 · Rick Collignon

"Be still, Francisco," Hipolito said. "None of us has changed, have we? Even as tired old men, we sit and argue as if fifty years was no more than a moment. I think all this village has become is what we are. You, Cristóbal, and you, Francisco, and myself."

"No," Cristóbal said. "It's more than that. Beneath this place is something else."

"Maybe we brought it here with us," Hipolito said. "What does it matter, anyway? It's still not too late. The three of us can make this village as we wish. You, Cristóbal, should have learned that much by now."

Cristóbal stared up at the ceiling without seeing. He could feel Percides' hand warm on his chest. It occurred to him that the last time he had heard Hipolito speak this way was just before he was dragged away from Las Sombras. He was happy that one of the benefits of old age was that people asked little of him.

"What do you want?" Percides asked.

"We want Cristóbal to come with us," Hipolito said. "To take one last walk together."

Percides gasped. Then she began to laugh and Hipolito could see how young she was. "My grandfather doesn't leave this house," she said, staring at Hipolito as if what he had said must have been a mistake. "You are all old men."

"Cristóbal," Hipolito said. "Pablo Medina and his brothers have taken your grandson Emilio to the church. The Medinas claim Emilio is a thief, and they mean to ask the priest's blessing to hang him."

For a few seconds, there was not a sound in the room. Percides felt as if she had been struck a heavy blow. She bent over and wrapped her arms around her belly and fought back a surge of nausea. Then she stepped away from the bed and, dropping her arms, she cried Emilio's name.

At that moment, Felix began to howl. His fists were clenched and his eyes were squeezed shut, his face red and streaked with tears. His heels kicked wildly against the bed, and the noise was so sudden that Flavio's heart caught in his chest and then began to race so fast that he, too, almost began to yell.

"I don't want anyone to hang Emilio," Felix shrieked. "I don't want to hear no more." He opened his eyes wide and looked at Flavio. "Let's go, Flavio," he wailed. "I don't want to stay here." Flavio could feel his own eyes begin to fill, and panic began to seep into his throat. Guadalupe was sitting calmly on the bed staring at him. Her hands were folded together, and there was a small smile on her face.

"By late afternoon," Guadalupe said, "the clouds hung low on the foothills and swirled with black, and water began to pour from the skies."

11

W hen I woke up this morning," Delfino said in the backseat
of the squad car, "the sun was shining, and I thought this day would
be like any other. I drank a little soda pop with my eggs, and then
I fed my pigs." He kicked at the blanket he was wrapped in
and hugged the santo to his chest. The blisters on the back of his
body rubbed raw against the seat. "This has been a bad day," he said,
his voice turning to the air. "Flavio and Felix should have known
better."

Nick Oliver had driven north away from Ramona's house, and
now, after a couple of miles, he had left the village behind. On each
side of the road was only stunted sagebrush and dried-out fields of
alfalfa. Oliver shook his head and cursed. Then, barely listening to
Delfino babbling behind him, he U-turned in the middle of the
highway and headed back the way he'd come.

"We're almost there, Mr. Vigil," he said, more to ease his own mind than Delfino's. He had no idea where the Guadalupe clinic was or even if there was such a thing. He'd left the Montoya house in too much of a hurry, and he could picture himself driving this same stretch of highway over and over again with a man who should have been cared for hours ago.

He glanced over his shoulder. Delfino's legs were moving beneath the blanket, and his eyes were pressed shut. His face was blistered and damp, and a line of blood ran from his mouth. "Jesus," Oliver said and looked back at the road. He reached for the radio and then cursed again and slammed it back when all he got was static. Behind him, Delfino began saying each of his pig's names aloud and explaining that his family had always kept pigs, even his grandfather, Gabino Vigil, who treated them poorly and had a disposition much like his neighbor's dog. Then, without even pausing for a breath, he went on to say that of everyone in this village, it was he, alone, who'd had the courage to fight this fire and that years ago things weren't this way.

"Then," Delfino said, "this was some kind of village. People knew what they were, and there was never no trouble. This place has been turning to shit for a long time."

Oliver slowed the squad car as he neared the village office. The parking lot was empty, and a chain was looped through the handles of the front door. "Where the hell is Lucero?" he muttered, and a feeling of helplessness rose in his stomach. He had absolutely no idea what to do.

"It doesn't hurt so bad now," Delfino said, and his voice was a little stronger. "But I can't breathe so good. I breathed fire in that fire and it tasted like ice. How can that be?"

"Rest yourself, Mr. Vigil," Oliver said. "Don't talk so much."

"If I ever see those two viejos again," Delfino said slowly, "I'm going to beat them both with a stick, especially Felix. He always thought he was better than everyone else and his beans tasted like spit." For a moment, Delfino fell quiet. Then he began to cough so badly that Oliver flinched and his jaw tightened. Then, a half mile later, he heard Delfino die. It wasn't much of a noise Delfino made—just a sharp intake of air as if he had seen something that surprised him and then a sigh so long and slow that Oliver knew nothing would ever follow it. He found himself holding his breath, and when he let it out, he eased his foot from the accelerator and pulled off the road.

As soon as he stopped, the interior of the car flooded with the sharp odor of Delfino's burns. Mixed with it was the smell of mold and dust from the blanket Oliver had taken from Ramona's bed. A fine mist of ashes was falling from the sky, and a light film was building up on the windshield. Oliver covered his nose and mouth with his hand and, breathing through his fingers, leaned his head out the window.

Across the road and set back a ways was an old abandoned adobe. The windows were boarded up behind splinters of broken glass, and the door was wide open and hung askew off of one hinge. The plaster on the walls had fallen off in large flat slabs, and the roof was so bellied that it looked as though the place was about to fall in on itself. Weeds and sagebrush grew everywhere. Scattered in the midst of them were junked vehicles and strewn piles of warped lumber. Old pickups, their beds torched off ages ago, their wheels only rusted rims, had sunk into the dirt at odd angles. Sun-blistered sedans without hoods sat low to the ground, and where the engines had been were dark holes grown in with brush. The place looked as though it had been that way forever, and Oliver couldn't imagine it being a house where people had once lived their lives. A soft breeze drifted through the open windows of the squad car, and the smoke it brought with it was so heavy that Oliver squinted to keep his eyes from burning.

He dropped his hand from his face and reached absently for a cigarette. He stuck it in the corner of his mouth and then sat staring quietly straight ahead. There was a wall of smoke like a storm not far from where he was parked that stretched the entire width of the valley.

"I don't know where I am," Oliver said softly, and for a moment he forgot about Delfino and watched in awe as the smoke lifted orange from the earth and then swirled gray and black as it rose higher and higher. He had never seen anything like it, and he wondered how in God's name this fire could be moving so fast. Down the road, he could make out the sign to Felix's Café and, beyond that, Tito's Bar and the lumberyard. It was impossible to tell exactly where the fire line was, but Oliver could see that it had moved well past the cemetery and was on its way to town. He knew that by now the fire would have washed over Ascencia Flores' house and was burning across the valley itself. Half this village is gone, he realized. He took in a deep breath and let it out slowly. Then he reached in his pocket, took out a match, and lit his cigarette. A few vehicles passed by him heading north out of town, and he could see someone walking toward him in the middle of the road. He tossed his match out the open window, and when all he could smell in the car was burning tobacco, he swung around and looked in the backseat.

The blanket had come off of Delfino and was lying on the floor. The old man was on his side, with his knees drawn up to his stomach. He looked swallowed up in his overalls, not much bigger than a child. His good eye was open and dead still. Beneath it, there was a trail of clean skin. Both of his hands were wrapped around the santo, which was pressed so tight against his chest that the Lady's face was buried in his clothes. For a second, Oliver wondered if Delfino had been talking to her all that time and not to him. He twisted in his seat a bit more and laid the back of his hand against

Delfino's mouth. Although heat was still coming from the old man's face, there wasn't a hint of breath. Oliver moved his hand to the santo, his fingers brushing the back of her body, and then he thought that she was probably better off where she was. He pulled his arm back and looked at the two of them lying together on his backseat.

"I'm sorry," he said. "You deserved better than this, Mr. Vigil." He tried to find some meaning in how a man as old as Delfino could drown in a fire and afterward walk miles to Flavio Montoya's house only to die holding the carved figure of a doll in the backseat of a police car.

He remembered driving his youngest daughter to the hospital one cold winter night. She, too, had been wrapped in a blanket and carried a small doll. It had been in the hours just before dawn. His wife and oldest daughter had left a day earlier to visit relatives. It was the only time Oliver had ever been alone with either of his daughters, and they had eaten their dinner awkwardly in silence. She had gone to bed early that evening and awakened after midnight crying and flushed. Her fever had been so high that when he'd bathed her in cold water, she stood thin and shivering in the bathtub and steam had come from her skin. He carried her from the house in a panic and laid her on the front seat of the squad car. As he drove the empty, snow-crusted streets of Las Sombras, the top of her head had pressed hot against his thigh and he had listened to her whimpering, knowing in his heart that she was going to die.

An ache now gripped Oliver's chest, and in his mind, he could see his two daughters standing close together and how they always seemed lost and out of place when he was near them.

"I have two daughters," he said to Delfino. "They're good girls. Their mother's name is Theresa. I loved her once, but that was a long time ago." Delfino's hands had relaxed their grip on the santo so that Oliver could see her face. Her features were stained black from soot, and there were thick blotches of red on her face. Her hands were together at her chest, and she was smiling slightly, staring up at Oliver. "Tell me," he said to her. "Tell me anything."

A thread of cigarette smoke drifted into his eyes, and he jerked his head back, starting up a cramp between his shoulders. He grunted softly and eased back down a little in his seat. Then he shook his head and smiled. "I'm having a talk with a dead man and his doll," he said out loud. He wondered what Sippy Valdéz had done with his Tío Petrolino. Maybe he could give Delfino to Sippy, and that way Delfino would have a little company.

"I've been in this village too long," he said. He took the cigarette from his mouth and flicked it out the widow. Then, after one last look at Delfino, he swung around in his seat and saw Ambrosio Herrera standing mute and drunk in the road just a few feet away.

Ambrosio's face was slack and his eyes were bloodshot and haggard. He was carrying two paper bags full of his things, and he was dressed in his boots and cowboy hat and a white shirt that was disheveled and stunk of whiskey. His mouth hung open and he was breathing thick and heavy, staring at the police officer without speaking. A pickup drove by going a little too fast. It swerved off onto the shoulder and then cut back sharply onto the road so that a cloud of ash and dust and smoke swirled around Ambrosio, and he staggered a few feet as if blown by a great wind. One of the bags fell from his arms, and wrinkled underwear and socks and colorful plastic toys spilled out onto the road. He stared down at them blankly and then looked back at Oliver.

"I am leaving this place," Ambrosio said so softly that Oliver didn't know what he had said or even what language he had said it in. "This storm is too big and I have been in the wrong village for too long. My home has never been here." He stopped talking and his eyes fell on the lights flashing silently on top of the police car.

He stared at them, swaying gently back and forth and wondering if there was to be a parade.

Ambrosio had drunk seven beers with Fred Sanchez and so many shots of whiskey that the bar in front of them had been littered with small empty glasses. By mid-afternoon, they were both so drunk that they began to argue loudly and incoherently about the color of chile and why the seeds, which were so small, held so much heat. When Ambrosio said it was because all true chiles came from a small pueblo in Mexico, Fred, who no longer knew what they were talking about, pushed him off his barstool. Tito, who had awakened that morning in the same bad mood he'd been in the past thirty years, had then thrown them both out of the bar. They had stumbled outside, blinking their bleary eyes at a world covered with ash and a sky black and churning. They had thought a storm bringing snow had come to the valley, and while Ambrosio had stood gaping, Fred had cursed and, with his shoulders slumped, gone home to cut firewood for his stove.

Ambrosio had made his way slowly up the road to Felix's Café. He had walked with his arms wrapped tightly around his chest and his body trembling from the cold. When he came to the small restaurant, he had stood for a long while staring at the outside of the place. Then, he bent over, picked up a large stone, and threw it through the plate-glass window. The sound of breaking glass had made him feel even colder and so he fell to his knees and began to weep. Through his tears, he could see the empty tables inside the café and the floor he had mopped for so many years. He remembered fondly the cracked linoleum in the kitchen and cooking beans with Felix, who had always treated him well. He knew everyone in the village and all of their families. But it had suddenly occurred to him that he cared for none of them, especially Felix, who had never treated him with respect and spoke Spanish like an animal might.

"I am quitting you," Ambrosio had yelled, waving his arms and rising to his feet. "Mexico is my home and my family waits for me. I have given you my best years, and I hope this blizzard buries you in snow and cold." He picked up another rock. It went through the hole the first had made, and he stood wobbling in his tight boots. Then he had begun to cry again. "Forgive me, Felix," he said. "You were my only friend and you have given me so much." Then Ambrosio had stumbled back to his small trailer and filled two paper bags with his things. As he walked up the highway, he had sung a song about love and sadness.

He was still staring at the flashing lights on the squad car when the bottom of the second bag broke and what was in it fell to the pavement. He groaned and clutched the empty bag to his chest. Then, with some difficulty, he sat down in the road and began to stuff his things back into his torn bags. "My life has always been like this," he slurred out, and then his hands fell still and he began to sing again softly.

Oliver pulled out another cigarette and sat smoking inside the car. He thought he should say something to the man sprawled in the middle of the road, but he knew that he would have better luck speaking to a tree. He wondered again where Lucero had gone to and why there was such an utter lack of emergency crews in the village. Overhead, he could hear the far-off drone of a plane, but it was so distant that it seemed to have nothing to do with anything. He let the cigarette drop from his fingers and pushed open his door. He walked over to Ambrosio and pulled him to his feet. Then, thinking this was a bad idea, he half carried the man around the car and helped him into the front seat.

Ambrosio was still singing, but his voice had fallen to a murmur. He sat with his head hung low and his hands folded in his lap. His face was wet from tears. Oliver closed the door gently and went back out on the road. He gathered up all of Ambrosio's things and stuffed them in the backseat with Delfino. For a moment, he stood outside the car looking at his passengers, and then, after letting out a long breath of air, he climbed in with them and switched on the ignition.

"Cuidado," Ambrosio mumbled. "There is wind and cold and too much snow."

"I remember," Flavio said. "I just don't know what it is I remember." He was standing in the open doorway of Ramona's house, and he could see the smoke rising from down in the valley. That smoke was my house, he thought, and Martha's little garden and her letters to me and the apple trees my father planted which were full of bees every spring. He remembered one of the letters he had found in the box that had once held Martha's shoes.

"To my husband," it had read. "Be careful, dear Flavio, and I love you so much." At the time, he had passed over it quickly, thinking it said little, but now he realized that those few words contained everything his wife had ever wished to say to him. He looked up at the smoke that was his life, and he was filled with the ache of joy and sadness. "I miss you," he said out loud, and his voice was choked and thick. Out on the highway, he saw the state police car driving fast back into town from the north, and he wondered what the police officer, whose name he had already forgotten, was doing driving Delfino back and forth over such bumpy roads. He said a little prayer for his old friend and hoped that he was asleep and resting easy in the backseat. Behind him on the sofa, he could hear Felix snoring lightly. Flavio cleared his throat.

"I remember, Felix," he said again. "But I don't know why." And then, though Felix was dozing, Flavio heard him say in a tired voice, "How could you, Flavio? We were just little boys."

Rosa Montoya and her grandson stood on the edge of the road looking down at the valley. It was late in the day and still warm, even though it was late in the autumn. The sky was a myriad of dark colors and in the ditch, not far from where they stood, water was running beneath the grass and twisted weeds. Down the hill was the García house and, beyond that, the church. The front door of Guadalupe's house was wide open, and Flavio had only glanced that way and then moved his eyes quickly away to where his own house sat. The windows in his house were dark, and his father's truck was parked alongside the small apple trees that were no more than saplings. Flavio knew that his father would be sitting by himself in the kitchen. He would be drinking slowly from a bottle of whiskey and staring straight ahead in the dark room as if he had lost something and no longer knew what it was.

"Your father is home from work," Rosa said as she reached out a hand and placed it on Flavio's shoulder. "He works so hard for you and your brother. And Ramona, también."

"My sister's not here, anymore," Flavio said.

"I know that, hijo," Rosa answered him. "She has gone to a city to be a great artist. But after she learns all there is to know, she will come back to us. You should be proud, Flavio."

Every so often, Flavio would stumble across some of his sister's things, a piece of her clothing or a cloth glove or one of the drawings that she kept under her bed. Even though Ramona had been gone only a few months, the things she had left behind were covered with dust and fine cobwebs. Flavio thought that his sister had gone to a place far away where he could never be. He would leave the things he found where they were so that she would have them if she were ever to return. But, in truth, although Flavio could still hear the sound of Ramona's voice and see the hard line of her mouth, he had forgotten the color of her eyes and the shape of her face. He knew in his heart that his grandmother was wrong. Like his mother, Ramona had left the village and her family so that her life would be full of other things.

"Let me tell you a story, hijo," Rosa said, and her hand brushed the side of Flavio's face. "One night, Alfonso Vigil came to our house and he and your grandfather sat outside. It was in the summer when the days are too long. Alfonso had spent the day drinking with his brothers. At that time, I was a new wife and your father was just an infant, too young even to sit up by himself. I brought your grandfather and Alfonso a plate of hard tortillas and chile and the small bottle of whiskey that your grandfather would sometimes sip from in the winter. Alfonso then, too, was a young man, but he walked slumped over. The skin on his face was mottled and hung loose, and his arms were so long and bony that they reached down to his knees. He had looked this way even as a child, and it was rumored that his mother had fallen into a deep state of sadness for a year after his birth.

"I sat in the grass with your father in my arms and listened to them talk. When they fell quiet, each would take a small drink from the bottle. Just before dark, Alfonso stretched out his arm and touched your grandfather's shoulder and in a voice heavy with whiskey, he said, 'Epolito, when I was a little boy, I saw a witch and his animal walk into this valley.' Here, Alfonso grunted softly. 'The witch's hair was red like hot embers, and his eyes were blue like he had been born too soon. No one else from the village saw this witch. What it wanted, I never knew.' Alfonso brought his hand into his lap and folded his hands together. He shook his head and let out a long sigh. 'I can still see this witch, and high up on my arm is the bite mark where his beast bit me.'"

It was early in the spring when Alfonso saw the witch. His father had sent him to clean debris from a ditch close to the foothills. There was still snow in the shadows behind trees, but the ground had thawed and was mud and small channels of water ran everywhere. The ditch that spring was choked with dead branches and the garbage Norberto Mascarenas sometimes threw in it. By the time the sun had risen over the mountains, Alfonso's feet were wet and cold and his head was hot. As he dragged a limb tangled with one of Norberto's old boots from the ditch, he heard the sharp sound of hoofs striking against stone.

"'When I looked up,' Alfonso said, and he was staring straight ahead now, the bottle in his hand forgotten, 'all I could see was sun. Then I saw the witch standing a few yards away from me. At first, I didn't know it was a witch. I thought it was someone I knew pulling a horse and that my eyes were just blinded. Then I saw that he was dressed in layers of rags and that his hair and beard burst red from his head and that at the end of the rope he was holding was an animal I had never seen before.' Alfonso shook his head slowly and let out a long breath of air. 'I tell you, Epolito,' he went on, 'it looked like a sheep that was too big had somehow mated with a bird and what came out was a surprise even to God. Its legs were thin, and its hips rose as high as a man's head and there were patches of fur, like wool, that stuck out in bunches. Its head was all strange angles, and its jaw moved back and forth slowly as if its teeth hurt or it was chewing tobacco and thinking about something. I knew that what I was seeing couldn't be.'"

At first, Alfonso merely stared in astonishment at what had appeared before him, and then he began to laugh. At that moment, as if offended, the witch began to yell loudly in a high-pitched voice.

Then he began to wave his arms wildly about and kick his feet as if he were dancing. The laughter froze in Alfonso's mouth, and a deep chill ran through his body. Then, the beast that had been complacently chewing nothing, suddenly stepped forward, lowered its head, and bit Alfonso on the arm.

" 'And to make things worse,' Alfonso said, 'after it was done biting me, it spit on me. And not a little spit either, but a lot of spit like it had been saving it for a long time to give to someone it didn't like. Eee, I never would have thought that an animal could spit, and if it could, why would you keep it? It was at that moment that I knew that what I saw was a witch and its beast.' "

Alfonso had grabbed his arm and screamed. He could feel blood staining the sleeve of his shirt, and he watched as the witch picked up a large stick and struck his animal on the head. When the witch turned back to Alfonso, Alfonso screamed again and threw himself into the ditch. He crawled out on the other side and scrambled madly up the loose rock on the hillside. When he ran into the branches of a large juniper, he hid crouching and trembling behind it. He stayed there until his clothes had dried and until the sun was directly overhead. Then, still dazed and shaken, he crept back down the hill. When he came to the ditch, he found the witch gone and in the mud were the deep tracks of its demon.

" 'I never saw that witch again,' Alfonso said, 'and sometimes, at night, I wonder if I saw it at all.'

"It had grown dark by then, hijo," Rosa said, "and all I could see was the shadows of your grandfather and Alfonso. Your father was asleep in my arms, and every so often he would whimper softly. I heard your grandfather grunt, and then he said that maybe Alfonso had only dreamed the witch. For a little while, Alfonso didn't speak, and then he took a drink of whiskey and lowered his head. He said that he had never thought of himself as a man who could see things that weren't there, and if he could, they should have the decency not to bite and spit and then disappear as if it were nothing. At this, your grandfather stirred in his chair and said that it was growing late and that the next day he was to go to his cows early. Alfonso stood and thanked me for the hard tortillas and chile, and your grandfather and I sat for a little longer and listened to the sound of Alfonso walking home."

While Rosa had been talking, Flavio had edged closer to her until the length of his body rested against hers. She pulled him tighter to her, and in a voice that was somewhere else, she said, "So you see, mi hijo, that is why Ramona will come back to us. Someday she will remember she once lived in a place where babies are born in snowbanks and roosters fly in front of stones and witches come walking from the mountains. This is your sister's place, hijo, even if she doesn't know that now."

It was not quite dark, and from far off came the muffled echo of wood being chopped. It sounded to Flavio like hoofs on hollow rocks, and he was glad that he wasn't alone. He thought Alfonso's story only seemed one more reason for Ramona not to return. He raised his head and looked up at his grandmother. "Have you ever seen the bite on Alfonso's arm?" he asked.

"No, Flavio," Rosa said, shaking her head slowly. "I have never wished to see Alfonso's arm without his shirt."

"What did the witch want?"

"Who knows what anyone wants?" Rosa said. "Maybe the witch was lost and came here by mistake. Or maybe what your grandfather said was true and what Alfonso saw was his alone. I don't know, hijo." Rosa suddenly took in a sharp breath, and her hand tightened on Flavio's shoulder. "Look," she said, "Guadalupe García is here."

Down the hill, Guadalupe was standing just outside her door, looking at where Rosa and Flavio stood. Flavio watched her raise her hand shyly as if to wave. "We should go now, Grandmother," Flavio said and took hold of Rosa's hand.

"I have watched her all her life," Rosa said softly, "and now she is a woman growing old."

Flavio pulled at his grandmother's hand, and she moved with him a few steps. He thought he heard Guadalupe calling from her house, but when he glanced there, she had already gone back inside and there was only the empty doorway. "Let's go, Grandmother," he said and his voice was frightened.

Rosa turned her head and looked down at her grandson. Then she stooped before him and placed her hands on both sides of his face. "Don't worry, mi hijo, you will never lose me. You are my grandson and I love you. And I am so proud of you." She smiled and stroked his face. "I, too, was once in that house. It was long before Guadalupe was born, and when I was taken away by my father, she was left by herself. My place has always been with you, Flavio." She didn't say anything for a few seconds, but looked at her grandson quietly until his breathing slowed and he forgot that he had been frightened. "Come, hijo," she said, and she stood up. "Let's go to your father and make sure that his dinner is warm."

More than seventy years later, Flavio stood in the doorway of Ramona's empty house and, as if for the first time, he heard the words his grandmother had spoken that evening. He could see the highway and the exact place where the two of them had stood. For a second, time wavered in Flavio's mind and he wasn't sure where he was.

"We walked across the valley in the dark to my house," he said softly and closed his eyes so as to see better. His grandmother had heated lamb and chile that night and then warmed two tortillas and covered them with a soft towel. While she had cooked, Flavio and his father had sat at the table. Every so often, Lito's eyes would rest on his son and then he would move them away and look elsewhere. After the dishes had been washed and the kitchen swept, Rosa had taken her grandson to his room and wished him goodnight. It had been the first time that Flavio had slept in his own house since the death of his mother, and sleep had not come easy. He could hear his father sitting in the kitchen, the scuff of his boots on the floor, the shifting of his body in the chair. Outside, he could hear dogs barking. By then, Alfonso Vigil was an old man, and Flavio had wondered if the mark on his arm still ached and if he, too, was lying awake listening to the noises in the village.

"Enough," Flavio breathed out and turned back into the room. He stepped over the santos and walked past Felix and into the kitchen. At the sink he turned on the tap and then cupped his hands and splashed his face again and again with cold water. When he straightened up, he wiped his face dry with the sleeve of his shirt and looked out the window. He could no longer see the foothills. They were blanketed with smoke and a line of fire was dancing along the far edge of Ramona's alfalfa field.

"It's hard to believe my own eyes," Flavio said. "This morning I was irrigating that field and now it's on fire." He watched as the flames jumped the ditch and began making their way toward the small sad plants that he had neglected all summer. "I should have watered you all these months," he said, "and maybe none of this would have happened."

A cramp of hunger knotted up his stomach, and he realized that he had eaten nothing all day. He pulled open one of the cabinet doors above the counter and then stepped back, startled, when a nest of black sticks and chewed cardboard and rodent droppings toppled out. When it struck the counter, a cloud of dust rose and he could smell the rancid odor of mold and urine. Cursing, he brushed the mess onto the floor with the side of his hand, and then reached into the cupboard and took out a small tin can. He wiped it on his pants and peered down at the label. It was a can of little hot dogs.

Flavio wiped the can again against the side of his leg and, looking at it fondly, carried it into the living room. He sat down on the sofa beside Felix, who had fallen asleep hunched over, his face resting on top of his knees on the sofa. Felix's back shuddered with each breath he took, and small noises were coming muffled from his mouth. Flavio put his hand on Felix's shoulder and shook him a little. "Wake up, Felix, and we'll eat a little something."

For a second, Felix's breathing almost stopped, and then his lungs gasped in a quick breath and he creaked his head sideways. "I was dreaming, Flavio," he said and, groaning, lifted the upper part of his body. "I was dreaming that Delfino was here with one of his pigs and it made little barking noises like a dog."

Flavio dug in his pocket and pulled out his knife. "Delfino was here," he said, "but none of his pigs." He slid the knife blade through the tin on top of the can and began cutting in a circle.

"Where did he go?" Felix asked, and then he saw the can in Flavio's lap. "Eee," he said, and suddenly his head stopped shaking and his hands fell still. "I always liked those red hot dogs I used to eat them wrapped in a tortilla with some ketchup." He watched as Flavio pulled back the lid and then took one out and ate it. "The last time I remember eating," Felix said, "was eight years ago, and then it was a burrito with chicharrón that Ambrosio made for me. He was good at keeping the floors clean, but not so good with my food. I think my pots made him nervous. If I told him to get me a few cups of flour, he would go outside and stand there singing his stupid songs as if he hadn't heard me. Who knows why I kept him around as long as I did. That chicharrón burrito tasted like it was full of small stones."

Flavio took out another hot dog and gave it to Felix. "Thank you, Flavio," Felix said, and then the two men sat together quietly eating.

After a while, Flavio said, "Felix, Guadalupe García was my tía."

Felix grunted and small bits of meat flew out of his mouth. "That explains everything."

"I'm glad to hear you say that," Flavio said as he took out the last hot dog and gave it to Felix. "Because even if she was my aunt, I still don't understand."

Felix shoved the hot dog into his mouth and let it sit there, sucking out the juice. Finally he shrugged. "Don't ask me," he said. "She was your tía, not mine. Maybe I am a García, but I was never those Garcías. You should know these things if she was your family." He wiped the grease from his face with the sleeve of his shirt. "Those were good hot dogs, Flavio," he said.

Flavio leaned back against the sofa and shut his eyes. He thought that if it were any other day, he'd take a nap. When he woke up, he would sit outside under his apple tree and drink a little coffee and look at the mountains. Then it occurred to him that he didn't have an apple tree anymore or even a cup to hold his coffee.

"Felix," Flavio said, opening his eyes. "Ramona's field is on fire."

Felix's body jerked slightly. "Oh sí? That's too bad, Flavio. I remember that field when your grandfather would irrigate. The alfalfa was as high as our heads."

"Yes," Flavio said as he bent over and put the empty tin can on the floor. "I think it would be better if we leave here, Felix," he said then and pushed himself to his feet. He took hold of Felix's arm and helped him stand, and the two of them walked slowly across the room to the doorway.

"I don't want to go out there," Felix said. "My belly hurts." He dropped a hand to his stomach. "It's not safe for us out there, Flavio. We are just two old men of no use."

"We can't stay here," Flavio said. "The fire is already in Ramona's field," and he pulled gently on Felix's arm.

"Maybe Delfino will put out the fire."

"Delfino is not fighting this fire anymore."

"Wait, Flavio. Let me catch my breath and then we can go."

Flavio eased his grip on Felix's arm and let him sag against the door frame. Then he turned around and looked at Ramona's paintings hanging in dust on the walls. In the kitchen, he could see the sink where his grandmother had cooked and washed dishes and later where Ramona would often stand and stare out the small window daydreaming. He brought his eyes back to the living room and looked down at the santos scattered on the floor. All of them seemed to be looking back at him.

"Wait here for a moment, Felix," he said. He took a few steps back into the room and gathered the Ladies in his arms. He carried them all to the couch and set them there next to each other. And then he touched each one. The last one he touched was the one his nephew, Little José, had carved.

The grin on her face reminded him of someone who was never quite sure of where she was, but was happy to be there. Her eyes were wide and a drop of red paint that had fallen from José's brush stood out on one cheek. Her hands were together, not so much in prayer, but as if they were clapping. Flavio frowned at her.

"Little José made you," he said. "With his knife, he sat with Ramona and worked until he found you."

All the other Ladies stood together quietly, their eyes looking down. Flavio leaned forward and picked up the santo that José had carved.

"Venga," he said to her. "You can come with me. We'll take a little walk with Felix."

12

As Hipolito and Francisco and Cristóbal made their way through the rooms of this house," Guadalupe said, "Percides pleaded with her grandfather to let her go with him to the church. Cristóbal held tightly onto Francisco's arm, and even though Percides tore at her hair and begged him to listen, he did not say a word to her."

Percides said that she would help Cristóbal walk down the hill and that she would be his eyes. She said that no one would dare harm Emilio if she were there. She said that if she were left behind, she would go crazy with fear. At the shrillness and the desperation in her voice, all the babies in the rooms of the house began to cry, and Percides screamed back at them until the walls themselves rang with madness and confusion.

Two of Percides' uncles were eating cold beans and tortillas in the kitchen when Hipolito entered the room. They had come in from the weather outside and still wore their hats. Mud and water ran far up their legs. When they saw Hipolito and heard the noise from within the house, the talk died in their mouths and the ladles they held floated above the table forgotten in their hands. Hipolito hurried to where they sat, bent his head, and whispered to them, as Francisco and Cristóbal and Percides staggered into the room.

Percides' face was swollen with anguish and her hair was wild. Her dress was ripped from where it had caught on a nail, and her knees were scraped and bleeding from falling.

"Grandfather," she shrieked. "Please don't leave me here. I will drown in this house if you leave me."

"Quiet, hija," he said hoarsely over and over again until his granddaughter fell still and her body only shuddered. "I will see this priest, whoever he is," Cristóbal said to her, "and I will tell him that I will burn this village down. I will curse the very dirt in the walls of his church if he does not give Emilio back to us. Do you understand, hija? You must stay here. There is no place for you with us. I swear to you that I will be home before dark."

Percides stood in the open doorway of the García house. The air was gray with rain and mist and drops of water dripped from the lintel above the door, threaded through her hair, and ran down her back. Her two uncles stood on each side of her and, as Hipolito had asked, they held her arms so tight that their fingers pressed deep into her flesh. Percides watched as Hipolito and Francisco and Cristóbal made their way slowly through the mud and down the hill. All three walked closely together, the arms of each wound around the others' so that when one slipped, he would not fall. She watched until they reached the church and, there, became no more than shadows. They paused for a moment outside the heavy door as if catching their breaths, and then the three of them together pushed it open. They stepped inside one after another, and never in her life did Percides see any of them again.

"I bet the priest will help," Felix said. He was lying back on the bed with one arm flung over his eyes, and the sound of his voice startled Flavio.

In spite of his uneasiness, Flavio had once again been lulled into the story Guadalupe was telling. His eyes were half closed, and he had almost forgotten the burned santo facing the wall and how deep he was inside the García house. The only fear he knew was Percides', not his own. Felix, too, had gradually fallen quiet. After his fit of howling had passed, he had lain back on the bed and covered his eyes. For a while, his chest had occasionally shuddered, but eventually he had calmed until, now, he was once more saying the same stupid things he always said.

"Don't you hear anything?" Flavio said. He wondered if he and Felix had even been listening to the same story. "How can the priest help if Emilio gets hung from the cottonwood tree?"

Felix moved his arm and lifted his head slightly. "That's what you say," he said. "I think the priest helps Emilio."

"The priest does not help Emilio," Guadalupe said, her voice flat and tired. "He was a weak man, and what happened at the church that day was too much for him." The light from the lantern fell full on her face, and shadows moved in the hollows beneath her eyes, in the creases beside her mouth. Behind her, Flavio could see Emilio's bones buried in the wall. From across the room, they looked yellow and brittle and more like the fingers of an old man.

"But maybe this time it's different," Felix said, and at the sharp edge in his words, Flavio jerked his eyes away from the bones and looked at his friend. "This time," Felix went on, "you can make it so the priest rescues Emilio."

Guadalupe shook her head. "I don't understand you," she said. "Which time?"

"Eee," Felix breathed out. "This time. You could tell the story so that the priest helps Emilio and then they all go back home and eat some food with Percides. Maybe even the burro could be there, and after they eat, they could take little burro rides."

For a moment, Guadalupe and Felix stared at each other without speaking. Then, Guadalupe said softly, "You want me to change the story of my family?"

"Just so the end is different," Felix said. "It would be just a little change."

"But then it would not be true. And it would make everything I've told you a lie."

"So?" Felix said, and he pushed himself up on his elbows and looked at Flavio. "We don't care, do we, Flavio? We don't care what we believe."

What Flavio couldn't believe was that Felix was actually having an argument with Guadalupe García. It didn't even occur to him that something true could be changed. If Guadalupe finished her story he could leave and then forget all about it. There was just a small pool of oil in the bottom of the lantern. The wick had begun to smoke, and the top of the chimney was stained black and there was the odor of kerosene in the room. He looked at Guadalupe and she stared back at him.

"The priest was a weak man," Flavio said. "He would never help anyone." Felix gazed at him for a while, and then he let out a little moan and flung himself back on the bed.

"The inside of the church was dark," Guadalupe said. "The light that came in the narrow windows was gray and dead and only made the room darker. Emilio lay on the floor near the altar. He had been beaten, and blood ran from his nose and out his ears. Three fingers on one hand were broken and twisted. In the church with him was the priest, Father Patricio, and three of the Medina brothers whose eyes were black and saw only what they wished. They had all come to this valley together, and they had brought nothing but emptiness."

Father Patricio had been huddled in his room when he heard the church doors flung open and then the sound of Pablo Medina and his two brothers dragging the García boy across the floor. He had let out a soft groan and then leaned closer to his stove. The priest's skin was so hard and creased from years of weather that, although he could feel the heat on his face, it seemed to go no deeper and only made the things inside Father Patricio even colder. He was a tall, thin man, worn down to bone, and the robes he wore were threadbare and hung loose on his frame. His gray hair was long and ragged from neglect. He often suffered from chills that racked his body and from sudden lapses of memory that would cause him to stare off vacantly as if he could see things no one else did. When he heard the sound of a bench falling over, he closed his eyes and hoped that whoever had entered would go quickly and leave him in peace.

Father Patricio had been priest in so many places before coming to Guadalupe that now, on the verge of his old age, they had become all mixed with one another so that they might have been only dreams. When he had first come to the valley, the village had rejoiced that it finally had a priest to call its own. Women had wept openly and brought even their grown children for him to bless. At each mass the church was so full that men stood outside the open doors on the hard-packed adobe. For a while, they tried to ignore that their priest would often forget the words of the Liturgy or that sometimes he would fall still for so long that, one by one, they would go quietly, leaving Father Patricio to stand lost by himself. At other times, it seemed as if the priest could not stop talking. He would tell them about all the places he'd been and the things he'd seen, and his stories would frighten the children so badly that they would be carried from the church crying. At night, they would sleep fitfully and cry out from their dreams. After a while, few came to mass or at any other time and the church became a place where the priest lived. What he did there, no one knew.

Outside Father Patricio's window, the clouds had fallen so low that the priest could no longer see the mountains. The few scattered houses down in the valley had fires going, and the smoke that poured from their chimneys hung flat and thick just above the roof lines.

"I have been in this place twenty years," he said out loud, "and I don't know where I am."

Inside the church, something fell heavily to the floor and the priest's body jerked. As he looked toward the door, it was suddenly pushed open and a cold rush of air fell upon him. A man stood in the doorway with water dripping from the brim of his hat. The high boots he wore were caked with mud.

"It's been a long time, Father," he said, and then he smiled when the priest said nothing. "Have you forgotten so easily? You and I came here together, Father. It's me. Pablo Medina."

Behind the man, just before the altar, Father Patricio could see two of Pablo's brothers, who stood looking down at the floor. Someone lay at their feet moaning, and the priest's first thought was that some member of their family had been injured. But why they had brought him here, he didn't know. He raised his eyes and looked back at the man in the door.

"Father," Pablo said. "There has been some trouble with the Garcías."

When Pablo Medina and his brothers and all of their families had come to Guadalupe, they were deeded land that sat at the far south edge of the valley. It was almost all foothill covered with loose rock and scrub oak. The rest was hard washed clay where not even grass would grow. Some of the Medinas grumbled among themselves that it was because their skin had been darkened with Indian blood that Hipolito Trujillo had given them such poor land. But Pablo, like Hipolito before him, would stare out quietly at the valley. He could see how much water was in the creeks and all the fields of pasture, and he knew that what they had been given was more than enough.

They settled at the base of the foothill and, soon after, began to haul timber out of the mountains. They built a small sawmill and milled planks and skinned vigas and smoothed latillas out of slender aspens. And then they traded these things to villagers for small parcels of land or livestock. To some, they traded only the knowledge of a debt that would one day be owed. After twenty years, their fields were full of cows and their fence lines stretched over a third of the valley and now rested uneasily against those of Cristóbal García.

"I am not a greedy man," Pablo would often say to his brothers, or to anyone else who would listen. "But when I offer the Garcías a fair trade for something they only neglect and then they don't have the decency even to let me into their house, what am I to think? I know that I should not be saying such things, but everyone in this village knows that the Garcías have far too much. And besides, they live in this valley as if none of us were even here."

Pablo would pass around his pouch of tobacco and, with fingers thick from hauling timber, he would make a cigarette. Then he would shake his head and go on. "I just want to know what kind of people these are who have never come to the church but bury themselves in the sagebrush like savages. I've been told that inside

that house the García children run naked and breed with one another and that the women are passed from bed to bed. I know, too,
the stories about Cristóbal García who speaks to the dead and of
the santo that he made and painted with his own blood." Here,
Pablo would look at those he was talking to and smile a little. "I
have lived in a few other places," he would say, "and in none of
them would things like this have been permitted."

As time went by, Pablo's words had grown more and more bitter.
He began to claim that he had found a number of his calves
butchered and left to rot in the Garcías' fields. He said that someone
was cutting his fence lines and that at night he could hear the sound
of his lambs screaming from their corrals. Those he talked to would
listen fitfully, and at least one would have his own story to tell. Pablo
was careful to blame no one for these things. But sometimes he
would fling his arm in the direction of the García house, and those
around him would look that way. Little by little, what had lain quiet
for so long began to weigh heavy on everyone in the valley.

"I don't know where Pablo Medina's hatred came from,"
Guadalupe said. Her head was bent now and she was staring down
at her open hands. Her hair was all about her face. And sometimes,
her voice would fall so low that Flavio thought she wasn't speaking
at all. He was pushed up against the wall and lay with his chin resting on his chest and his legs stretched out on the banco. The room
was warm and clouded with smoke from the lantern. Felix had
fallen asleep close beside Guadalupe with his arm over his face. A
soft sound came from his mouth as he breathed.

Flavio looked up at the santo. Through the smoke, all he could
see was her dark shadow on top of the trastero. I would never hate
anyone, he thought, and then there would never be any trouble. He
closed his eyes and, in his mind, he could see Pablo Medina stand-

ing at the far edge of the valley. He was not a big man, but slight and wiry. His arms were too long, his hands were callused and thick. His hat was pulled low, and he stood without moving, gazing toward the García house. The fences had been cut, and strands of wire were strewn and curled on the ground. A heavy rain began to fall, and Pablo bowed his head against it. He began to walk slowly, and behind him came two of his brothers. Flavio could hear Guadalupe talking softly, and his eyes began to burn. A knot grew in his chest, and he pressed on his tongue hard with his teeth so that he would not begin to cry.

"My great-grandmother told me," Guadalupe said, "that the Medinas were frightened of us and that they spread this fear throughout the village. But I think it was something worse. I think that when Pablo Medina came here he could see into the very soul of this place. And what he saw was not a thing he cared for. To him, my family was no different from a tree that needed to be cut or a fence line that had to be moved. We had lived within ourselves for too long, and Pablo Medina knew this."

The person lying broken on the floor of the church wasn't much older than a boy. He lay on one side of his body with his knees drawn up to his chest. His nose was bent and bleeding, and blood had run from one ear and down his neck. He held one hand clutched at the wrist, and Father Patricio could see that three of the boy's fingers had snapped and now hung slightly askew. The knuckles on each finger were flattened and scraped to bone as if they had been crushed by a rock. The boy's clothes were wet and full of mud, and already a dark stain of blood and water was seeping into the floor.

"I don't know this boy," Father Patricio said. He was holding tightly onto Pablo's arm, and his knees were weak.

"His name is Emilio García," Pablo said. "He is a bastard, and there is no one in that house who will speak for him."

Father Patricio leaned over and squinted his eyes. "What has happened to him?" he asked. At the sound of his voice, Emilio's eyes moved, and he looked up at the priest.

"Only what he deserved," Pablo said. "He is a thief. My bother Manuel found him by the carcass of one of our calves. The boy had cut the fence and then had slit the animal's throat."

Emilio moved his legs away from his chest and lifted his head slightly off the floor.

"No," he said to Father Patricio, and bits of blood came from his mouth. "I was with my own cows." His voice was clogged and shaking, but his eyes were clear and didn't waver from the priest's face. Blood had dried on the floor where his face had rested, and his broken hand was shaking badly. Then the boy grimaced and began to breathe quickly. One of his legs jerked back up to his chest and he laid his head down. "They were together," he said in a voice full of pain, "and they called for me to come."

"You should be quiet now," Pablo said. Then his foot snaked out and stung Emilio's shoulder. "You are a thief and a García, and no one has time to listen to your lies." He looked up at his two brothers who stood facing him. "There's more," he said. "Tell the priest, Manuel."

Manuel was the oldest of the Medina brothers. He resembled Pablo so closely that the two were often mistaken for each other. Like his brother, his eyes were dark and his hair and beard were streaked with gray. His arms hung almost to his knees and his hands were large. There was a bruise high up on his cheekbone that was still raw, and a thin line of blood had run into his beard. Andamo Medina stood beside him, staring off at nothing. He was built heavier than his two brothers, and his head was misshapen and one side of his face did not move. He had been injured a few years earlier when a large branch from a pine tree had snapped and fallen on him. It had caved in part of his skull above one ear and punctured one eye. Andamo had not spoken a word since the accident, and the lid over his empty eye was scarred and sealed shut.

"Andamo and I found the boy crouched beside our calf," Manuel said. "He had just come from Miguel Esquival's pasture, where we could see four lambs that had been butchered. In a field not far away, a horse belonging to the Cortez family was running so scared that it floundered in a ditch and broke two of its legs. The boy has spent the day killing senselessly." Manuel turned his eyes away from the priest. His voice fell to a whisper. "He has taken food from the families of this village just as it faces winter. There is no greater wrong."

The four of them stood, with the boy at their feet, in the gray light that came through the church windows. Water ran on all the glass and made shadows that wavered on the floor. Though the doors were closed, Father Patricio could feel a cold breeze slice through his robes and touch his skin. He twisted his hands in the cloth to warm them, and a drop of moisture came from his nose and fell to the floor. "It is too cold here," he said to no one.

"Winter is coming," Pablo said. "Soon there will be snow. The village will be buried in cold, and you will need someone to bring wood for your stove and meat and beans and flour for tortillas."

"I will need these things, yes," the priest said absently as he looked back down at the boy. "Why is he hurt so?"

"Because he fought us," Pablo said, and he and Manuel looked at each other. "Like a madman, he fought us."

Father Patricio lifted his eyes and looked at Pablo. "Why have you brought him here? I can do nothing for him."

"You are the priest of this village even if this church stands empty," Pablo said. "We have come for your blessing."

"Then I bless you," Father Patricio said, waving his hand. "And I bless the boy. Now take him home to his family where he will be cared for," and he turned to go back to his stove.

"Have you heard nothing?" Pablo said. His hand tightened on the priest's arm and he drew him close. "Do you remember, Father, your life before this one? We found you in Las Sombras in the stench of that place, in a small room with three other priests like you. I took you from that place, and I brought you here, Father. I gave you this church and a warm stove to grow old by. You have a debt to pay me. And today we've come to ask for it."

Father Patricio's head was bent awkwardly toward Pablo, and he stared off as the man spoke. Though the priest's eyes were open wide, he no longer saw the inside of his church or heard the boy moaning at his feet. He could feel his heart beating slow and faint and the thin layer of ice that lay around all of his bones. "I don't re-member that life," he said.

"I do," Pablo said and for the first time there was anger in his voice. "And it is not the life that anyone in my family will ever have."

"Let me go to my stove," Father Patricio whispered. "It is too cold in this room. If I sit for a little—"

For a few seconds Pablo stared at the priest without speaking. Then he let out a long breath of air and, nodding his head, he let go of Father Patricio's arm. The priest shuffled slowly back to his room. He closed the door behind him and sat down beside his stove. For a little while, he stared out the window, and every so of-ten a spasm of cold would shoot through his body. He could hear no noise from inside the church, and he prayed that the Medinas had left. Then the doors of the church were pushed open and Hipolito Trujillo, Francisco Ramírez, and Cristóbal García walked inside.

Across the room from Guadalupe, Flavio's eyes were shut, and he lay still on the banco, his legs stretched out. On the bed beside her, Felix's hand lay on her thigh, and sometimes he whimpered softly in his sleep. By now, the chimney to the lantern was stained black with soot and the only light it cast fell upon Guadalupe. Her voice had grown hoarse from the smoke in the room, and occasionally, when she paused, it was as if she could hear the echo of her grandmother's voice coming from the walls of the house, as if both of them knew the same words.

"Hipolito and Francisco and my grandfather had not spoken a word to each other as they walked down the hill. The ground had turned to mud and everything about them was gray and damp and their breaths hung white in the air. Though they held each other so tightly that their hands ached, still Francisco's feet slipped from under him and he fell, wrenching his knee badly. Hipolito and Cristóbal helped him to stand and with each step, Francisco would cry out in pain."

When they came to the church, they paused to catch their breaths. Even then, Hipolito thought in his heart that everything could be made right. He looked at Cristóbal and Francisco beside him, and for a brief second, he remembered them as young men. The fifty years that had passed seemed like nothing.

"This place has always been ours," he said, though he was out of breath. "Do you remember? We were the first ever to see this place."

Francisco stood with his weight on one foot. He grunted and shook his head. It had grown colder, and mixed in with the rain now were large flakes of snow. He thought of his wife and his grandchildren and of the fire in his stove. He wondered how, at his age, he had come to be standing outside the church in such weather. On top of that, he had had dealings with the Medinas and he knew them to be hard men who only saw things one way. He knew that whatever was going to happen inside the church would not be easy.

Cristóbal stood breathing heavily. The muscles in his legs ached and cramped from so many years in bed. He was trembling from the cold, and whenever he turned his head, all he could see were the shadows of things moving away from him. Worse, his head was bare and he could feel snow beginning to fall. "There is snow falling," he said.

"It is mostly rain, Cristóbal," Hipolito said, glancing up at the sky. "It is still too early for snow."

"It snowed for days when you left me," Cristóbal said. "It snowed until it buried me." He suddenly realized that he had left the santo in his room, and he saw her standing beside his bed lost and confused in his absence. He could not remember the last time he'd gone anywhere without her. To ease his own mind he said softly, "Don't worry yourself. I will be home soon." Then he took in a deep breath and turned his head toward Hipolito. "Where is my grandson?" he whispered harshly.

"Here," Hipolito said. He took Cristóbal's hand and placed it flat on the door. "Come, Cristóbal," he said, and then he smiled. "I am so proud that you are with me."

Pablo and Manuel were sitting on the step before the altar. Both looked up when Hipolito and Francisco and Cristóbal pushed open the heavy doors and walked inside the church. Their brother, Andamo, was standing off to the side, and he did not even move his head at the creaking of the hinges. He was staring down at Emilio and every so often his foot would scrape the floor and touch the boy.

"Light the lamp, Manuel," Pablo said as he watched the three old men slowly make their way between the rows of benches. He could see that Francisco was dragging one leg painfully and that Hipolito carried himself with the same arrogance that had once so offended his family. He did not recognize Cristóbal and had no idea who this man was until Manuel reached out and gripped his arm.

"It's Cristóbal García," Manuel hissed, and then he crossed himself.

"No," Pablo said sharply. "It is just another old man. Cristóbal García is only a story people tell to keep us in our place."

"I tell you, it's him," Manuel said, and his hand tightened on his brother's arm. "You said no one in that house would dare come here. He sees the dead, Pablo. This is not what I bargained for."

"I don't care who he is," Pablo said. He jerked his hand free and grabbed Manuel's shoulder. "Look at him, Manuel. He cannot even walk without help. This man can only frighten children. Now light the lamp and go to the window and watch for the others."

"We should leave," Manuel said under his breath. "No good can come of this," and then, after one last look at the three old men, he rose quickly. He lit the lantern on top of the altar and hurried over to the window on the side of the church. He cupped his hands and leaned his forehead against the glass, but outside all he could see was the village layered in darkness.

"All this time," Guadalupe said, "Emilio García lay on the floor."

A part of him thought that if he kept still and did not move, Pablo and his brothers might forget about him.

His nostrils were clogged and his breath was quick and ragged. Blood had dried on his face and neck, and his ear was swollen and burned with heat. Although there was little pain in his hand, the sight of his fingers bent backward and the pale sheen of bone and tendon at the knuckles, twisted his stomach in nausea. He had no memory of what had happened to him in the fields. He could see himself standing beside his ditch with a shovel and watching the clouds fall low on the mountains. Before he had left the García house that morning, Percides had pulled him aside and told him in a whisper that she had found a small room where no one ever went. It was a room that had no windows. She had swept it clean and brought blankets to lay on the floor. If you like, she had said, her eyes wide and her mouth bent in a smile, this time I will let you undress me. Emilio had been thinking about that when he'd heard his name called. He had turned his head slowly and seen Pablo smiling and walking toward him with his brothers just behind.

What happened after that, Emilio didn't know, until he found himself dragged into the church and thrown on the floor. Now, every so often, he could feel Andamo's foot press against his body. For a reason he couldn't grasp, that frightened him more than anything else. When he saw his grandfather walking toward him, he clenched his eyes shut and almost began to cry.

Hipolito and Francisco and Cristóbal stopped a few feet before Pablo. Their clothes were wet and the cold inside the church sat upon all of them. Francisco looked down at the boy, and when he saw how badly the boy had been beaten, his breath caught in his chest. He closed his eyes to steady himself and realized that what was happening was far worse than he had imagined. Hipolito stood beside Cristóbal gazing only at Pablo. His eyes did not waver.

"Why have we stopped?" Cristóbal asked, and he stretched out his arm and moved it about blindly.

"We are here, Cristóbal," Hipolito said. "We are inside our church."

"Then where is this priest?" Cristóbal said loudly. "Where is this priest who has my grandson?"

At the window, Manuel groaned and shook his head. Through the glass, he could suddenly see lights. They were far down the valley and in all directions and they hung in the air as if not moving.

"They are coming, Pablo," he said softly, and then, his voice shaking, he looked at his brother and spoke the words again.

Pablo stood slowly and said, "There is no priest, old man. There is only me."

"We have come to take the boy home, Pablo," Hipolito said. "You and your brothers had no right to do this."

"Where is my grandson?" Cristóbal yelled. "I have not come here to talk."

Emilio stretched out his arm and brushed the side of his grandfather's leg. "Grandfather," he said. Cristóbal pulled his hand free from Hipolito's and knelt down. His hands fell upon Emilio's shoulder and moved up to his face. He could feel the heat coming from his skin and the blood crusted on his face. "What have they done to you?" he said harshly.

"I don't know, Grandfather," Emilio said and his eyes filled with tears. "My hand is broken and I can't remember so well."

"Come, Emilio," Cristóbal said, pulling at Emilio's shirt. "Percides is waiting for us. Come, hijo, let us go home."

"Your grandson is a thief," Pablo suddenly screamed. "He has slaughtered my neighbor's livestock and he's gotten only what he deserves."

Cristóbal's hand stroked the side of Emilio's face and he looked up at where he had heard Pablo's voice. "I don't even know who you are," he said softly, "but if I hear you speak again I will send all of my family to your house and everything you have I will take and burn. I curse you and all of your children and even the walls of this church for allowing a thing like this to happen." Then he turned his face back to his grandson and touched the boy's hair. "Hipolito," he said, "help me. I cannot do this alone."

"There is nothing here for you now, Pablo," Hipolito said. "Take your brothers and leave." He put his hand on Cristóbal's shoulder and lowered himself to his knees. "Vamos, Emilio," he said. "The three of us have come to take you home."

And then, for a reason no one ever knew, Andamo clenched his hands together in a fist and raised them high over his head. He took one step forward and then brought them down with all of his strength across Francisco's shoulders. Something broke in Francisco's back, and he fell as if shot on top of Hipolito and Cristóbal.

For a moment, no one moved. Andamo stood with his arms loose at his sides as if he had done nothing. Manuel, his mouth gaped open, stared from the window. He could not believe what he had just seen, and a cold emptiness suddenly flooded his heart. Pablo could see that the blow had broken Francisco's back and that the old man was struggling to draw a breath.

"Help me, Manuel," Pablo said harshly. Then he kicked out his foot and struck Hipolito on the side of the head and he did not stop kicking until there was not a sound that came from the three men on the floor.

"Not long after that," said Guadalupe García, "the church filled with men from this village. They came from every house, and among them were the sons of Hipolito and Francisco, though none of them knew that their fathers had been there. I don't know what Pablo said to them through that night. I can hear his voice raging in my head, but I can't hear his words. I only know that in the morning, Emilio was carried from the church and a rope was placed around his neck.

"It had rained all that night while Pablo spoke. Water lay over the mud, and the cottonwood tree was black from moisture and its limbs sagged. The mountains were lost in clouds, and mist hung in the air just above the valley. In this house, Percides had fallen asleep in a chair and her two uncles at the table. She woke slowly. Outside she could see that dawn had come to the village. For a second, she thought that while she had slept Emilio and her grandfather had returned and that they had gone to rest before waking her. She could feel the heat from the cookstove and when she stretched out her legs a soft sound came from her mouth. She stood slowly and walked to the door. Then she let out such a wail of anguish that her two uncles awoke and then froze beside the table.

"I think that the last thing Emilio ever saw as the horse was led out from under him was Percides running down the hill to him. Her hair was flying and a few times her feet slipped out from under her and she fell. Then she would scramble to her feet and Emilio would hear her calling his name. By the time she came to the cottonwood tree, the men from the village were walking away, their faces hidden, their shoulders slumped from the weather. Inside the church, Father Patricio sat sleeping by his stove. And somewhere together were Hipolito and Francisco and Cristóbal García."

13

"I miss my son, Flavio," Felix said, and then he belched softly. He was sitting in the front seat of the pickup. His hands were shaking in his lap and his head was trembling. His back was so hunched now that the top of his head came no higher than Flavio's shoulder. A breeze was blowing through the cab, and mixed in now with the smell of smoke was the sour odor of hot dogs.

"I don't miss my son when he was big," Felix went on. "I miss him when he was just a little boy. Did you know that sometimes he used to help me in my kitchen? I can remember this like it was yesterday."

Every so often, as Felix would quietly leave his bedroom, he would be startled to find Pepe standing in the hallway outside his door. In a hushed voice, Felix would bend low and tell his son to be quiet. Then, he would dress him in his small overalls and, leaving

Belinda asleep in bed, they would walk together to the café. The inside of the restaurant would be dark and still, and through the windows Felix and his son would see the stars hanging above the mountains. A small bulb hung outside over the door. If it wasn't burned out, it would throw a yellow light onto the highway, and the road would look old and empty and abandoned. Felix would hold Pepe's hand so that he wouldn't bump his head on the tables, and every morning the boy would talk incessantly in his high, lilting voice, telling his father things he was still too tired to hear.

Inside the cab of the pickup, Felix turned his head and peered up at Flavio. "I miss those mornings with my little boy," he said. "I don't know why I woke up after so long just to be sad. I think it was better being asleep. At least then if you feel bad, you don't know it." When Flavio said nothing to that, Felix stretched out his hand and touched his friend's leg. "Are you listening, Flavio?" he asked.

Flavio was staring blankly out the windshield, and though he could feel the hand trembling lightly on his leg, he hadn't heard a word Felix had said. The fire was not far from Ramona's house, now, and the alfalfa field was waist high in flames. He had left the front door wide open, and smoke was pouring out the doorway. Inside, all he could see was a dark haze, but he could picture the santos huddled closely together on the sofa, looking out the doorway at his truck. A steady wind had begun to blow, and ash and small embers were landing on the hood of his pickup and swirling through the leaves of the cottonwood trees. Although he knew it couldn't be much past mid-afternoon, already the day seemed to be growing dark. Beside him on the seat was the small santo Little José had carved. She stood staring straight ahead, and there was a lopsided grin on her face as if she were looking forward to taking a little ride after being cooped up inside the house for so long.

"Flavio," Felix said again. "Why are we just sitting here? Little pieces of fire are falling on your truck."

Flavio shook his head and pushed himself up on the seat. He looked down at his ignition and saw the same thing he'd seen when he had first tried to start the pickup. "My keys are gone, Felix," he said, and then he wondered at how little this surprised him.

"Look in your pockets, Flavio," Felix breathed out. "Maybe you put them in there by accident."

"I looked in my pockets," Flavio said. "Besides, I never take my keys out of my truck. My keys live in my truck." He bent over awkwardly and looked down at the floor again. All he could see were dried clumps of mud and the rusted handle to his jack sticking out from under the seat. He sat back up and then, after a few seconds, looked over at Felix.

"Don't blame me," Felix said. He pulled his hand back and placed it in his lap. "They're not my keys."

"You were alone in my truck," Flavio said. "Maybe you took them and forgot." Suddenly, he could picture Felix grabbing the keys out of the ignition and then, for a reason not even Felix would know, throwing them out the window.

Felix looked down at his hands and tried to fold them together. "I don't know nothing about your keys," he said. "Why is it my fault when things go wrong? Maybe you lost them somewhere in Ramona's house. Or maybe that policeman took them. Who knows who he was, anyway. Maybe he took your keys when we weren't watching."

Flavio let out a long, tired breath. "Why would he take my keys?" he asked.

"How should I know?" Felix said. "You think I know everything?" He looked at the santo on the seat beside him as if he'd never seen her before. "Why is she coming with us, Flavio?" he asked. "She looks like she's been drinking too much whiskey. She looks like she wants to go to a party with a bunch of other borrachos."

"My nephew José made her when he was little," Flavio said.

Then he felt a rush of sadness when he thought that all his nephew had ever been in his life was little. He looked down at the Lady and put his hand on top of her head. He could feel the thick clumps of paint beneath his palm, and he remembered the first time he had seen her.

José had been gone from the house that day, when Flavio had walked into the kitchen. She had been standing in the middle of the table. For being so small, she seemed to take up the whole room, and for a second Flavio thought that she might wave her arms and begin to sing.

"Ramona," he had said. "What is that?"

Ramona had been at the sink, and when she saw the expression on her brother's face, she began to laugh. The small room seemed to fill with light, and the breeze coming through the screen door was warm on his face. When Ramona finally stopped laughing, she dried her hands and wiped her face and then, still smiling, she had leaned back against the sink.

"She was waiting in the wood all these years, Flavio," Ramona said. "And Little José found her there. She's so beautiful, isn't she, Flavio?"

"But what is she, Ramona?" Flavio had asked, and then he and his sister both looked at the santo.

"I don't know," Ramona said. Sunlight was coming through the small window above the sink, and the breeze stirred the curtains and pulled gently at his sister's hair. "All I know is that our nephew made her and when I look at her, she makes me happy."

Outside Flavio's pickup, the wind suddenly gusted, and it beat down the flames behind Ramona's house, sending up a whirlwind of smoke and cinders. Flavio brought his hands to his face and rubbed at his eyes. "I am missing too many things, Felix," he said.

"Yo también," Felix said hoarsely.

Flavio grunted softly and let his hands rest on the steering wheel. "You are so lucky, Felix," he said, "to have such a son as Pepe. All these years while you sat sick in the café, he took such good care of you."

"Did I tell you?" Felix said. He reached out again and touched Flavio's leg. "When he was little, he would help me with my tortillas. He would beat on them hard with his spoon and all the time he would talk and talk. Sometimes I thought my little boy would make me crazy with his talking. He would sprinkle water on my tortillas and wrap them in towels, and I would let him put the spices in my beans. When we were done, we would make a little breakfast and go sit by the big window in the café. It would still be dark out, and while my son ate, I would smoke a cigarette and we would wait for the village to wake up." Felix fell quiet for a moment, and then he took in a deep breath and it shuddered slowly out from his mouth. Then he raised his eyes and looked out the windshield. "We should go, Flavio," he said. "This fire is getting too big."

The brush and thin saplings behind the old chicken coop were bowed and moving from the heat of the fire. Smoke was coming from the grass that ran from the edge of the alfalfa field up to the house. My sister's house is going to burn, Flavio thought, and her paintings that she cared so much about, and the Ladies on the sofa, and the bed where my grandparents slept.

"My whole family has come from this house," he said softly. "My father was born here." The front door moved a little in the wind, and for a second, Flavio thought he saw a figure standing just inside the doorway. He leaned forward and wiped at his eyes, and then whatever it was he had seen was gone.

"Flavio," Felix said.

"I know," Flavio answered, and after one last look, he pushed open the door to his truck. He walked around the front of the pickup and, above him, he could hear the dry, brittle sound of leaves blown in the wind. He pulled open Felix's door, and the two men looked at each other.

"This has been a bad day, Flavio," Felix said. His face was gray, and saliva had dried white at the corners of his mouth.

"Yes," Flavio said. He could see that Felix's head had stopped trembling and that his hands were still. For some reason, this worried him more than anything. "Venga, Felix," he said. "We'll take a little walk and find someone to give us a ride."

"Where, Flavio?"

"I don't know," he said and almost smiled. "Let's go see."

"My legs have cramps in them, Flavio," Felix said. "I don't want to walk anymore. We should take your truck."

"We've lost the keys, Felix," Flavio said. "Come, I'll help you. The highway is not so far." He reached in the cab and took Felix's hand.

Felix squeezed hard on Flavio's fingers and then he pulled Flavio's hand to his chest and held it there. "We never saw her again, did we, Flavio?" Felix asked him. His eyes were damp and bloodshot and the scratches on his face were red and crusted. His clothes were filthy and one elbow, white and all bone, stuck out where his shirt had been torn.

Flavio stood leaning into the truck and holding on to Felix's hand. He thought that his old friend looked frightened and lost and far too small inside the cab. "Felix," he said softly.

Felix moved his eyes away and looked past Flavio. "We thought she was dead," he said, "and we never went back there again, did we, Flavio?"

For a moment, Flavio didn't speak, and then he closed his eyes and shook his head. "No," he breathed out. "We never went there again."

Flavio had jerked awake and in his mouth was the heavy taste of kerosene. His eyes were burning from the smoke in the room. Across from him, he could see that Felix was sitting up and that he was crying softly. His head was bent and, every so often, he called out Flavio's name. Guadalupe still sat on the bed beside him, but her head was now resting facedown on her knees. Her hair spilled white down her legs, and her hands were folded beneath her. She was so still that Flavio thought she was dead. Just then, the flame in the lantern spit and died out, and the room fell into darkness. For a few seconds, there was not a sound. Then Felix began to wail out Flavio's name, and the small room filled with the noise of two boys crying.

Later, Flavio would remember vividly how he woke in the room where Emilio García's bones were buried in the wall and where Guadalupe had once played while her great-grandmother, Percides, lay dying. Then, he would remember running wildly into the kitchen with Felix howling behind him and holding tightly on to the back of his shirt with both his hands. But how he and Felix had managed to find their way through the maze of rooms in the García house, neither one of them ever remembered.

For weeks after that day, Flavio would have vague dreams of too much darkness, and in it would be the faint outline of things that had been left alone for a hundred years: tall, thin trasteros cloaked with dusty cloths and crooked benches that squatted low to the ground and small painted cradles that rocked unevenly on the adobe floors. He would dream of Felix crying without stopping, and he would hear the frantic scraping of his own footsteps that sounded to him as if all the rooms he was passing through were full of people he couldn't see. Flavio would dream fitfully of these things, and when he awoke they would stay with him for a little while until he wandered outside. There, like mist, they would be burned away by the sun or blown off by the wind. As autumn passed into winter that year, Flavio's dreams eventually began to fade. By the time the first heavy snow fell on the village in November, they had left him altogether without his even knowing it.

When Flavio and Felix came running out of the García house, their clothes reeked of kerosene and their hands and faces were smeared with soot and dust, and cobwebs clung to their clothes. The sun had set and the mountains were soft and still. The sky hung low above them and was streaked red. The air was cool and clean on their skin, and it tasted of woodsmoke and of apples that had lain on the ground for too long. At the top of the hill, Rosa was standing on the edge of the road. She was wearing a black dress and around her head was a shawl. When she saw the boys come from the house, she waved her arm and called their names. As they ran toward her, she took a few steps down the hill, and then she stopped and stooped down.

"Mi hijos," she said, and she hugged them both. "There's nothing to cry about now. You are safe with me." Then she pushed them both away from her gently and looked at them. "Look how dirty you two are," she said. "What will your mother think, Felix?" She wiped at their faces with the edge of her shawl and the cloth came away black.

"We were lost, Grandmother," Flavio said, and he almost began to cry again. "Why did you send us there?"

"Hush, hijo," Rosa said and touched the side of his face. "You were never lost. You just went somewhere for a little while and now you're back with me."

"I don't want to take her any more beans," Felix said. "I think she has enough beans." Then he glanced quickly over his shoulder as if he thought the house might be coming up the hill after him.

Rosa smiled and put her hand on Felix's shoulder. "Don't worry, Felix," she said. "You don't have to go there ever again."

"She looked like she was dead, Grandmother," Flavio said, and again he saw Guadalupe lying with her head facedown in her lap and not even a strand of her hair was moving. "She got all quiet, Grandmother, and then the light burned out."

"Eee," Felix said loudly and a shiver shook his body. "Don't talk about that. I think she was just tired and needed a little rest."

For a brief second, a shadow passed over Rosa's face and her features tightened. She took in a long, slow breath, and when she breathed it out, she smiled. "No, hijo," she said. "Guadalupe García is not dead. I would know it if she were. She is old and has had a hard life, and all that she told you was difficult for her. Later, I will ask your grandfather to go to her house and look in on her. Then we can leave her alone by herself."

"You should have been me, Flavio," Felix said, "when that light went out. I had to sit next to her and behind me Emilio's dead bones were sticking out of the wall, and I could hear that stupid santo moving around like she wanted to jump on my head." Felix's face was smeared black, and under his eyes were white swathes of skin from his crying. His hands were shaking a little and a thin line of clear mucus ran from one nostril.

"Santos don't jump," Flavio said.

"Maybe not all santos," Felix said. "Besides, who knows what they do when the lights go out. I tell you, when that light went out, I almost screamed like a little baby."

"You cried like one," Flavio said.

Felix's lower lip suddenly began to tremble, and he bit on it with his teeth. "How do you know?" he said. "I saw you. You were sleeping. I only cried because the story was so sad. I didn't cry because I was scared. I was never scared."

"Quiet, hijos," Rosa said, and she rose slowly to her feet. She straightened her dress and pulled the shawl tight around her head.

"Come," she said. "Your grandfather will be wondering where we've gone to. I have made a platter of enchiladas for supper and fresh tamales and sopapillas. Maybe you can eat with us, Felix, and then we will walk you home." She looked down for a moment at the two boys, and then she turned and began walking back up the hill.

At the edge of the road, Rosa paused and looked out over the valley. There was not a breeze blowing, and the village looked quiet and empty and still. From far off came the sound of a cow, and its low moaning seemed to hang in the air below them. Felix stood close beside her, so close that the folds of her dress touched the side of his face lightly. He was staring down at the ground and moving a small stone about with his foot. Flavio stood a few feet away and, like his grandmother, stared out over the valley.

He could see the García house with its rooms that sprawled everywhere. The door was open and the small windows were dark. Twisted sagebrush grew all about the place. Not far down the hill was the church. The walls were thick and heavy, and all four corners were buttressed as if it might fall. The roof was pitched and sagged in places from years of snow loads, and it was layered with old wood shingles. Behind the building, Flavio could see the high branches of the cottonwood tree. As he watched, a small flock of sparrows flew into it and disappeared among the leaves. Flavio's mouth hung half open, and his breath came slow and easy. The village that he had always known had become a place where young boys were hung from trees and where santos were carved in blizzards and painted in blood and where old men could become lost and never be found again.

He looked up at Rosa. "Why did you send us there, Grandmother?" he asked again.

"From the very beginning there has been a sadness in this place that few chose to even see," Rosa said softly. "It runs through the creeks and lies in the dirt and it comes with the wind in the dead of winter. We have lived with it so long that we don't know any different. I have a debt to pay both of my families, and someday I will ask both you boys to do a little something for me."

Felix raised his head and looked up at Rosa. "I don't like to do some things," he said. "Flavio is older than me. I think Flavio could do it by himself. Or maybe Delfino could help him."

"It's just a little thing, Felix," Rosa said and she smiled. "You are such a good friend to mi hijo, and it won't be for a very long time."

"When I'm nine?"

"Longer," Rosa said. "So long you won't even remember."

Nick Oliver was driving north up the highway when he caught a flash of light in his rearview mirror and heard the loud sound of an explosion. He cursed and hunched his shoulders. In the middle of the road, a half mile behind him, was a gigantic ball of black fire. It curled and twisted up into the air and then it blew out in a cloud of smoke.

"That was a propane tank," he said. "Right in the middle of town." He looked over at Ambrosio.

Ambrosio was staring dully out the windshield. His eyes were glazed and a thin thread of saliva ran from his open mouth. He could see black clouds rolling above the valley, and on the highway, ash was sneaking across the pavement. A wave of dizziness rose in his head, and for a second, everything he saw began to waver. A long sigh came from his mouth as he watched the village move about him in swirls of smoke.

"Guadalupe is dancing in the snow," he said, then he looked over at Oliver and spoke the words again in English.

"There is no snow, amigo," Oliver said. "There's only fire. Maybe you should sleep a little. This has been a bad day for everyone."

"In Mexico," Ambrosio said, "there is never cold and when it rains, the water is warm and forgiving." He looked down at his hands and moved one of his fingers, and then he vaguely remembered breaking all the windows at the café. In his mind, he saw snow and dirt blow in on the linoleum floors that he had always kept so clean. He began to cry again, and then he began to sing a song about a man whose heart was broken from loss. He closed his eyes and leaned his head back, and as he sang, he wondered where he was and how long it would take to get wherever he was going.

Oliver looked back at the road and then glanced again in his rearview mirror. All he could see now was an empty stretch of road behind him and a sky churned black with smoke. Off to his left, the fire was already a good mile ahead of him and beginning to turn back on itself. He could no longer see the foothills, and flames were washing across the fields. Out the side window he could see that down in the valley things were even worse.

There was nothing left of Flavio's house but charred walls. The apple trees around it were black and skeletal and smoking. The fire that had been started there had spread in all directions, and Oliver could see houses and trailers on fire. Flames were sweeping across fields of grass. A few head of cattle were climbing the slope toward the road, their mouths foaming, their eyes wild. They screamed and bit at each other as they ran. The mountains in the east looked as if a storm were raging there, and even with so much fire all about, the day was turning dark. Oliver's eyes were running with water and burning. It suddenly occurred to him that if he wasn't careful, he could get stuck in this village and never get out.

Just up the road was the village office. Lucero's beat-up vehicle pulled out from behind it and then slowed to a stop. Oliver hit his brakes, swung off the highway, and pulled up alongside. In the front seat with Lucero were two of his children. They were both young boys, and they looked small and skinny sitting beside their father.

They didn't even raise their eyes when Oliver stopped. But he could see that both their faces were puffy and blotched red from crying.

For a moment, neither man said a word. Lucero's arm was hanging loose out the window, and the flat of his hand was slapping gently against the door. "I'm leaving," he said finally. His shirt was soaked through with sweat, and the creases in his face were lined with soot and dirt. His eyes were bloodshot and the skin beneath them was sagging and discolored.

"I've got a problem here," Oliver said. He pulled out a cigarette and lit it.

The muscles in Lucero's face tightened, and his hand slapped hard on the car door. "I don't want to hear about your problems," he said. "I just lost my house, hombre. I got home to find my wife holding a water hose and my kids scared to death. You don't have no problems." One of his boys began to cry. Lucero half turned and put a heavy hand on his son's shoulder. "I don't want to hear you cry no more, Mario," he said. "You hear me, hijo?"

"Yes, Papa," the boy mumbled.

"You're too big to be crying like a little girl."

Oliver brought his cigarette to his mouth and looked out the windshield. An empty field stretched away from the edge of the parking lot. Sitting in the middle of it was an old adobe falling in on itself. The roof had collapsed and the walls had bellied out, swelling open the one small window and twisting the thick, wood door frame. For a second, it seemed to Oliver as if everything in this village was old and abandoned. It didn't surprise him at all that the emergency crews hadn't even bothered to come into the valley. He thought that this place had died a long time ago. Everyone seemed to know that, except the people who lived here. Thin reeds of grass were growing out of the roofing paper on top of the adobe, and the viga ends were rotted and as soft as wet paper. High weeds and stunted sagebrush grew all about the place, and strewn throughout were the carcasses of discarded machinery. Old village tractors and rusted-out ploughs and burned engines coated with oil and dirt and piles of gravel and black asphalt. Oliver could hear Lucero talking in a low voice to his son, and again, he brought his cigarette to his mouth. He inhaled deeply and then let out a long, slow stream of smoke.

Bordering the far edge of the field a quarter mile away was the rutted road that ran in front of Ramona Montoya's old house. One wall of the adobe was crawling with fire. The high branches of the cottonwood trees were swaying in the wind, and the leaves were trailing smoke. Flavio's truck was still parked beneath the trees. Oliver could picture the two old men sitting asleep inside the house while it burned about them. He shook his head and groaned softly. He took one last drag off his cigarette and let it drop out his open window. Then he looked over at Lucero.

Donald was staring past Oliver at Ambrosio, who had passed out a half mile before. "What are you doing with him?" he asked. "Is that the problem you got?"

"No," Oliver said. "I found him on the highway. He was too drunk to walk and I didn't want to leave him there." Ambrosio's chin was now resting on his chest, and he was snoring raggedly. Every so often his body would jerk and he would mutter loudly as if arguing with himself.

"He's a mojado," Lucero said. "His name's Ambrosio Herrera, but most people called him Bocito because when he gets drunk he won't shut up. He mops the floors at the café and sweeps garbage out of the lot, and he lives in a little shit hole of a trailer Felix gave him. He's been here so long he got to thinking he was one of us, but he's just a wetback out of Mexico." Lucero lifted his hand as if to wave something away. "What you should do is drive about four miles north and on the east side of the road you'll see the Sanchez ranch. I've been sending everybody there to wait this fire out. My wife and the rest of my kids left for there an hour ago, and I don't know anyone dumb enough to still be here. You take him out there and put him under a tree and let him sleep it off. He don't have nothing in this place anymore." Lucero leaned his head out the window and spat. His saliva was stained black, and Oliver could taste the grit in his own mouth. Lucero wiped his mouth with the back of his hand and then jerked his head back as if slapped.

"Why's he smell like that?" he asked.

Delfino had been lying for so long in the backseat that Oliver had almost grown used to the smell inside his vehicle. But now, as if for the first time, he caught the odor of burned clothes and singed hair and the thick scent of charred skin that was so strong he seemed to taste it rather than smell it.

"He doesn't," Oliver said and glanced back at Delfino fetaled up on the backseat like a child that had been forgotten. "I've got Delfino Vigil in my backseat," he said. His voice cracked and he coughed to clear it. "He got burned in the fire. I was trying to find some help for him, but he died on me."

Lucero didn't say a word. He stared at Oliver and his fingers rubbed gently on the metal of the door. Finally, he said, "You trying to make a joke or what? I saw Delfino get run over by this fire hours ago." The boy beside him slid a little closer to his brother. He turned his head away and looked out the far window.

Lucero was smiling slightly and his eyes were so red that they seemed to be bleeding. Although his face was dark and heavy, beneath his skin was a gray caste of fatigue or maybe sickness. Again, Oliver thought that all he had to show for a day of fire was a dead man in his backseat and a drunk Mexican who thought he was lost in a blizzard. A cramp started up in the back of his neck, and he swiveled his head trying to work it out.

Down the highway, smoke was billowing black and rolling up

the road. Oliver thought that maybe Ambrosio wasn't so wrong after all. It looked like a sudden winter storm had blown into the village from nowhere. The wind was howling and ash blew about like snow. Oliver realized that if it was any other day, his shift would have been over. Something stirred in the backseat, and he heard the santo fall from Delfino's arms to the floor. Beside him, Ambrosio spoke a name and then fell quiet.

"I don't have time for this, Lucero," he said. "All I need to know from you is if Delfino has any family."

Something shifted in Lucero's face. Suddenly, he looked older, his face drawn, his eyes flat and empty as if he'd lost more than just his house in this fire. He swung open his door and told his sons to stay where they were. Then he went to the back window of the squad car. He leaned over and cupped his hands. He stayed peering inside for a little while and then he straightened up slowly.

"He don't have no family," he said, without even looking at Oliver. "He lived by himself about a mile north in a little house just off the road. I don't know what you should do with him." He looked down at Oliver. "Where'd you find him?" he asked.

"In the old Montoya house," Oliver said, waving a hand toward Ramona's. "He was sitting inside with Montoya and that Felix García."

Lucero grunted. Then he passed his hand over his face and ran it up through his hair. Soot smeared across his face. "None of this makes any sense," he said.

Just then, the gas tank in Flavio's truck ignited and blew. The hood flew up into the windshield and the vehicle seemed to lift a few inches off the ground and then slammed back down. The cottonwoods above it were burning, and as Oliver and Lucero looked that way a heavy limb fell across the bed of the truck.

"That old man sure started something," Lucero said to no one. Then his eyes snagged on something moving and he saw Flavio and Felix walking through the high weeds not far off. Ash and smoke drifted around them, and after every few steps, they would stop and rest, their heads drooped down, their bodies leaning into each other.

"I see them, too," Oliver said. "They've been walking this way ever since I parked."

Lucero stepped back from the squad car. Still looking at Felix and Flavio, he said, "You should go."

"No," Oliver said. "I'll wait with you."

"There's no room in your car," Lucero said. "I can put them in my backseat." He looked back at Oliver and smiled. "That way I can slap them a little bit and you won't have to watch." He leaned forward and pounded the roof of the squad car. "Go," he said. "I'll be right behind you."

Oliver reached out and started his car. Beside him, Ambrosio began to sing softly "You sure?" he said to Lucero.

"What do you think I am?" Lucero said. "Go on, now. This is still my place even if there's nothing left. I'll see you at the Sanchez ranch and we'll drink a beer."

14

Eugenio's dead," Flavio said.

"No," Felix breathed out. "Not Eugenio, también."

"Oh sí," Flavio said. "He died almost a year ago. I think it was a year ago. Maybe it was a little longer."

Felix stopped walking. He creaked his head sideways and peered up at Flavio. "I thought Eugenio would never die," he said. "When I would see him, I would think he was like a little motorcar that didn't know how to stop."

They were standing in the shallow ditch on the other side of the road from Ramona's house. Weeds and dried-out sagebrush rubbed against their legs, and there were empty beer cans and rotted plastic bags lying on the ground. Flavio had one arm wrapped around Felix's waist. Tucked under his other arm was the santo his nephew had carved. She dug into the flesh above his elbow, and sometimes she slipped as if trying to squirm loose. Although they had only come some twenty-five yards, already both of Flavio's arms were aching and his heart was beating too fast. Sharp pains were shooting down into his belly and up into his chest. He could feel Felix's ribs thin and frail against his hand, and he wondered how Felix could manage to lean so heavily against him and sag away from him at the same time. He straightened his back and wiped the sweat from his face with his sleeve.

"Eee," Felix said. He shook his head and gazed down at the ground. Every so often, his legs would begin to shake. If Flavio had not held on to him tightly, he would have fallen. "I remember Eugenio when he was a little boy," Felix went on. "We were all classmates at that little school. Me and you and Eugenio and Delfino and Telesfor Ruiz and Josepha Pacheco." He fell quiet for a few seconds and then said, "¿Quién mas, Flavio?"

"Victoria Medina," Flavio said.

"Oh sí," Felix said softly. "Her, too." He began to tremble and Flavio pulled him closer as if to comfort him. Behind them, the walls of Ramona's house were burning. Flavio could feel heat pressing against the back of his shirt.

"Come, Felix," he said, trying to keep the urgency from his voice. "Let's walk some more and I'll tell you about Eugenio."

"I don't think I can, Flavio," Felix said. "Maybe you should leave me here and come back with some help."

"Eugenio fell off his daughter's roof," Flavio said as he pulled Felix a little bit forward.

"No." Felix took a small step.

"Yes," Flavio said. "He landed right behind his daughter, who was hanging out her laundry."

Eugenio Rivera had been a carpenter all his life and had never had much luck. He had lost fingers to saw blades on each hand. Vigas had rolled onto his feet, crushing his toes, and splinters of wood had pierced both his eyes. Once even a portal he had built collapsed, gashing his head and knocking him unconscious for two days.

"What surprised most people," Flavio said, "wasn't that Eugenio had died, but that it had taken so long. At the Rosary, Eugenio looked like he always did. He was dressed in his overalls, the ones with all the holes, and his heavy work boots. And one of his grandchildren threw in a hammer for his grandpa to take with him that hit Eugenio on the side of the head.

"Eee, pobrecito," Felix sighed. "Every morning, Eugenio would stop at my café and we would visit for a while."

Felix was still moving forward, but he was taking such small steps that they had crossed only a third of the field. And now, as Flavio paused to catch his breath, Felix stopped walking altogether. His breath was ragged and whistled from his mouth, and when he spoke, his voice was all air. He tried to turn his head and look up at Flavio, but the muscles in his neck had weakened. His head fell forward, his knees suddenly gave, and he pulled free from Flavio. He knelt there, his back badly rounded—and then, as if he had seen something there, he reached out and put his hand flat on the dirt.

"We would run through this field as children, Flavio," Felix said. "How did we get so old?" His voice was so low that Flavio didn't hear a word.

Across the road, the gasoline in Flavio's pickup exploded and a wave of heat blew over the field. Flavio staggered a few steps forward, and then he turned and looked back at where he had come. His truck was awash in flames that rose high up into the limbs of the cottonwood tree. The roof of Ramona's house and all four walls were burning, and beneath the fire the house seemed to waver in the heat. As he stared, openmouthed, the wind pulling at his clothes, Flavio thought that he had seen this before. Then through the noise of the fire, he could hear his sister's voice.

"Flavio," Ramona said. Her voice was choked and she leaned across the table. Her hands reached out and took his. "All these years, I've been looking for him. In my paintings. In the field where the alfalfa grows high by the ditch. I listen for his voice at dusk when the light is so frail you could fall through it. Sometimes I feel that if I look fast enough I'll see him. He's here, Flavio, but I don't know where."

Beneath the fire, like the shadows in all of Ramona's paintings, Flavio could see his sister's house. The front door blew back and forth, and the window where his grandmother would watch out for him was cracked and splintered, the paint on the frame peeled and scorched. The ceiling inside the living room would be crawling with fire and below it, on the sofa, the santos he'd left would be sitting close together. "I should have taken them all," he whispered. The wind suddenly gusted. A thick cloud of smoke rolled across the road and into the field. Flavio closed his eyes and, behind them, he saw his wife sitting at the table in her own kitchen.

"Martha," he said. She lifted her head and smiled at him. On the table was a pencil and a small piece of paper. Sunlight spilled in through the open window and fell upon the table.

"I'm writing you a letter, Flavio," she said. "So that you'll know."

"I've never known anything, Martha," Flavio said.

"How could you, Flavio? It was in the rustle of my mother's dress as she moved and in the breeze that blew through our apple trees. It was in all the things we never spoke to each other." She looked at him for a little while longer, and then her hand reached for the pencil and she began to write.

As Flavio opened his mouth to call to her, a heavy limb from the cottonwood began to sag. Then, with almost a groan, it ripped loose from the trunk of the tree and fell across the back of the pickup. Flavio opened his eyes and saw a myriad of sparks fly into the air and settle in the weeds across the road. Small fires began to flare along the edge of the road, and the wind began to fan them higher.

He hurried over to Felix and knelt down beside him. He put his hand on his old friend's back and shook him. "Felix," he said. "The fire is getting too close. We can't stay here."

Felix raised his head in a series of small jerks. His nose was bleeding and blood ran over his lips and down his chin. His eyes were glazed and full of tears. "Those old women messed with us, Flavio," he said. "We were just little boys who didn't know any better. Why would they do that to us? She was your grandmother, Flavio."

"I don't know, Felix," Flavio said. Behind him, he heard the tearing of another limb and heat crawled up his back. His own eyes were running with water and he wiped at them. "We have to go now, Felix," he said quickly. "Let me help you."

"No, Flavio," Felix said. "Just let me be."

Flavio wrapped his arm around Felix's waist. He rose to a crouch and then, both of them moaning, he stood holding Felix against his body. On the far side of the field was the village office, and Flavio could see Donald Lucero's vehicle by the highway. Parked beside it was the state police car. He hefted Felix a little higher.

"Mira, Felix," he said. "Donald is waiting for us." Lucero was standing outside his car, staring into the field. Then Flavio watched him turn back to the squad car. He slapped the car roof once and stepped back as it rolled forward and then swung out onto the highway. Donald watched it drive off, and then he walked to the rear of his vehicle. He leaned back against the high bumper and folded his arms. The wind blew at his hat, and he lowered his head and stayed standing there as if it were just any other day in the middle of the summer.

Felix straightened his legs slightly and rolled his eyes up. "That's Menard Lucero's boy," he said.

"He's waiting for us," Flavio said, but he felt a sudden misgiving. For some reason, he wished that the state police officer, even though he had only given Flavio trouble, had not been the one to drive off.

"I never liked that boy," Felix said, and now that he was complaining, his voice seemed a little stronger. "When he was little, he would steal my candy." He staggered a few steps forward. "And his papa wasn't much better. His neighbor, Porfirio, told me he used to make his children stand in the snow without their shoes."

"Did you know," Flavio said, pulling Felix along a little faster, "that Menard once knocked down Porfirio's wife?"

"No," Felix gasped. "I never heard that."

"It's true. I don't know how you forgot. She was just a little woman, and whenever Porfirio was sick in bed for too long, she liked to go into Menard's field and chase his cows."

Felix began to shake and Flavio realized that his old friend was laughing. "Eee," Felix said. "This village was something. Tell me, Flavio."

"Walk a little faster, Felix, and I'll tell you what happened."

As they made their way through the field, Felix would stumble along listening to the sound of Flavio's voice. Flavio told Felix everything he could remember in the eight years his friend had been asleep inside the café. And when Flavio's mind went blank, he would make up little stories, and it didn't matter to either of them if they made no sense. Flavio talked until his voice grew harsh from smoke and his throat ached.

They skirted carefully around the carcasses of abandoned machinery and rusted-out engines and piles of gray lumber. Flavio could hear the fire burning through the weeds behind him, and he held Felix tighter, afraid that if one of them fell they might never get up. They walked past the ruined adobe, and from inside came the frantic skittering of rodents and the flapping of wings like pages of a book being blown. Every so often, Flavio would glance up, blinking the sweat from his eyes. He could see Donald still leaning against the back of his vehicle. The sky above him was low and dark. The highway was empty, and ash snaked across the pavement. Far off to the east, veins of smoke clogged the canyons. On the ridges, small bursts of fire would flare up and then die out.

By the time Flavio and Felix staggered out of the field, Flavio's lungs were burning and his legs had no more strength. His mouth was bone dry and his lips were swollen and cracked from the heat. The santo slid out from under his arm and fell onto the asphalt. Flavio stumbled over her, kicking her a few feet away into the weeds. He lowered Felix to the ground and then knelt beside him.

"We're here, Felix," he gasped. Over the last fifty yards, Felix had sagged so low that Flavio had dragged him through the sagebrush. Felix's pants had torn and his knees and thighs were smeared with fresh blood and dirt. The cuts on his face were bleeding again, and there was a bruise high on his cheekbone.

"I lost my shoe, Flavio," Felix moaned. He was slumped forward on his knees, his arms stretched out. His foot, bare and white, was gouged with scratches.

"You don't need a shoe, Felix," Flavio said. "The highway is so close I can carry you."

"That's what you always say, Flavio," he said weakly. "You know what I think? I think if I ever see your grandmother again, I won't listen to a word she says. My grandmother used to make me sugar cookies and dolls with apple heads." For a few seconds, Felix lay still. Then his breath caught in his chest. He struggled a little to break it loose and a thin stream of air went to his lungs. Then he began to breathe so quickly that his back spasmed and he sucked dirt into his mouth.

"Cuidado, Felix," Flavio said frantically. "You'll hurt yourself." He put both of his hands on Felix's back to quiet him. Then Felix's leg began to shake and his bare foot kicked out, scraping the pavement. "Let me help you, Felix," and panic filled Flavio's heart. He turned Felix onto his side, and the old man rolled onto Flavio's knees. Felix's eyes were a maze of broken blood vessels. Flavio wiped at his face with his hand. "Felix," he whispered. "Don't do this to me now, Felix."

"I miss my son, Flavio," Felix breathed out. "I missed him from the day he was born." Then suddenly, he sagged down deep into Flavio and let out a long sigh. His legs eased to the ground and his arms fell away. And in his mind, Felix saw himself sitting in his café. It wasn't yet dawn, and all Felix could see out the front windows were the shadows of the mountains. In the kitchen, Pepe was rolling out tortillas. The radio was on low and Pepe was singing softly along with it. Felix leaned back in his chair and folded his hands on his stomach. Then he heard the sound of the café door opening. Standing in the doorway was a woman dressed in black. A shawl was draped over her head and fell far down her back.

"Felix," she said softly. It was the voice of Felix's wife, Belinda, and his mother and his grandmother. And it was the voice of Guadalupe García and Rosa Montoya. "Hijo," she said. "I've waited so long to see you."

Felix thought of all the things he could say to this woman whose voice sounded like his whole life. Then his mind emptied, and in a dream, he said, "If I had a little burro, I would ride over all these hills all the way to Albuquerque."

"I know you would, hijo," the woman said, and as dawn came to the village, inside the café the two of them smiled.

Donald Lucero was halfway across the lot when the sight of Felix lying dead in Flavio's lap stopped him. The old man's limbs were sprawled out and his face was bloodied and empty. Donald rubbed his eyes hard and groaned. His day had begun with Flavio and Felix and now it was ending with them. He felt as if something had slipped by him that he should have noticed. But what it was, he didn't know. He shook his head in confusion and then glanced off to the north. The fire was a mile away and beginning to swing east. He realized that he had about twenty minutes before it swept over the highway north and he would be stuck in the village. As he walked toward Flavio, he could hear the sound of his two boys crying.

The fire in the field had reached the door of the old adobe, and the thick grease on a tractor engine was burning. Heat and smoke brushed hot against Donald's face. He squinted his eyes and pulled his hat low. Then he stooped down, reached out, and slapped the side of Flavio's face. "Wake up, viejo," he said.

The front of Flavio's shirt was stuck to his skin with blood. His cracked lips were moving, and he was staring straight ahead and patting Felix's shoulder gently.

"Flavio," Donald said sharply. Again, he slapped the side of the old man's face. Flavio sucked in a mouthful of air and his head jerked back. He looked about, as if lost, and then his eyes fell on Donald. "Let's go, Flavio," Donald said. He dropped to one knee and slid his arms beneath Felix. Then, as if all that was left of Felix was air, he lifted him easily and rose to his feet. He looked back down at Flavio. "Get up," he said. "Or I swear."

Flavio's hat had blown off and was lying on the ground. He reached out, his hand shaking, and picked it up. Then he shoved it on and stood slowly. The side of Felix's head was resting against Donald's chest and his eyes were closed. For a second, Flavio thought that Felix was just resting and might wake up again. But then Donald hefted him a little higher. Felix's head fell back and his foot moved lifelessly.

"Did you hear me, Flavio?" Donald said. "I don't have time to wait for you."

"I don't want to go with you," Flavio said, still looking at Felix. He thought that all of his old friends were being carried away. And he didn't know where.

Donald stepped closer to him. "This was our village," he said. "Both of our families have lived here forever. How could you do such a thing?"

Flavio didn't say a word. He could see Donald's two boys turned around in the car looking back at him. Even with the noise of the fire and the wind tearing at it, he could hear how frightened their crying was. "Tell Pepe," he said to Donald, "that Felix always re-membered him."

"You think I'm going to leave you here," Donald rasped out. "You think I'm going to wake up at night with bad dreams because I left you in this fire? Get in my fucking car, jodido, or I'll drag you over to it."

Flavio moved a few steps away. He bent over and picked up the Lady. He brushed the dirt from her face and wiped away the ash. Some of the small sticks of her halo had snapped when she'd fallen. She looked even more lopsided than before. "I'm sorry," he said to her. "I never should have dropped you," and he began walking away.

"Flavio," Donald shouted.

"My nephew, Little José, carved you a long time ago," Flavio said softly. "He found you in the wood and he painted you with my sis-ter's paints." He could see Ramona and José sitting in his sister's house. They were sitting at the kitchen table and the sun was warm on the curtains. "Here," Ramona said, handing her nephew a knife. "But be careful, José, and take away only a little at a time. If you do that, you will see things in the wood that have been there forever."

As Donald backed away, he shouted Flavio's name again. The wind blew sparks against the side of his body, and something stored inside the old adobe blew. He took one more look at Flavio, and then he turned and carried Felix back to his car. By the time he reached the rear door, he was crying and he couldn't make himself stop.

"There's no one here but me," Flavio said. He was standing on the edge of the highway looking out over the valley. The road to the north and south of him was empty, and wherever he looked, all he could see moving were smoke and fire. "Eee," he whispered, shaking his head, "what a mess we started."

The mountains were buried under the smoke that hung over the whole village. Along the bottom of the valley, houses and trailers were burning, some of them already just twisted metal or charred adobe. Flavio heard the high frantic bellow of a cow; then he watched it lumber across the road and head south toward town. He wondered what had become of Delfino's pigs. He remembered telling Delfino that he would watch out for them. Now, it seemed as if he would not be able to keep even that one little promise to his old friend. He pictured them, worried and alone, inside their pen, staring out at the village along with him. The fire had swept through all of the bottom valley and was beginning to creep up the hill toward the church. The branches of the cottonwood were blowing wildly in the wind, and the old wood roof was leaking smoke. Behind him, the fire had come almost to the edge of the highway. Embers were falling on his shoulders, and the back of his neck was hot and raw. The only place untouched by what was happening was the old García house.

It sat, as it always had, on the hill above the church. Most of the rooms had fallen in and the vigas had rotted to dust. The mud plaster on what was left was long gone, and rain and melting snow had eaten away at the adobe so badly that loose dirt lay in mounds all about the place. The few windows intact were boarded up with blackened lumber. The house looked like every other old abandoned adobe in Guadalupe—a place where someone had once lived that was now turning back to dirt. He realized that while everything he had ever known was burning down, all he and Felix had done was dream the dreams that old men sometimes have.

"Felix was right," Flavio muttered. "We should never have listened. We both should have stayed asleep." An ember fell on the back of his hand and he brushed it away. Then he caught the pungent odor of burning cloth. He moved his hand over his shirt and down the front of his trousers. When he leaned over, he saw that the cuff of his pants was smoking. He bent down, groaning at the tightness in his back, and smothered it with his hand. Then, as he stood, he could see that the front door of the García house had swung open. For a while, he stared at it as it moved back and forth in the wind. A chill ran through his body, and suddenly, in so much heat, he felt cold. "I could never go there alone," he said. Then, holding Little José's santo tight against his chest, he began to walk slowly down the hill.

The spikes that had held the door shut had come loose from the rotted frame, and the top hinge was rusted through. As Flavio pulled the door open, the hinge snapped and the door twisted and fell off to the side. Down the hill, the fire had spread past the church and into the dry sagebrush. As Flavio gazed inside the García house, light from the flames spilled past him into the room.

His shadow fell across the floor and onto the heavy table that still sat in the middle of the room. The cast-iron stove where Guadalupe had once made tea and warmed tortillas was littered with large chunks of dirt that had fallen from the ceiling. The sides had rusted from water. Cut into the wall behind it were nichos, and each one was empty and spun with cobwebs. In the darkest corner of the room was the narrow opening that led to the rest of the house. Nearly all the rooms he and Felix had walked through so long ago were gone now. And, in his mind, he could see Guadalupe García still sitting where he had last seen her, buried beneath so much dirt and scattered with her were the bones of Emilio García. He had no idea what had brought him to this house, and a wave of sadness went through him. The room looked small and empty, and Flavio realized that was all it had ever really been. There had never been any life in this place. It had only been full of dead things and the noises they had made.

Flavio looked down at Little José's santo. She was looking into the room, her eyes wide, a grin on her face. "Venga," he said to her. "We should go." As he turned to leave, his shadow fell from the table. Standing in the center of it, light from the fire moving over her body, was the santo Cristóbal García had made. For a second, Flavio was so startled at the sight of her that he didn't move but stood there seeing her out of the corner of his eye. He thought that what he was seeing couldn't be and that, if he was smart, he would ignore her and just walk away. But then he remembered coming home from the fields one day to find on his living room floor the small box of letters Martha had left him. He turned back slowly. "I've seen you before," he said. "When Felix and I were just little boys."

Her shoulders were draped with cobwebs and dirt. Though her gown had been painted with ash and soot, the light from outside stained it red, as if Cristóbal's blood had run everywhere over her. Even from the doorway, Flavio could see the deep gashes on her body from the knife. Her head was bent slightly, and she was gazing down at the table. She looked smaller to Flavio than she had years before and a little lost, as if she had been alone in this house for too long.

"Why was I frightened of you?" Flavio said. She looked as though, if she were to move about, it would be slowly and with sadness. He could see her lying in Cristóbal's arms, and he realized that she was only what he had been. She had gone through her life with him, and the stories she knew were the same ones Flavio had heard. He stared at her for a while longer and then he stepped inside the room, went over to the table, and sat down on the bench. He took off his hat and rubbed the top of his head.

"To see you standing here," he said, letting out a long breath.

He placed José's santo on the table beside Cristóbal's. She stood there looking about as if expecting a party to begin or a marching band to come through the doorway. Flavio could see that the old santo's shoulders had been rubbed smooth after so many years. Beneath the dirt, he could see that the soot had faded and there was the color of cottonwood. As he reached out to touch her, the sleeve of his shirt brushed against something that rolled across the table. He picked it up and held it close to his face.

"I don't believe my eyes," he said. "It's Felix's little piece of wood." He had no idea who had left it for him or what it meant, but just looking at it made him feel happy. He rubbed his fingers over it and then tossed it up and down in his hand. "Eee. It's Felix's little piece of wood."

When Flavio stepped outside the house, under his arms were the two Ladies. The fire had jumped the highway and was burning down the hill. And below the García house, flames were dancing wildly over the roof of the church. In the air all there was to breathe was smoke. Flavio sat down against the wall of the house, the adobe hot against his back, and held the two Ladies in his lap. The three of them looked out over the village. They watched as the high branches of the cottonwood caught fire, and as the wind blew, ash and embers flew like snow.

"I am the last of this village," Flavio said. "And if I could see two of everything, then there would be two villages. In one would be fire and smoke and it would be a place where young boys are hung from trees and where men are buried in blizzards. And in the other will be grass as high as my waist and creeks full to bursting. And I would name both of these places Guadalupe, for neither of them would ever be lost."

The fire was rushing up the hill now, and as Flavio closed his eyes from the heat, he thought that in all his life he had never seen anything so beautiful.

Photo © Laura Shields

The author of *The Journal of Antonio Montoya* and *Perdido*, **Rick Collignon** lives in northern New Mexico.